Further praise for **Adriana Trigiani** and her fabulous novels

Queen of the Big Time

'Big dreams, small-town wisdom and star-crossed lovers make this as more-ish as "Mama's Wedding Cookies"' MAIL ON SUNDAY

'Nella dreams of escaping her family's farm, but discovers life – and love – doesn't always go to plan. This sweet, beautifully written story is a real tear-jerker' COMPANY

'This bittersweet tale of missed opportunities will have you racing through the pages, holding your breath in anticipation' GLAMOUR

'Like her bestselling *Big Stone Gap* trilogy, the result is an old-fashioned moral read, celebrating hard work, feisty women and the power of pure nostalgia' DAILY MAIL

Lucia, Lucia

'The perfect feel-good read' GLAMOUR

'A tender tale of being torn between family, career and love' COMPANY

'The author of *Big Stone Gap* triumphs again' HEAT

'A nostalgic tale told with warmth and humour – use a handkerchief as a bookmark' DAILY MAIL

The *Big Stone Gap* trilogy

'Evokes a world of rustic simplicity, wholesome wisdom and down-home charm. The ideal read' THE TIMES

'A charming, moving and beautifully observed tale' DAILY MIRROR

'It is hard to imagine a better book with which to be slung in a hammock on a sunny afternoon' WENDY HOLDEN

'As warm and sweet as Southern Comfort' ELLE

ALSO BY ADRIANA TRIGIANI

Big Stone Gap
Big Cherry Holler
Milk Glass Moon
Lucia, Lucia

Queen of the big time

Adriana Trigiani

POCKET
BOOKS

LONDON • NEW YORK • TORONTO • SYDNEY

First published in Great Britain by Simon & Schuster UK Ltd, 2004
This paperback edition published by Pocket Books, 2005
An imprint of Simon & Schuster UK Ltd
A Viacom company

1 3 5 7 9 10 8 6 4 2

Simon & Schuster UK Ltd
Africa House
64–78 Kingsway
London WC2B 6AH

www.simonsays.co.uk

Simon & Schuster Australia
Sydney

A CIP catalogue record for this book is available from the British Library

ISBN 0 7434 6227 0
EAN 9780743462273

Grateful acknowledgement is made to A.P. Watt Ltd on behalf of
Michael B. Yeats for permission to reprint 'When you are Old' by W.B. Yeats.
Reprinted by permission of A.P. Watt on behalf of Michael B. Yeats.

Printed and bound in Great Britain by
Bookmarque Ltd, Croydon, Surrey

In memory of my grandmother
Yolanda P. Trigiani

Queen of the big time

PART ONE

1924–1927

*T*oday is the day my teacher, Miss Stoddard, comes to see my parents. She sent them a letter telling them she wanted to come to our house to discuss "the further education of Nella Castelluca." The letter is official, it was written on a typewriter, signed by my teacher with a fountain pen, dated October 1, 1924, and at the top there's a gold stamp that says PENNSYLVANIA EDUCATION AUTHORITY. We never get fancy mail on the farm, only handwritten letters from our relatives in Italy. Mama is saving the envelope from Miss Stoddard for me in a box where she keeps important papers. Sometimes I ask her to show it to me, and every time I read it, I am thrilled all over again.

I hope my parents decide to let me go to school in Roseto.

Delabole School only goes to the seventh grade, and I've repeated it twice just so I can keep learning. Miss Stoddard is going to tell my parents that I should be given the opportunity to go to high school in town because I have "great potential."

I am the third daughter of five girls, and I have never been singled out for anything. Finally, it feels like it's my turn. It's as though I'm in the middle of a wonderful contest: the music has stopped, the blindfolded girl has pointed to me, and I've won the cakewalk. I've hardly slept a wink since the letter arrived. I can't. My whole world will change if my parents let me go to school. My older sisters, Assunta and Elena, stopped going to school after the seventh grade. Neither wanted to continue and there is so much work on the farm, it wasn't even discussed.

I was helping Mama clean the house to prepare for our company, but she made me go outside because I was making her nervous. She's nervous? I don't know if I will make it until two o'clock.

As I lean against the trunk of the old elm at the end of our lane and look up, the late-afternoon sunlight comes through the leaves in little bursts like a star shower, so bright I have to squint so my eyes won't hurt. Over the hill, our farmhouse, freshly painted pale gray, seems to dance above the ground like a cloud.

Even the water in the creek that runs past my feet seems full of possibility; the old stones that glisten under the water look like silver dollars. How I wish they were! I would scoop them up, fill my pockets, and bring them to Mama, so she could buy whatever she wanted. When I think of her, and I do lots during the day, I remember all the things she doesn't have and then I try to think up ways to give her what she needs. She deserves pretty dishes and soft rugs and glittering rings. She makes do with enamel plates, painted floorboards, and the locket Papa gave her when they were engaged. Papa smiles when I tell him about my dreams for Mama, and sometimes I think he wishes he could give her nice things too, but we're just farmers.

If only I could get an education, then I could get a good job and give Mama the world. Papa says I get my brains from her. She is a quick study; in fact, she taught herself to read and write English. Mama spends most nights after dinner teaching Papa to read English, and when he can't say the words properly, Mama laughs, and then Papa curses in Italian and she laughs harder.

I feel guilty being so happy because usually this is a sad time of year, as the green hills of Delabole turn toffee-colored, which means that soon winter will come and we will have the hog killing. Papa says that if we want to eat, we must help. All the chores around the killing used to bother me; now I don't cry much. I just stay busy. I help stretch the cloth tarps where the innards lay in the smokehouse before they're made into sausage, and line the wooden barrels where the scraps go. I have taught my sisters how to separate the innards and rinse them in the cool stream of the springhouse. There's always plenty of help. Papa invites all his friends from Roseto, and we make a party of it. The dinner at the end of the day is the best part, when the women make tenderloin on the open pit and Papa's friends tell stories of Italy. It helps to laugh because then you don't think about the dying part so much.

"Nella?" Mama calls out from the porch.

"Over here!" I holler back.

"Come inside!" She motions me over and goes back into the house.

I carefully place my bookmark in the middle of *Jane Eyre*, which I am reading for the third time, and pick up the rest of my books and run to the house. It doesn't look so shabby since the paint job, and the ground around it is much better in autumn, more smooth, after the goat has eaten his fill of the grass. Our farm will never be as beautiful as the houses and gardens in town. Anything that's pretty on the farm is wild. The fields covered in bright yellow dandelions, low thickets of tiny red beach roses by the road, and stalks of black-eyed Susans by the barn are all accidents.

Roseto is only three miles away, but it might as well be across an ocean. When the trolley isn't running, we have to walk to get there, mostly through fields and on back roads, but the hike is worth it. The trolley costs a nickel, so it's expensive for all of us to ride into town. Sometimes Papa takes out the carriage and hitches our horse Moxie to take us in, but I hate that. In town, people have cars, and we look silly with the old carriage.

Papa knows I like to go into town just to look at the houses. Roseto is built on a hill, and the houses are so close together, they are almost connected. When you look down the main street, Garibaldi Avenue, the homes look like a stack of candy boxes with their neat red-brick, white-clapboard, and gray-fieldstone exteriors.

Each home has a small front yard, smooth green squares of grass trimmed by low boxwood hedges. There are no bumps and no shards of shale sticking up anywhere. Powder-blue bachelor buttons hem the walkways like ruffles. On the farm, the land has pits and holes and the grass grows in tufts. Every detail in Roseto's landscape seems enchanted, from the fig trees with their spindly branches to the open wood arbors covered with white blossoms in the spring, which become fragrant grapes by summer.

Even the story of how Roseto became a town is like a fairy tale. We make Papa tell the story because he remembers when the town was just a camp with a group of Italian men who came over to find work in the quarries. The men were rejected in New York and New Jersey because they were Pugliese and had funny accents that Italians in those places could not understand. One of Papa's friends saw an ad in a newspaper looking for quarry workers in Pennsylvania, so they pooled what little money they had and took the train to Bangor, about ninety miles from New York City, to apply for work. At first, there was resistance to hiring the Italians, but when the quarry owners saw how hard the immigrants worked, they made it clear that more jobs were available. This is how our people came to live here. As the first group became established, they sent for more men, and those men brought their families. The Italians settled in an area outside Bangor called Howell Town, and eventually, another piece of land close by was designated for the Italians. They named it Roseto, after the town they came from. In Italian, it means "hillside covered with roses." Papa tells us that when the families built their homes here, they positioned them exactly as they had been in Italy. So if you were my neighbor in Roseto Valfortore, you became my neighbor in the new Roseto.

Papa's family were farmers, so the first thing he did when he saved enough money working in the quarry was to lease land outside Roseto and build his farm. The cheapest land was in Delabole, close enough to town and yet too far for me. Papa still works in the quarry for extra money sometimes, but mainly his living comes from the three cows, ten chickens, and twelve hogs we have on the farm.

"Mama made everything look nice," Elena tells me as she sweeps the porch. She is sixteen, only two years older than me, but she has always seemed more mature. Elena is Mama's helper; she takes care of our two younger sisters and helps with the household chores. She is thin and pretty, with pale skin and dark brown eyes. Her black hair falls in waves, but there is always something sad about her, so I spend a lot of time trying to cheer her up.

"Thanks for sweeping," I tell her.

"I want everything to look perfect for Miss Stoddard too." She smiles.

There is no sweeter perfume on the farm than strong coffee brewing on the stove and Mama's buttery sponge cake, fresh out of the oven. Mama has the place sparkling. The kitchen floor is mopped, every pot is on its proper hook, and the table is covered in a pressed blue-and-white-checked tablecloth. In the front room, she has draped the settee in crisp white muslin and placed a bunch of lavender tied with a ribbon in the kindling box by the fireplace. I hope Miss Stoddard doesn't notice that we don't have much furniture.

"How do I look?" Mama asks, turning slowly in her Sunday dress, a simple navy blue wool crepe drop-waist with black buttons. Mama's hair is dark brown; she wears it in a long braid twisted into a knot at the nape of her neck. She has high cheekbones and deep-set brown eyes; her skin is tawny brown from working in the field with Papa.

"Beautiful."

Mama laughs loudly. "Oh Nella, you always lie to make me feel good. But that's all right, you have a good heart." Mama pulls a long wooden spoon from the brown crock on the windowsill. She doesn't have to ask; I fetch the jar of raspberry jam we put up last summer from the pantry. Mama takes a long serrated knife, places her hand on top of the cool cake, and without a glitch slices the sponge cake in two, lengthwise. No matter how many times I try to slice a cake in two, the knife always gets stuck. Mama separates the halves, placing the layers side by side on her cutting board. She spoons the jam onto one side, spreads it evenly, and then flips the top layer back on, perfectly centered over the layer of jam. Finally, she reaches into the sugar canister, pulls out the sift, and dusts the top with powdered sugar.

ZIA IRMA'S ITALIAN SPONGE CAKE

1 cup cake flour
6 eggs, separated
1 cup sugar
1/4 teaspoon almond flavoring
1/4 cup water
1/2 teaspoon salt
1/2 teaspoon cream of tartar

Preheat the oven to 325 degrees. Sift the cake flour. Beat the egg yolks until lemon-colored. Gradually add the sugar. Blend the flour and almond flavoring in the water and add to the egg yolk mixture at low speed. Add the salt and cream of tartar. In a separate bowl, beat the egg whites until they are frothy and stand in peaks. Fold the egg yolk mixture into the whites just until blended. Pour the batter into a 10-inch ungreased tube pan. Bake for one hour or until cake springs back when lightly touched in center. Let sit in inverted position until cool.

"Now. Is this good enough for your teacher?" Mama asks as she lifts the cake onto her best platter.

"It looks better than the cakes in the bakery window." I'm sure Mama knows I'm lying again. As nice as Mama's cake is, I wish that we were serving pastries from Marcella's, the bakery in town. There's a pink canopy over the storefront and bells that chime when you push the front door open. Inside they have small white café tables with matching wrought-iron chairs with swirly backs. When Papa goes there and buys cream puffs (always on our birthdays, it's a Castelluca tradition), the baker puts them on frilly doilies inside a white cardboard box tied with string. Even the box top is elegant. There's a picture of a woman in a wide-brimmed hat winking and holding a flag that says MARCELLA'S. No matter how much powdered sugar Mama sprinkles on this cake to fancy it up, it is still plain old sponge cake made in our plain old oven.

"Is the teacher here yet?" Papa hollers as he comes into the house, the screen door banging behind him.

"No, Papa," I tell him, relieved that she has not arrived to hear him shouting like a farmer. Papa comes into the kitchen, grabs Mama from behind, and kisses her. He is six feet tall; his black hair is streaked with white at the temples. He has a wide black mustache, which is always neatly trimmed. Papa's olive skin is deep brown from working in the sun most every day of his life. His broad shoulders are twice as wide as Mama's; she is not a small woman, but looks petite next to him.

"I don't have time for fooling around," Mama says to Papa, removing his hands from her waist. I am secretly proud that Mama is barking orders, because this is my important day, and she knows that we need to make a good impression. Roma and Dianna run into the kitchen. Elena grabs them to wash their hands at the sink.

"I helped Papa feed the horse," Roma says. She is eight years old, sweet and round, much like one of the rolls in the bakery window.

"Good girl," Mama says to her. "And Dianna? What did you do?"

"I watched." She shrugs. Dianna is small and quick, but never uses her dexterity for chores. Her mind is always off somewhere else. She is the prettiest, with her long chestnut brown hair streaked with gold, and her blue eyes. Because Dianna and Roma are only a year apart, and the youngest, they are like twins, and we treat them as such.

"Everything is just perfect." I give my mother a quick hug.

"All this fuss. It's just Miss Stoddard coming over." Assunta, the eldest, is a long, pale noodle of a girl with jet-black hair and brown eyes that tilt down at the corners. She has a permanent crease between her eyes because she is forever thinking up ways to be mean.

"I like Miss Stoddard," Elena says quietly.

"She's nobody special," Assunta replies. Elena looks at me and moves over to the window, out of Assunta's way. Elena is very much in the shadow of the eldest daughter; then again, we all are. Assunta just turned nineteen, and is engaged to a young man from Mama's hometown in Italy. The marriage was arranged years ago; Assunta and the boy have written to each other since they were kids. We are all anxious to meet him, having seen his picture. He is very handsome and seems tall, though you really can't tell how tall someone is from a photograph. Elena and I think the arrangement is a good idea because there is no way anyone around here would want to marry her. Assunta doesn't get along with most people, and the truth is, most boys are scared of her.

"Teachers are the same wherever you go. They teach," Assunta grunts.

"Miss Stoddard is the best teacher I ever had," I tell her.

"She's the *only* teacher you ever had, dummy."

She's right, of course. I have only ever gone to Delabole School. For most of the last year, I've helped Miss Stoddard teach the little ones how to read, and when school is dismissed, she works with me beyond the seventh-grade curriculum. I have read Edgar Allan Poe, Jane Austen, and Charlotte Brontë, and loved them all. But now Miss Stoddard believes I need more of a challenge, and she wants me to go to a school where I will learn with others my age.

Assunta leans on the table and eyes the cake. Mama turns to the sink. Papa has gone into the pantry, so Assunta seizes the moment and extends her long, pointy finger at the cake to poke at it.

"Don't!" I push the platter away from her.

Assunta's black eyes narrow. "Do you think she'll be impressed with sponge cake? You're ridiculous." I don't know if it's the way she is looking at me, or the thought that she would deliberately ruin a cake for my teacher, or fourteen years of antagonism welling up inside of me, but I slap her. At first, Assunta is surprised, but then delighted to defend herself. She hits me back, then digs her fingernails into my arm.

Mama pulls me away from her. Assunta always ruins everything for me, but this is one day that cannot be derailed by my sister. "What's the matter with you?" Mama holds on to me.

I want to tell my mother that I've never wanted anything so much as the very thing Miss Stoddard is coming to talk to them about, but I've made a habit of never saying what I really want, for fear that Assunta will find some way to make sure I don't get it. Mama never understands, she can't see what kind of a girl my sister really is, and demands that we treat each other with respect. But how can I respect someone who is cruel? My parents say they love each of us equally, but is that even possible? Aren't some people more lovable than others? And why do I have to be lumped in with a sister who has no more regard for me than the pigs she kicks out of the way when she goes to feed them in the pen? Assunta is full of resentment. No matter what her portion might be, it is never enough. There is no pleasing her, but I am the only one around here who realizes this.

Elena, who hates fighting, hangs her head and begins to cry. Dianna and Roma look at each other and run outside.

"I should tell your teacher to go straight home when she gets here, that's what I should do," Papa says. Assunta stands behind him, smooths her hair, and smirks. She tells Papa I threw the first punch, so it is I who must be punished.

"Please, please, Papa, don't send Miss Stoddard away," I beg. I am sorry that I fell for Assunta's jab, and that the whole of my future could be ruined by my impulsive nature. "I am sorry, Assunta."

"It's about time you learned how to behave. You're an animal." Assunta looks at Mama and then Papa. "You let her get away with everything. You'll see how she ends up." Assunta storms upstairs. I close my eyes and count the days until Alessandro Pagano comes from Italy to marry her and take her out of this house.

"Why do you always lose your temper?" Papa asks quietly.

"She was going to ruin the cake."

"Assunta is not a girl anymore. She's about to be married. You musn't hit her. Or anyone," Papa says firmly. I wish I could tell him how many times she slaps me with her hairbrush when he isn't looking.

Mama takes the cake and goes to the front room.

"I'm sorry," I call after her quietly.

"You're bleeding," Elena says, taking the *moppeen* from the sink. "It's next to your eye." She dabs the scratch with the cool rag and I feel the sting.

"Papa, you musn't let her meet Mr. Pagano before the wedding day. He'll turn right around and go back to Italy."

Papa tries not to laugh. "Nella. That's enough."

"He has to marry her. He has to," I say under my breath.

"They will marry," Papa promises. "Your mother saw to it years ago."

Papa must know that the deal could be broken and we'd be stuck with Assunta forever. Bad luck is wily: it lands on you when you least expect it.

Papa goes out back to wash up. I put the jar of jam back in the pantry. Elena has already washed the spoon and put it away; now she straightens the tablecloth. "Don't worry. Everything will be fine," she says.

"I'm going to wait on the porch for Miss Stoddard," I tell

Mama as I push through the screen door. Once I'm outside, I sit on the steps and gather my skirts tightly around my knees and smooth the burgundy corduroy down to my ankles. The scratch over my eye begins to pulse, so I take my thumb and apply pressure, something Papa taught me to do when I accidently cut myself.

I look down to the road that turns onto the farm and imagine Assunta in her wedding gown, climbing into the front seat of Alessandro Pagano's car (I hope he has one!). He revs the engine, and as the car lurches and we wave, her new husband will honk the horn and we will stand here until they disappear onto Delabole Road, fading away to a pinpoint in the distance until they are gone forever. That, I am certain, will be the happiest moment of my life. If the angels are really on my side that day, Alessandro will decide he hates America and will throw my sister on a boat and take her back to Italy.

"Nella! Miss Stoddard is coming!" Dianna skips out from behind the barn. Roma, as always, follows a few steps behind. I look down the lane, anchored at the end by the old elm, and see my teacher walking from the trolley stop. Miss Stoddard is a great beauty; she has red hair and hazel eyes. She always wears a white blouse and a long wool skirt. Her black shoes have small silver buckles, which are buffed shiny like mirrors. She has the fine bone structure of the porcelain doll Mama saved from her childhood in Italy. We never play with the delicate doll; she sits on the shelf staring at us with her perfect ceramic gaze. But there's nothing fragile about Miss

Stoddard. She can run and jump and whoop and holler like a boy. She taught me how to play jacks, red rover, and checkers during recess. Most important, she taught me how to read. For this, I will always be in her debt. She has known me since I was five, so really, I have known her almost as long as my own parents. Roma and Dianna have run down the lane to walk her to our porch; Miss Stoddard walks between them, holding their hands as they walk to the farmhouse.

"Hi, Nella." Miss Stoddard's smile turns to a look of concern. "What did you do to your eye?"

"I hit the gate on the chicken coop." I shrug. "Clumsy. You know me."

The screen door creaks open.

"Miss Stoddard, please come in," Mama says, extending her hand. I'm glad to see Miss Stoddard still has her gloves on; she won't notice how rough Mama's hands are. "Please, sit down." Mama tells Elena to fetch Papa. Miss Stoddard sits on the settee. "This is lovely." She points to the sponge cake on the wooden tray. Thank God Mama thought to put a linen napkin over the old wood.

"Thank you." Mama smiles, pouring a cup of coffee for Miss Stoddard in the dainty cup with the roses. We have four bone china cups and saucers, but not all have flowers on them. Mama gives a starched lace napkin to her with the cup of coffee.

"Don't get up," Papa says in a booming voice as he enters the room. Papa has changed out of his old work shirt into a navy blue cotton shirt. It's not a dress shirt, but at least it's pressed. He did not bother to change his pants with the suspenders, but that's all right. We aren't going to a dance, after all, and Miss Stoddard knows he's a farmer. I motion to Dianna and Roma to go; when they don't get the hint, Elena herds them out.

Mama sits primly on the settee. Papa pulls the old rocker from next to the fireplace. I pour coffee for my parents.

Miss Stoddard takes a bite of cake and compliments Mama. Then she sips her coffee graciously and places the cup back on the saucer. "As I wrote you in the letter," she begins, "I believe that Nella is an exceptional student."

"Exceptional?" Papa pronounces the word slowly.

"She's far ahead of any student her age whom I've taught before. I have her reading books that advanced students would read."

"I just finished *Moby-Dick*," I announce proudly, "and I'm reading *Jane Eyre* again."

Miss Stoddard continues. "She's now repeated the seventh grade twice, and I can't keep her any longer. I think it would be a shame to end Nella's education." Miss Stoddard looks at me and smiles. "She's capable of so much more. I wrote to the Columbus School in Roseto, and they said that they would take her. Columbus School goes to the twelfth grade."

"She would have to go into town?"

"Yes, Papa, it's in town." The thought of it is so exciting to me I can't stay quiet. How I would love to ride the trolley every morning, and stop every afternoon after school for a macaroon at Marcella's!

"The school is right off Main Street, a half a block from the trolley station," Miss Stoddard explains.

"We know where it is." Papa smiles. "But Nella cannot ride the trolley alone."

"I could go with her, Papa," Elena says from the doorway. She looks at me, knowing how much it would mean to me.

"We cannot afford the trolley twice a day, and two of you, well, that is out of the question."

"I could walk! It's only three miles!"

Papa looks a little scandalized, but once again, Elena comes to my rescue. "I'll walk with her, Papa." How kind of my sister. She was average in school and couldn't wait to be done with the seventh grade. And now she's offering to walk an hour each way for me.

"Thank you, Elena," I tell her sincerely.

"Girls, let me speak with Miss Stoddard alone."

The look on Papa's face tells me that I should not argue the point. Mama has not said a word, but she wouldn't. Papa speaks on behalf of our family.

"Papa?" Assunta, who must have been eavesdropping from the stairs, comes into the room. "I'll walk her into town." Elena and I look at each other. Assunta has never done a thing for me, why would she want to walk me into town?

"Thank you," Papa says to Assunta and then looks at me as if to say, *See, your sister really does care about you.* But I am certain there must be some underlying reason for Assunta to show this kind of generosity toward me. There must be something in it for her!

"I am starting a new job in town next month," Assunta explains to Miss Stoddard. Elena and I look at each other again. This is the first we have heard of a job. "I am going to work at the Roseto Manufacturing Company. I have to be at work by seven o'clock in the morning."

Elena nudges me. Assunta has been keeping secrets. We had no idea she was going to work in Roseto's blouse mill.

"School begins at eight," Miss Stoddard says.

"I'll wait outside for them to open the school. I don't mind!" Miss Stoddard smiles at me. "Really, I'll stand in the snow. I don't care!"

"Nella, let me speak to your teacher alone." Papa's tone tells me he means it this time, so I follow Elena up the stairs and into our room.

"Can you believe it? I'm going to school!" I straighten the coverlet on my bed so the lace on the hem just grazes the floorboards.

"You deserve it. You work so hard."

"So do you!"

"Yes, but I'm not smart." Elena says this without a trace of self-pity. "But you, you could be a teacher someday."

"That's what I want. I want to be just like Miss Stoddard. I want to teach little ones how to read. Every day we'll have story hour. I'll read *Aesop's Fables* and *Tales from Shakespeare* aloud, just like she does. And on special days, like birthdays, I'll make tea cakes and lemonade and have extra recess."

Assunta pushes the door open.

"When did you decide to work at the mill?" Elena asks her.

"When I realized how small my dowry would be. Papa's money is all tied up in cows. I don't want Alessandro thinking he got stuck with a poor farm girl." Assunta goes to the window and looks out over Delabole farm. "But he *is* getting stuck with a poor farm girl, so I have to do my part."

I never thought about a dowry, but it makes sense. Of course we have to pay someone to take Assunta off of our hands. Who would take her for free?

"I'm sure Alessandro isn't expecting—" Elena begins.

Assunta interrupts her. "How do you know what he expects?"

The funny thing is, I've read all of Alessandro's letters to Assunta (she keeps them hidden in a tin box in the closet), and I don't remember a single word about any expectations of a dowry. But now is not the time to point that out. If she knew I read her private mail, she'd do worse than scratch me.

"Alessandro is a lucky man." Elena and Assunta look surprised. "You're very kind." I smile at Assunta. "You didn't have to offer to walk me to school, but you did and I appreciate it."

"You will have to work for the privilege." Assunta crosses her arms over her chest like a general and looks down on me.

"The privilege?"

"I'm putting you to work for me. You will make all the linens for my hope chest. And when I pick my house in town, you will make all the draperies. And for the first year of my married life, or until I decide otherwise, you will be my maid.

You will cook, do our laundry, and clean my house. Do you understand?"

So there it is: the catch. Assunta wants a maid. I'd like to tell her that I will never clean her house, or sew for her, or do anything she asks of me, because from as far back as I can remember, I have hated her. I pray every night that God will stop this hate, but the more I pray, the worse I feel. I cannot be cured. But I want to be a teacher, and no matter what I have to do to reach that goal, I will do it. I don't want to stay on the farm my whole life. I want to visit the places I read about in books, and find them on maps that I have studied. I can't do any of this without Assunta's help. "It's a deal," I tell her. Assunta smirks and goes back downstairs.

"She should walk you to school just because she's your sister. How dare she make you pay for that?" Elena is angry, but she knows as well as I do that in this house, Assunta is the queen, and we serve her. If I have to scrub a thousand floors to go to Columbus School, the exchange will be worth it.

Every year, Papa chooses the last Saturday in November for the hog killing. We've always been lucky with the weather; it's not too cold and usually it's sunny. Early this morning, the men killed the hogs by clubbing them, then scalded them in the large pots to get all the hair off. The afternoon was spent doing the hardest part, the butchering of the meat. Papa and the men will separate out the best parts, which will become smoked hams and roasts. Then they carve away the meat they cure into bacon. The rest will be made into sausage. No part of the hog is wasted, not even the feet, which Mama pickles and puts up in jars. When the work is done, everything is shared among the men who have come to help us. There is even some meat left over for Papa to sell to the butcher in town.

My sisters and I have worked hard preparing the smoke-house for Papa, and now we help Mama with the meal. The big supper, an outdoor picnic, is everyone's reward for a hard day's work. Mama has slow-cooked the tenderloin over an open pit for most of the day. The wives have made roasted sweet potatoes, a salad of fresh red peppers, corn pudding, and fresh bread. For dessert, the ladies made all kinds of pie, sweet raspberry, pumpkin, or tapioca cream with egg-white peaks. My favorite is rhubarb and Mama made two.

The children are in the barn playing hide-and-seek. I used to organize the *bocci* games after supper, but I'm too old now. It's nice to have company on the farm, it fills up our house and fields with laughter, news, and conversation, which I can't get enough of.

I look up and see that there are no clouds in the twilight sky as I set the table. Elena lights the oil torches. With darkness settling around us, she points to the sun as it sinks behind the slate hills like a deep pink peony. "Look at the sunset!"

"Someday I'll have a hat that color." I laugh and place the last of the tin plates on the table.

There is a definite nip in the air, but the heat from the

open pit will keep us warm, along with our long wool stockings and sweaters.

"You should change your clothes for dinner." Elena sizes me up in my work clothes. She already went inside and changed into her best skirt, a pale blue wool circle with a matching sweater Mama knit for her.

"Do I have to?"

"It would be nice. Go ahead. I can finish setting the table."

I never used to get dressed for dinner. This is another sign that I'm now officially a young lady. On my way upstairs, I pass Mama and the ladies in the kitchen. They speak in Italian, and Mama throws her head back and laughs, something I rarely see her do. I wish Papa wanted to move to town, where Mama could have friends around her all the time. We are all so much happier when we have visitors; we feel a part of things.

I go up to my room and take my burgundy corduroy skirt out of the closet. I have a pretty pink calico blouse to wear with it. The sweater Mama knit for me is burgundy, so it's a perfect match. I climb out of my overalls, covered with smudge from the open pit. I go to the washbasin and scrub my face and hands. I brush my hair, putting some powder on the ends to take out the smell of the smoke. I put on my slip and stockings, and then pull on the blouse, buttoning it carefully. The pink color looks nice against my skin.

The door pushes open. "What are you getting all dressed up for?" Assunta asks as I button my blouse and straighten the collar.

"Mama said we should look our best for dinner."

"You better not spill anything on that skirt," she barks. Assunta goes to the closet and pulls out her best dress, a simple green wool chemise with long sleeves. She takes her silk stockings out of the top drawer of the dresser. "And be careful with your blouse too," she says without looking at me. I don't know why she takes it upon herself to order us around; we already have one strong mother, we don't need another. I look in the mirror, wishing I had rouge or powder. I look so plain.

"You're not pretty at all," Assunta says, practically reading my mind, as she pulls on her stockings. "It's not your fault. You got the worst features of Papa and Mama. That's just the way it is." Assunta steps into her dress. She motions for me to zip up the back, so I do. "At least you're not too thin or too fat, just medium. Of course, there's nothing very memorable about that, either."

As Assunta prattles on about what I don't have, I feel my confidence melt around my shoes like hot candle wax. But instead of rallying my spirit and aspiring to the height of my own self-confidence, I crumble. Deep down I believe that Assunta is right: I am not pretty. This isn't the first time I've thought about it, but it's the first time it seems true. Maybe that's because I'm not out in the field playing with the other kids; now I'm expected to be a proper young lady. It didn't matter when I played *bocci* if I was pretty, it only mattered that I was good, that I could win. But proper young ladies are supposed to be pretty, and I'm not. I sit down on the bed.

"There's no sense crying about it," Assunta says flatly. "There's nothing to be done. Some girls are pretty and some girls aren't." Assunta turns and looks at herself in the mirror.

"I know I'm not a beauty," I tell her. She looks surprised that I would admit this. "But there are other things about a person to treasure. Like their wit. Their kindness. Their concern for others. Qualities you wouldn't appreciate because they have lasting value."

Instead of snapping at me and turning my observation into an argument, Assunta grabs her sweater and looks at me. "You're strange," she says. She takes her sweater off the shelf and goes. I hear her clop down the stairs in our mother's old shoes, and remind myself that my sister only says terrible things because she wears Mama's hand-me-downs and no one has ever found her special. Alessandro Pagano doesn't count because she is being forced upon him, it's not like he chose her. Part of me wants to tell her that even though she has fancy ideas about life in town, she's just a farmer too, but if I got in a fight with her, Papa would make me stay in my room all night, and then I would miss the chance to be with our company, something I wait for all year.

I lean into the mirror to look into my eyes, and instead of squinting at my image, I lift my chin a bit and smile. Yes, there are freckles and a nose with a bold tip, but my eyes are nice and my teeth are straight, and though my cheeks are full, my jawline is strong. I'm not so bad, I remind myself. *The most important element of being a lady is posture and carriage,* I hear Miss Stoddard say in my ear. I stand up straight and let my shoulders fall naturally. This instantly lengthens my neck and I look better.

When I walk down the stairs, I'm careful not to clomp stomp, but skim the wooden stairs silently, like a dancer. When Miss Stoddard walks between the school desks, you never hear her feet hit the floor; she swishes past and you get the clean scent of sweet peaches as she goes.

"Aren't you pretty!" Elena claps her hands together when she sees me as I enter the kitchen. "Here." Elena reaches into her hair and pulls out a pink satin ribbon. She arranges it in my hair, then points to my reflection in the glass of the pantry door. "You're a beauty."

"Thank you, Elena."

"It's the little things that make such a difference," she says, fixing a curl over my ear.

Mama lines us up and gives each of us a quick kiss, then rattles off the instructions of how we will serve the meal. Besides pouring drinks and otherwise serving our guests, there's a big buffet table near the table we set, and Mama wants us to replenish it whenever we see an empty platter. She hands Dianna the basket of hot bread. I grab a clean cloth to serve the rolls.

Papa comes from the barn with the men, a laughing army, pleased with themselves after a day of hard work well done. They gather around the table, filling the long benches on either side. Papa loves to have company, especially male company. It must be so hard for him, surrounded by girls all the time. I know he wishes he had a son to take over the farm.

We do our best to help him, but on days like this, it must be particularly difficult, as most of the men bring their sons along.

Papa stands at the head of the table, gives his guests a word of thanks for their help, and invites them to take their plates to the buffet table and fill them. The men make a line down either side of the table without breaking their conversation for a second. They return to the table and sit, chatting in Italian mixed with English. Dianna and I stand by to serve the bread.

Papa winks at us, our cue to serve, so we start with the first man to his right. The man is making Papa laugh; he has a handlebar mustache and big hands. Dianna holds the basket as I place the roll on the end of his plate.

"*Bellissima!*" he says as he looks at Dianna. When he looks at me, he smiles politely. I wonder what it would be like to be beautiful, so beautiful a man has to tell you so when he sees you for the first time. Dianna doesn't hear the compliment, or notice the slight I feel, but she's too young to understand what her beauty means.

We weave in and out among the men, placing the bread. When I reach the end of the table, I place the last roll and turn to go back to the kitchen.

"You're working hard," says the last guest in the last seat at the end of the table.

"Everyone works hard around here." I look at Papa's guest and realize that I've never seen him before. He doesn't look like the other men. Most of them are Papa's age, but this man is much younger, just not as young as me. I would say he's at least twenty. He has sandy brown hair and a wide smile with perfect teeth. Mama always says to look at a man's teeth, which are the key to his general health. I must be looking at him for too long and maybe with too much admiration. He butters his bread.

"Something wrong?" He looks tall, and his shoulders are broad, but his hands are not like the other men's. The fingers are long and tapered; there are no calluses or cuts, like on Papa's hands.

"Oh no," I tell him quickly.

"What's your name?" he says pleasantly.

"Nella."

"Ah. Rhymes with *bella*."

"Oh, but I'm not the pretty one in my family."

He laughs. "Maybe you just can't see it."

"Oh no, I can see it. I have a mirror in my room. Well, it's not just my room, I share it with Elena and Dianna and Roma. Assunta gets her own room because she's the eldest. But she keeps her clothes in our closet because we only have one closet." I don't know why I am compelled to tell this man every detail of our living arrangements, what does he care, but it's too late now. At least he seems mildly interested, or maybe he's just polite. He motions for me to sit down, so I do.

"I'm an only child. I wish I would have had a brother to share things with." The way he smiles at me makes me look into his eyes, which are as blue as the sapphire in Mama's locket.

"But not four of them. I never get a moment's peace."

He laughs. "Not a moment, huh?"

"Hardly ever. Half the time when I'm reading, I have to stop because there's some chore to be done or I have to look after my little sisters."

"You like to read?"

"It's my favorite thing to do."

"Me too. Are you in school?"

"At Delabole. But it only goes to seventh grade, and I'm already fourteen, so I repeated it twice. My teacher tutors me, but she thinks I need to be in a classroom with my peers. She wants me to go to Columbus School."

"You must be smart if she wants you to continue in school."

"I've always gotten As."

"I graduated from Columbus School."

I was right. That means he's at least eighteen. "What's it like?"

"Excellent teachers. I was well prepared for college."

"You're in college? I want to go someday."

"What do you want to be?"

"A teacher." My heart begins to race. Saying my dream out loud is so exciting to me, and saying it to a college man makes it even more thrilling. "What do you want to be?" I ask him. He looks at me, a little surprised that I would want to know.

"I don't know yet."

"Why not?"

"There are lots of things I'm interested in," he says and shrugs.

"You should eat. Your food is getting cold," I tell him as I stand. I look beyond to the black field behind our barn and wish I could run into the dark night. I feel trapped and so sad that I'm only fourteen and I won't ever know this young man as I would like. I need to find a graceful way to exit. I remember Miss Stoddard and throw my shoulders back.

"Nella, Papa needs coffee," Assunta tells me nicely, and I am so relieved, as I would hate for her to embarrass me in front of this man with the beautiful hands.

"Right away," I tell her.

As I walk quickly back to the kitchen, I can feel his eyes following me. I take a deep breath when I get inside. My heart is pounding now.

"Slow down," Mama says as she passes me with a fresh platter of pepper salad. "There's no rush."

"What's the matter?" Elena takes one look at me and the empty bread basket and can see something has happened.

"Nothing."

"You're all red."

"It's windy," I lie. "Do me a favor?"

"Sure."

"Papa wants coffee. Can you take it to him?"

"Yeah. But something's wrong. What is it? You can tell me." Elena lifts the coffeepot off the stove with a flannel mitt.

"There's a boy at the end of the table, the farthest seat from Papa. Will you find out his name?"

Elena laughs. "Is he a sheik?"

"No . . . I mean, yes." Ever since Elena and I went to the

movie house and saw Rudolph Valentino in *The Sheik*, she swears I have not been the same. "He's just nice," I tell her, and as soon as I say it, my face flushes the color of Papa's best red handkerchief.

"He must be more than nice. You're shaking," Elena says quietly.

"It's the sound of his voice. It's very deep and soft and I don't know how to say it . . . it thrills me."

"I understand." Elena smiles. I am so glad I can tell her things, even when I'm not exactly sure what I'm feeling. "Let me see what I can find out." Elena turns to go outside. I stop her.

"Don't say I said anything," I whisper.

"Don't worry."

Two ladies come out of the pantry carrying Mama's rhubarb pies, and as much as I love it, I won't go outside to get a slice. I'm afraid if I look at the blue-eyed boy again I might cry. I have never been overwhelmed by a boy. This must be what love at first sight feels like. If it is, it's awful. I feel sick and nervous and sad. I've met the boy I want and I cannot have him. He's too old and would never wait for me. He would have to wait four years at least, until I'm eighteen. Four years. It might as well be a hundred.

I've had little crushes, but for the most part, the boys at Delabole School are silly. They hardly study and have no interest in books and learning; they only go because their parents make them go.

I wonder how Elena will approach him. I don't want to

know everything about him, just a few things: his name, where he lives, and exactly how old he is. I wish I would have asked him what his favorite book is, because you can tell a lot about someone by the books he reads. As soon as I get my courage up, and the flush of my cheeks dies down, maybe I'll go back outside and talk to him again. I will forget for a moment that Papa would think I was too young for him, and play the part of a lady. In fact, I will pretend I am Miss Stoddard, and that I have an education. I wonder if he thinks I'm pretty. He must, he said I was *bella*. I take the *moppeen* and go into the pantry. I wipe off my face and sit on Mama's step stool and wait. It seems like hours before I hear the screen door slam.

"Nella?" Elena calls out.

"In here," I whisper.

"There's no need to hide." She comes into the pantry and sits on a step stool. "Here's what I found out. His name is Renato Lanzara."

"What a beautiful name."

"Isn't it? He is twenty-one years old."

"Twenty-*one*!" My heart sinks in my chest. He might as well be forty, he's too old for me.

"And you'll love this: he lives in town. His father is the barber."

"Why haven't I ever seen him before?" I wonder aloud.

"Nella, he's seven years older than you. That's a lot."

I don't want to go outside anymore, and I've lost my nerve for talking to him. I don't even care about sitting around hearing the grown-ups tell stories of Italy or the sweet slice of rhubarb I'm missing. I just want to go up to my room and be alone.

"He had to go." Elena breaks the news gently, but I am so disappointed I can't speak. "But he said to tell you that he enjoyed meeting you."

"He did?" I am amazed.

"And then he said to tell you something only you would understand."

"What was it?"

"He said, 'Tell Nella not to forget the rhyme.' " Elena fixes the bow in my hair. "What rhyme?"

"It was nothing," I tell her. As much as I love Elena, this is one secret I'd like to keep to myself. "Nella rhymes with *bella*," he'd said. He thinks I'm beautiful! He sent me a message. A message just for me! With this news, my ambition returns and races through me like a fever. I don't want to sit in this pantry another moment. Not only will I stay up late and listen to stories and eat pie, I will wash every dish and pot and pan after our guests leave. I don't ever want to go to sleep, I want to stay awake and think of Renato Lanzara, the handsome boy from town with the exquisite name.

CHAPTER TWO

J follow Assunta on Delabole Road, a few paces behind her. She carries a small lantern as we make the turn onto the main road to town. The sun is not yet up. It is strange to start my first day of school in the dark, as I used to be able to run down the lane to Delabole School five minutes before Miss Stoddard rang the bell and be on time. In the distance, the hills of jagged gray slate slag look forbidding as the sun makes a ribbon of light over the mountains far away.

"Hurry up," Assunta says impatiently.

"Sorry," I tell her, picking up my pace. Assunta is particularly peevish because she doesn't want to go to work. She'd rather come from a family that could provide a proper dowry. "Wish we could take the trolley."

Assunta stops, turns, and looks at me. "All you do is dream. Get your head out of the clouds. We can't afford the trolley and we never will. Wishing doesn't help the situation."

"Sorry."

"And stop saying you're sorry. You say it so much I know you don't mean it."

I stay quiet and follow Assunta the rest of the way. "This is Division Street," she says matter-of-factly. "It separates Roseto from Bangor. People in Bangor don't like the Italians, so don't talk to them. You'll soon understand who the Johnny Bulls are."

Papa explained to us about the Johnny Bulls; they're Welsh businessmen who came over from England, bought up the slate quarries, and hired Italians at a pittance to work in them. Last year, when the rain ruined our corn, Papa worked all summer in the quarry. Usually, though, Papa takes extra work in the winter, when there are only the cows and horse to tend to. It's backbreaking work, and two of our cousins have died in the quarry. Most miners die from falls into the pit or injuries they get when dynamiting the slate walls. "Will there be Johnny Bulls in school?" I ask.

"Probably. Just be aware. Don't pay them any mind."

Assunta never seemed concerned about my safety before, so her tone surprises me. Maybe there is a little patch of pink velvet on her black heart, maybe she isn't all bad.

Garibaldi Avenue springs to life as the sun peeks over the Blue Mountains. As we walk down the wide avenue and pass the houses, I hear children laughing and talking while their mothers cook breakfast. Lights twinkle in front windows. I can see inside most houses and their well-appointed front rooms. We just got electricity at the farm, but in town, they've had it for almost ten years. We still have an outhouse, but here they have indoor bathrooms.

I wonder what it would be like to take a bath in a deep white enamel tub where the water tumbles out of the spigot without having to pump it or carry it from the spring-house. Imagine not bathing in the old tin tub set in the middle of the kitchen near the stove where it is warm. Imagine soap shaped like roses instead of the slab of lye we use. Imagine taking a bath in a room with the door closed! Imagine fluffy towels like they advertise in the Sears catalog instead of big squares of flannel Mama hemmed by hand. Imagine having your own bathwater that you haven't shared with your sisters! It must be heavenly to have your own batch of hot water.

Assunta stops in front of Marcella's bakery. "Wait here," she tells me. She goes inside. I look at a wedding cake in the window, a series of perfect round layers stacked on top of one another, separated by Greek columns of spun sugar. The cake is covered in white butter-cream frosting. Whimsical marzipan cherubs dance up the sides. At the very top are a tiny bride and groom; their ceramic hands hold a lace heart between them. I study the cake and memorize every detail, from the silver lace doily on the pedestal that holds it, to the rococo ruffle edges of tinted lavender frosting that support the cherubs as they climb up the cake. I hear the bells on the door as Assunta pushes it open.

"Here." She hands me a small box. "Papa wanted you to have a cream puff with your lunch."

"Thank you," I say as I tuck it carefully into my lunch pail. Dear Papa. He wants me to have a special first day of school, and I feel bad because there must not have been enough money to buy Assunta a cream puff on her first day of work. "Look at the cake," I say. "You and Alessandro should have one just like it!"

Assunta smiles. "Maybe we will."

My sister walks me to the front door of the Columbus School, a large, square brick building that sits back in a field off Garibaldi Avenue. Assunta pushes open the door. "Wait inside until the bell rings. It might be a while before someone gets here since school doesn't start for an hour. They're expecting you, so give them your name in the office. They'll tell you where to go. I'm working at the end of Front Street, that's one block from here. If you need anything, I take lunch from noon to twelve-thirty. I'll pick you up at three-fifteen. School is out at three, so wait right here."

"I will," I promise. I watch Assunta walk up the block. Once she is gone, I go into the school. How wide the corridors are! I walk down the main hallway. The *terrazzo* floor, with its black, white, and gold flecks, has been waxed and almost glitters. I breathe in the smell of fresh pine and waxy wood and chalk. I can see the shadow of my reflection in the shiny pink tile on the walls. A series of doors that lead to classrooms line the sides of the hallway, and I peek in each one on my way to the office. How pristine every detail is—the clean chalkboards and the desks in neat rows.

"What are you looking for?" a man's booming voice bellows.

I jump at the sound. "The office," I stammer, turning around to face him. When I look up at the man, I realize that he's a friend of Papa's. I recognize his handlebar mustache from the hog killing. "Mr. Ricci?"

"You're a Castelluca," he says with obvious surprise.

"Yes, sir. I'm Nella."

"Well, I'm the janitor here. Your pop never said one of you was coming to school here. Did you take the trolley?"

"We walked. My sister Assunta is working at the blouse factory on Front Street."

"Walked! That's almost three miles."

"It wasn't so bad."

"You have a long wait until the bell rings. Come with me." Mr. Ricci takes me into the boiler room, where he has set up a small table and chairs. He pours some hot milk from one thermos and a splash of hot coffee from another into a cup for me. He puts two heaping tablespoons of sugar into the cup and stirs it. He gives me the cup and makes the same for himself, only with more coffee. I reach into my lunch pail and give him the box with the cream puff.

"From my papa," I tell him. "He would want to thank you for looking out for me." Mr. Ricci opens the box and smiles.

"We'll share." Mr. Ricci cuts the cream puff in two, giving

me the larger piece. "I have a daughter about your age in school here. Concetta. We call her Chettie."

"I'm in ninth grade, at least agewise. I went to seventh in Delabole."

"Chettie will show you the ropes. You got a good teacher too. Miss Ciliberti."

"She's Italian?"

"Oh yes. You have four Italians teaching here. Too bad I didn't bring Chettie out to the hog killing. You two could have gotten to know each other."

"I'm sure she'll be a good friend," I say. He smiles at me just like Papa does when I say something that pleases him.

Mr. Ricci doesn't say much more. He finishes his coffee and pastry, and then he goes about his chores. When the bell rings, I go to the office, where they sign me in. Mr. Ricci was right: I am sent to Miss Ciliberti's class at the end of the hallway. As I walk in, the students are laughing and talking around their desks. I go to the teacher and give her the envelope from the office.

"Nella Castelluca?" Miss Ciliberti smiles, but it is not a warm smile like Miss Stoddard's. It's more businesslike. Her dark brown hair is bobbed close to her head. She is a small woman with a determined jaw.

"Yes, ma'am."

"So, you're skipping eighth grade?"

"Yes, ma'am. I'm fourteen. But I've gone ahead and read all the required books through grade eight."

"Such as?" she asks impatiently.

"*Walden* by Henry David Thoreau. *The Three Musketeers* by Alexandre Dumas. *Pride and Prejudice* by Jane Austen. *Wuthering Heights* by Emily Brontë, *Jane Eyre* by Charlotte Brontë—"

"Fine. Enough." She holds up her hand and smiles pleasantly. "We'll see how you keep up." She jots a few notes on the envelope. "Take the last seat in the second row."

The girls sit in two rows on one side of the room, and the boys in one row on the other. We outnumber them, but that's to be expected. Most boys have to work in the quarry as soon as they are old enough. In all, there are about thirty of us in the ninth grade.

When I sit down, a round-faced girl with chin-length curly black hair taps me on the shoulder. "I'm Chettie." She smiles. "My pop said you need a tour guide."

I smile appreciatively at her. As I look around the room, I see that the kids are more polished than me. One girl wears a plaid wool jumper with a drop waist. I wear my best skirt and a white blouse, but as I survey the room, I see it's not good enough. I'll have to convince Papa to let me buy some tartan plaid to make myself a jumper. I am the only one with a lunch pail, which I quickly shove under my seat.

Miss Ciliberti begins the lessons with mathematics—not my strongest subject, but I do my best to follow the lesson. When the bell rings and Miss Ciliberti dismisses us for lunch, I am relieved. This school is much harder than Delabole, and Miss Ciliberti has very little patience. If someone doesn't know an answer right away, she moves on to the next student without as much as a second glance. There will be no lemonade and tea cakes under the tree at recess. I doubt they even have recess here.

"Where are you having lunch?" Chettie asks.

"I could eat anywhere. Outside, I guess."

"Outside? Nobody eats outside."

"Where do they go?"

"Home."

"Home? That's three miles away for me."

"Well, we all live a few blocks from here. You want to come home with me?"

"Sure. I won't be any trouble. I have my lunch." I show Chettie the pail.

"That looks like something Pop takes to the quarry. He works in the quarry all summer when school is out."

"My pop uses this pail when *he* works in the quarry. He's a farmer but goes in whenever we need the money."

"I don't like my father to work there."

"Why not?"

"Have you ever seen the quarry? It's the scariest thing, just this giant pit filled with black water, and the men have to get in these boxes and they're lowered into the hole to work."

"Papa doesn't talk about it much. And he's never taken us there." Little does my new friend know, we haven't gone anywhere, not even Allentown or Easton. We stay on the farm.

"Pop doesn't say much about the quarry either," Chettie admits. I can already tell we have lots in common. How lucky to meet her on my very first day of school. This will make everything so much easier.

As we walk to Chettie's house, she takes time to introduce me to her friends, who are nice enough but look me up and down suspiciously.

When I mention this to Chettie, she replies, "They'll get nicer when they know you better. After all, it's not like you're a Johnny Bull. You're Italian too."

Chettie takes a sharp turn onto a stoop on Dewey Street. "This is it. The Ricci palazzo." She laughs. When she opens the screen door, she hollers for her mother, who yells back from the kitchen. The house has more furniture than ours, their settee is covered in burgundy velvet, and there are rugs that are old but clean. In an alcove hangs a cupboard with a small pine table underneath. A set of delicate teacups and saucers are arranged on the shelves, and on the table is a white ceramic bowl filled with green apples.

Chettie calls to me, "Come in here, Nella."

I continue to the end of the hallway to a bright kitchen filled with children younger than we are. "I am the oldest of the brood," Chettie says, grabbing a roll stuffed with salami. She sits down and helps her mother feed the little ones who sit around the table. I start to count them. "There's six of us." Chettie saves me the trouble. "A handful."

"I need a maid," Mrs. Ricci says ruefully. She is petite, with brown hair streaked with gray. She has soft brown eyes and a big smile, just like Chettie's.

"Let me help." I put my lunch pail down in the corner and sit next to a little boy. "Here." I fill a spoon with *pastina* and direct it toward his mouth.

"Oreste hates to eat," Chettie warns me.

"Is that true?" I ask him. The way I say it makes him smile. "Please? For me? I'm your new friend Nella."

"Nay Nay?" he says.

"You can call me Nay Nay."

"Hey, Ma, look, Oreste is eating." Chettie points.

"Well, it's a Monday miracle. Thank you, Nella. And welcome to our house." I can tell Mrs. Ricci means it. I feel like I'm part of the family already. I knew I'd love school, but I had no idea lunch would be fun too.

When Assunta comes to pick me up, I try to tell her all about the school and my new friend Chettie, but she cuts me off when she's heard enough. "When Alessandro comes, I want to live in a house on Dewey Street. I wouldn't mind starting out in one half of a two-family home. There's a red-brick one on the end of the street that's pretty. It has green awnings and a shade tree." She treats me to one of her rare smiles. "I could be happy there, I think."

The walk seems much shorter going home, and I realize that I'm not the only Castelluca with dreams of living in town. I hope Alessandro Pagano is a good provider, because Assunta will want Oriental rugs and teacups and copper pots and pans. I'll bet she'll make him buy striped awnings so the front porch has shade when the sun is hot.

"Where do you go to Mass?" Chettie wants to know as we walk back to school from lunch. I've been helping her and her mom every day at lunch for a month now, and they are so grateful, they give me a hot meal, so I don't have to carry a pail anymore. I much prefer Mrs. Ricci's hot minestrone soup and fresh bread to a cold sandwich. Chettie and I sprinkle grated cheese on our soup and dunk the bread into the broth. On Fridays, Mrs. Ricci lets us have birch beer, a sort of root beer soda, with our lunch. "Aren't you Catholic?"

"Yes," I tell her, blushing, because our family only makes it to church on Christmas and Easter. We can't afford the trolley for the whole family, and besides, Sunday is a day of chores for us. "The cows don't know it's the Sabbath," Papa says. "They still have to be milked." How do I explain this to Chettie without making my family sound like a bunch of godless heathens? "We work on Sundays. Chores have to be done every day, rain or shine."

"But you *have* to go to church. You have to make the time."

"Why?"

"Because if you don't you'll go to hell, and I'm not visiting you in hell." Chettie laughs. It's a wonder to me that we have become such fast friends. Chettie could be friends with anyone though; she's funny and everyone likes her. And while she has a cute smile, she's not a great beauty. But being funny is much better than being beautiful; I can see that already. "Why don't you come to my church?"

"The big one on the hill?" I ask her.

"Our Lady of Mount Carmel. It's brand-new. They hung the bells in the tower last year."

"It's pretty," I say, wishing I could go to church with Chettie, but I don't have a dress coat and a felt hat to wear to such a fancy place. Maybe I could borrow Mama's gloves!

"We were Presbyterians for a year until they got the Catholic church built."

"Really?"

"Yeah. For a long time, the bishop of Philadelphia wouldn't build a Catholic church here because he didn't like the Italians. He was Irish. So the Italians became Presbyterians because the Presbyterians were willing to build a church, and they did, on the other end of Garibaldi Avenue. When the bishop found out, he rushed to get Mount Carmel built and even sent a nice Italian priest, Father Impeciato, to run the parish and to keep us happy."

"That sounds so crazy." I laugh.

"It was. My papa says it's all about the money. He says the bishop figured out how much collection money he was missing when the Italians turned Presbyterian and that's why he built the church. Mama thinks it's terrible when Papa criticizes the Church, but that's how he feels."

I imagine Mr. and Mrs. Ricci debating about the Church and the neighbors joining in for a lively discussion. That sort of conversation could only happen in town. "When I'm on the farm in Delabole, I feel like I'm missing something. It's so quiet on the farm, nobody ever drops in, it's always arranged. Here, you have conversations on the street, you hear people laughing. You have nice stores. The bakery. The butcher shop. The grocery store. Places to go, like church. People everywhere. You can go for days on the farm and only ever see your own family."

"Not here. Every night after dinner we walk through town. Everyone does. It's called *La Passeggiata*, but Papa calls it 'stretching our legs.' "

"That must be wonderful."

"It is. That's when you hear all the gossip, like which husbands have girlfriends—we call them *comares*; they visit on Saturday nights while the wives sit home waiting—and which wives spend too much at the butcher, and funny things, like Mrs. Ruggiero, who goes to Philadelphia to get her hair done and gets her poodles done at the same time in the same style. Stuff like that."

"Do you think you'll live here forever?" I ask her.

Chettie thinks for a moment. "Yes, because I'm the oldest. The oldest always has to stay near the parents."

"Why?"

"Because being the oldest puts you in the chain of command. Isn't Assunta like a boss?"

"Yes, always has been."

"See? She knows she would have to run things if your parents weren't around or, God forbid, got sick or something. It's a curse to be the oldest. I wish I wasn't."

This is what I love about Chettie: besides the fact that she makes me laugh and I can tell her anything, she is sensible. She sees order in the world, and she fits her dreams into that order. She doesn't have high hopes or expectations that can never be fulfilled. She's practical. Practical is the best thing to be; when you aim too high, you will be disappointed. I wish I was more like her. I haven't told her about my crush on Renato, but I'm eager to know if she thinks it's a crazy dream to like someone who is so much older, so I ask her, "Have you ever been in love?"

Chettie laughs. "Not yet. I don't think so anyway. What's 'in love'? Butterflies in your stomach, bees on your brain? I get the vapors when I think of Anthony Marucci. I like him, but he'd never go for me. Not now, at least."

"Why?"

"Because he likes the girls from West Bangor."

"Are they special?"

"Let's put it this way: they are much friendlier than the Roseto girls, if you know what I mean. But then, when it's time, Roseto boys marry us."

"My sister is betrothed to an Italian."

"From the other side?" Chettie shakes her head. "That never works. My mama's sister married a man from the other side and he spent all of the family's savings on a roofing business. Then they had to move in with us, and then he and my pop got in a fight and they ended up going to Philly, where, guess what, he started another business, and now they're making the *sòldi* hand over fist, Mama says.

Can you believe it? You gotta watch the ones from over there."

"They can't all be bad. We were all from the other side at some point."

"I just don't trust them. I'm sorry." Chettie shrugs. "How about you? Do you like a certain boy?"

"I only met one I liked."

"Only one? Is he in our class?"

"No. He's older."

"How much?" Chettie's eyes narrow.

"Seven years," I say quietly, afraid of her reaction.

"Seven years? He's twenty-one! That's old."

"I know. It's hopeless."

"What's his name?"

"Renato Lanzara."

"You love Renato Lanzara?" Chettie grins. I notice she likes to say his name aloud as much as I do.

"Why? Do you know him?"

"Every girl in Roseto is in love with him. Probably every girl in Bangor, West Bangor, Pen Argyl, and Martins Creek too. I might as well warn you now, the Martins Creek girls are very determined. *Marca-john*, you know Roman Italians. They are tough. You picked a real popular boy."

"Of course I did. It makes an impossible situation worse, which is something I'm very good at."

"Now you have to come to church with me."

"To pray that these impure thoughts leave me?"

"No, because you'll see him there. Sometimes Renato

sings with the choir. He sounds like an angel," Chettie promises.

I wish I had money for the trolley today, because I can't get home fast enough. Miss Ciliberti posted our marks, and mine were the best in the class. She gave the students a big speech about how I come from a farm and had no access to books and learning and yet somehow figured out how to learn anyway. She said, "If Nella Castelluca can do it, anyone can." I don't think I've ever been so proud. Finally, something I am good at. Finally, something I can have that is all my own.

By the time Assunta and I reach the farm, it is dark outside. Mama has lit the lamp on the porch, and we can hear laughter from the kitchen as we climb the steps.

Elena meets us at the door. "Hurry! Papa has good news!"

Assunta and I follow her to the kitchen.

"What is it, Pop?" Assunta puts her satchel down and sits on the bench. In this light, Assunta is looking older; she has dark circles from the long hours at the factory. I hope Alessandro gets here quickly, before Assunta's beauty hits the rocks.

"I got a contract with Hellertown markets. They have four stores, and I am going to provide their eggs and milk. They came out to see me, and took one look at our Holstein cows and said, 'Mr. Castelluca, you got the job.' There are lots of farmers around, and they give out many contracts, but after years of trying, I finally got one."

"Congratulations, Papa!" I throw my arms around him. No

more hitching the wagon and taking his milk and eggs around to beg vendors to buy his supply. And no more disappointment when he returns with most of what he was trying to sell.

"They are coming in with modern machinery and will set me up," Papa continues. Mama stands back and smiles. "It will be a lot of work, but at least we will reap the benefits of it. I may even have to hire some help." Mama claps her hands together when she hears this. I am sure she would like to sleep late for once in her life and not worry about milking the cows before they start their mooing at dawn.

"Well, Papa, you're not the only one with good news. I got my marks," I tell my parents proudly.

"How did you do?" Mama asks.

"I'm first in my class."

"Good. Good." Mama looks down the report card. "Look, Papa."

"Maybe someday we can afford the trolley for my girls." Papa smiles.

"Just on Sundays, Pop," I tell him.

"Why Sundays?"

"I want to go to Mass."

"Mass?" Papa is surprised.

"You heard her." Mama smacks Papa gently with my report card. "Mass. She wants to go to church. We should all go to church. And we'll have no excuse if you hire some help around here." Mama looks at me. "Good for you."

Mama is a good Catholic; she prays the rosary every night,

baptized us all, and makes us say grace before meals. She is reverent, but has never made Papa feel bad that chores take precedence over Sunday Mass. Mama thinks God understands the workingman and his duties. In the spirit of helping the family, I promise Papa that I will walk to Mass on Sundays. "Save the money," I tell him.

"Well, I'm not going to church with you," Assunta says wearily, rubbing her knuckles. "You'll have to bribe one of the others to go with you. Five days a week walking to and from town is enough for me. Of course, when I move to Roseto, that will be different. I'll be the holiest, most devout woman you've ever seen. I'll be so religious I'll grow wings. But not until I live in town." Assunta takes her coat and hat and goes up the stairs.

"I'll walk with you," Elena promises.

"What about dinner?" Mama calls after Assunta.

"I'm too tired to eat," she calls back.

"You may go to Mass as soon as the machines are installed, but I still need your help this Sunday," Papa tells me. "The next two weeks I am going into the quarry. They have a rush job and posted signs in town. Carlo Ricci came to see me, and we're both going to take the work."

"I don't want you to do it." Mama puts her hand on Papa's shoulder. He takes her hand and smiles.

"Alessandro is arriving at Eastertime. We'll have a wedding to pay for. You want to have guests? A fancy dress? I need the work." Papa goes to the cupboard and brings out the wine and a few glasses. "Now, we toast our good fortune. Roma, go get your sister."

Roma runs up the stairs while Papa pours the wine. Elena passes the full glasses around. Dianna smiles because this means someday there may be enough money to send her to school. And for Mama, dear Mama, it means that she won't have to work from morning until night. Papa gives each of us a glass; for the little ones, he adds water to the wine. Assunta and Roma join us around the table. "*Salute!*" he says and takes a drink. We all follow suit.

"We should thank God," Mama says, looking at me.

"Yes, we should." Suddenly, I am the religious center of our family. If only Mama knew that the only reason I want to be in church is to be closer to Renato Lanzara. I'm sure people believe in God for less reason than that.

"I'll tell you what. If God gives us good weather and a nice profit this year, even I will go to church," Papa announces.

Mama rolls her eyes. "Such a good Catholic."

The spring of 1925 is the most beautiful we have ever seen. As the snow melts, the muddy ground beneath turns the palest green, and when you look far away to the Blue Mountains, the silvery-gray coat they have worn all winter melts away to reveal a soft blue that in time will become as dark as a night sky.

Everyone in our house is on edge, because Assunta received a letter that Alessandro Pagano will arrive in Philadelphia on March 15. Mama has scrubbed the house from top to bottom three times this week. She goes to the smokehouse every morning to select the best *prosciutto* to serve her future son-in-law. Papa chides her for her perfectionism, but Assunta is grateful. Alessandro has seen her picture, but if he doesn't like the rest of us, he doesn't have to marry her. This is why Elena and I are ironing every tablecoth, napkin, and curtain; in fact, anything made of fabric, including the *moppeens* we use to wash the dishes, has been pressed. Mama has been baking cookies, cakes, and pies for three days. She says every corner must sparkle, and every hem must be starched. Alessandro must see that he is marrying into a family of quality or he can turn around and go right back to Italy.

We know that Alessandro comes from a good family. He is the third son of eight children. He is from Mama's hometown, Rimini, on the Adriatic Sea. Papa is also from the Bari region, farther south than Mama's people.

Papa and Mama married in Italy, then came to America, following some cousins who settled in Pen Argyl. Their marriage was not arranged, which was unusual. A mother and father usually choose a spouse for their child, striking a deal with a good family. This way, everyone knows what they are getting. A good match means two nice people can come together and the union will make both families stronger. Even Chettie's parents were arranged. Mama and Papa fell in love on their own, but Papa soon won Mama's family over. Mama never wanted the farm life, but she took it on because she loves Papa.

Yesterday, Papa took the train to Philadelphia to pick up Alessandro. Assunta has stayed behind with us, to make sure all final details are tended to. Mama has been working so hard she fell asleep at the kitchen table right after she finished putting lace on the nightgown for Assunta's wedding trousseau.

"Mama?" I gently shake her. "Mama, you fell asleep. Go to bed," I tell her.

"Did you sweep the walk?" she asks groggily.

"Everything is done," I promise her.

Mama gets up slowly and climbs the stairs to her room. I put out the lights and follow her. When I get to my room, I change into my nightgown in the dark, so as not to wake the girls. They are as exhausted as Mama, and soon it will be morning and there will be more chores. Assunta's room will become Alessandro's, so she is bunking with us. All five of us in one room. It reminds me of the cold winters when we would huddle together to stay warm, only now we come together for a different reason.

I climb into my bed next to Roma, whom I nudge closer to the wall to make room for me. I lie on my back and feel every muscle and bone in my body ache. Besides making the house ready, we did all of Papa's chores this morning. I marvel at how hard he works. I don't know how he does it, day in and day out, and then has the ambition to work in the quarry. I guess he loves us so much he would do anything to give us what we need. I wonder if I'll ever love anyone that much.

I turn to go to sleep and hear Assunta sniffling. Soon the sniffles give way to quiet weeping. At first I lie in the dark and listen, not saying anything.

"Assunta?" I finally whisper. "Are you all right?"

She doesn't answer.

"Assunta?" I get up out of the bed and kneel next to her. "Are you sick?"

She shakes her head.

"What is it then?"

Assunta twists the sleeve of her nightgown over her fist and wipes her eyes. "I'm scared."

"Scared? Of what?" But somehow I already know the answer. She's afraid to leave home, Mama and Papa and even us, though we irritate her. She's afraid that when she sees Alessandro for the first time, she won't like him and then everyone in both families will be sorely disappointed.

"What if he doesn't like me?"

I didn't even think of that! She's worried he won't like *her*? I've known my sister all my life, but oh, how she surprises me. "I wouldn't worry. He's seen your picture and written to you."

"But a picture isn't real."

"Sure it is. You can tell a lot by a picture." Of course, I won't tell her that Elena and I have examined Alessandro's picture a million times and we can't tell if he's tall or short. You never know if the photographers put a large vase or a small vase on the table next to the chair where they take the picture. His stature could be an optical illusion.

"Don't worry. He'll like you," I promise her.

"Why?"

"Well, you are very determined," I begin. It takes me a moment to compliment her, as I am so used to complaining about her. But I think very hard. "And you have lovely long hair. It's as black as night, Mama always says. And you have pretty eyes and your feet aren't too big for your height."

"Thanks," she says softly. "It's just . . . I thought I'd be happy when he came. But now I wish he'd turn around and go home."

"No you don't."

"No, really I do. I don't know him." Assunta begins to weep again.

"If you don't like him, you don't have to marry him. Mama said so."

"She doesn't mean it." Assunta sobs.

"She means it. And I'll tell you what, if you don't like him, you tell me and I'll tell Mama and Papa and I'll lock you in this room and I won't let you out until he's gone."

"You'd do that for me?"

"Yes, I would. No woman should marry a man she doesn't love. Not ever." I give her a hug, which I haven't done since I was small. I go to my bed and get in it, giving Roma another nudge. She rolls over close to the wall.

Assunta's tears soon give way to the gentle breathing of sleep. I lie on my back, surveying the ceiling of this room as I have for so many nights when sleep won't come. Even though Assunta is bossy and mean, deep down I know I will miss her when she marries Alessandro Pagano. After all, we've been a family all these years, and she was a big part of us. Often she was the big heaving angry part of us, but part of us nonetheless. I hope Alessandro is a good man. And I hope she'll have the strength to create a new family for herself, one where she'll be happy, if happiness is even in the cards for Assunta Castelluca. I make the sign of the cross and turn my plea into a quick prayer. Chettie would be pleased.

"They're laughing and talking!" Dianna runs into the parlor the next morning. "He's taller than Papa!" I look out the window and see Papa walking down the lane with Alessandro Pagano, who looks exactly like his picture. Assunta, wearing a simple white linen sheath and Mama's sapphire locket, looks lovely standing in the kitchen doorway. Her shiny black hair hangs straight to her waist. She exhales a sigh of relief.

"Assunta, go upstairs," Mama directs.

"But Mama . . ."

"Go." Assunta goes upstairs. "There is a proper way to be introduced. It's not right for a lady to wait for a man. He waits for her."

Dianna and I look at each other. Is Mama kidding? Alessandro has waited all these years, and now we're going to make him wait even longer?

Papa opens the door and shows Alessandro into our house.

"Mr. Pagano, this is my wife, Mrs. Castelluca."

"I am pleased to meet you," he says slowly, then gives Mama a package out of his satchel. "This is from your sister Elena." Tears spring to Mama's eyes as she sits and opens the package, a stack of small lace doilies.

"Now, now, Celeste, stop the tears. Mr. Pagano has come a far distance and he's hungry," Papa says softly to Mama. Papa knows better than anyone how much Mama misses her family in Italy, so he is extra kind to her whenever they are mentioned.

"Shall I go and get Assunta?" I ask Mama.

"Not yet." Mama shoots me a look like she'd take a switch to me if she could.

"Come, Alessandro, first we have supper, and then you'll meet our beautiful Assunta."

In what seems like the longest midday supper in history, Mama offers Alessandro every delicacy she knows how to make. Elena and I serve him as though he is a duke. He has fine table manners, and after the long journey he has quite an appetite. He eats orange slices dressed in olive oil and pepper, shavings of Parmesan cheese with *prosciutto*, a salad of black olives and dandelion, a soup of *tortellini* in a chicken broth, sliced ham in fresh bread with butter, and all the wine he can drink.

I think he's handsome. His face is angular, with a large nose and full lips. He has jet-black hair combed with a neat side part. His ears are big but close to his head. His neck and shoulders are strong. His hands, big and calloused, are like Papa's; the nails are trimmed and neat, though. Evidently Assunta wasn't the only one gussying up to impress her intended.

Elena motions for me to fetch water from the well with her, while Mama laughs with Alessandro at news he shares from Italy.

"What do you think?" I ask Elena.

"He's good-looking enough. She'll like him," Elena says practically.

"He seems quiet."

"That's fine. You know she'll do all the talking anyway. " Elena pumps water into a bucket. "I think they'll be a good match. She'll be able to boss him around and he won't even notice it. I hope he makes enough money for her. He'll be importing nuts and candy from Italy. Is that a good business?"

"It doesn't matter. Papa needs help here on the farm."

"But Assunta wants to live in town."

"First get them married. Then all the details can be worked out."

"I hope they never arrange me." Elena hands me the first pail.

"Me either."

"It's too upsetting. I'd rather stay home with Mama and Papa all my life."

"Me too," I lie. Really, I would rather live in town and marry Renato Lanzara. But I can't tell Elena that. I can't tell anyone but Chettie, because my Renato is as elusive as her Anthony Marucci.

As we carry the water back to the house, I imagine the day when we won't have to haul water, milk the cows, stack the hay, and kill the hogs. Maybe one day when I'm a teacher, Papa will sell the farm and move into town, where we can join the other fine families who stroll up and down Garibaldi Avenue after supper stretching their legs. Maybe Delabole farm is just the beginning of our story and not our destiny.

"Girls, come inside!" Mama motions to us from the porch. As we approach, she says quietly, "We're going to introduce Assunta to Alessandro."

Elena and I almost drop the pails, but the thought of having to haul more from the springhouse makes us extra careful. We put the buckets by the door on the porch and follow Mama inside. Roma and Dianna sit on the settee with their hands folded as Papa pours wine into the small silver goblets Mama keeps in a velvet case.

"Elena, please go and get your sister," Mama says.

I look at Alessandro, who inhales deeply through his nose. The sound of Elena's footsteps going up the stairs is loud, like the ticking of a great clock. Soon Assunta appears in the doorway.

"Alessandro, I would like you to meet my daughter Assunta," Papa says in a voice that booms and then falters. Mama begins to cry. Alessandro turns and looks at the girl who has been promised to him, and we all can see that he is well pleased. Assunta, who never smiles, beams at him as though he is the most handsome man she has ever seen, and in doing so, she becomes so beautiful that even those of us who know her well cannot believe the transformation. Love changes people. It has taken a stranger coming from Italy to show us exactly how.

CHAPTER THREE

*F*ather Impeciato is a stern priest with a long face and thin lips that form a single straight line. Under his vestments he wears a silver pocketwatch on a long link chain that he routinely fishes out of his pocket and checks as the organ plays the processional. His Masses begin precisely at eight o'clock in the morning. He has been known to throw out parishioners who arrive one minute after he has made it to the altar. Chettie believes he has eyes in the back of his head, as he spends most of the service with his back to the congregation yet seems to know if we move, whisper, or yawn, because suddenly he will pivot around and glare directly at the sinner who has offended him.

I find priests and the nuns who tend them strangely

otherworldly. Perhaps it's the black habits, the veils and vestments that obscure the person underneath, but whatever it is, it separates us from them. Maybe it is the design of the church itself, the great distance between the pews and the altar, or the forbidding marble Communion railing that makes the priest seem miles away. It is all so grand: the high ceilings, the crouching angels, the glass-eyed statues lurking in dark alcoves, the stations of the cross detailing Christ's suffering at the end of His life, and especially the lifelike crucifix that hangs over the altar. It seems designed to frighten us into good behavior. It must be working, because Our Lady of Mount Carmel is filled to capacity for every Mass.

All of the rituals seem eerie to me too, from the smoking urns Father Impeciato waves around on a chain to the icy-cold holy water in the font that we bless ourselves with coming and going. The stained-glass window over the altar shows souls in torment, reaching up to the Blessed Lady, who looks down on the sinners in the fiery pit from a safe spot on a cloud. She holds the baby Jesus, who looks out at us, not down at the sinners. I don't know what kind of savior looks away from those who are suffering, but this Jesus does.

This morning on the farm, we all got up early to have a final breakfast with Assunta before her wedding. It was very calm, even though Mama was pressing our new dresses, which I helped her sew until the last moment. Assunta was surprisingly serene. She packed, dressed, and ate her breakfast without saying much. It's as though she had already moved on to her new home in town.

As we stand in the back of the church awaiting the organ music, Papa gives Father Impeciato an envelope. Father Impeciato understands that as a farmer, Papa cannot attend Sunday Mass on a regular basis because of his chores, but the Holy Roman Church is happy to take Papa's donations, his eldest daughter's wedding service included.

Assunta Maria Castelluca and Alessandro Agnello Pagano chose April 12, 1925, as their wedding day. April 12 is also Mama and Papa's wedding anniversary, so they chose it to honor our parents. All of Assunta's life she bragged that she would have twelve bridesmaids, but alas she only has Elena. Alessandro asked a cousin from Philadelphia to stand up for him. He is an oily fellow, with his wavy brown hair parted in the center and slicked down with pomade, and a wolfish grin. When he smiles, there's a gap between his front teeth. Papa told us to stay away from him. Papa must know something about him that we don't.

Assunta looks pretty in her drop-waist satin gown of shimmering ivory with a train that can be bloused into a bustle and bow for the reception. She wears a headband of tiny white roses, made by Mama in the early hours of the morning. Assunta carries three calla lilies, though she asked Papa if she could have a dozen. Assunta never gets exactly what she wants, but today she makes do without complaining.

As Assunta and Alessandro kneel before the priest, I think back to the moment they first met. Assunta was on her best behavior. Alessandro still has no idea of the Mount Vesuvius within her, the red-hot rages, or her violent tantrums. When she blows, it will come as a terrible shock to him. Elena said she wishes he had shown up ten years ago because we would have been spared years of torment. Clearly, when the prize is worth it, when she is getting something she truly wants, Assunta is capable of complete transformation.

I am wearing a pink satin dress Mama made for me. It's a straight sheath with a wide band across the hips; the skirt falls straight over the knee. Mama covered small buttons and sewed them up the band to give the dress some interest. Now that I'm fifteen, I would have liked a split tunic like the older girls wear, especially one with full dolman sleeves (cap sleeves are too girlish for me), but Mama would not hear my argument. I wear short white kid gloves, which Chettie thinks gives the whole ensemble some sophistication. I hope so.

There's a nice crowd in church, since Papa knows so many people from the days when he would deliver milk and eggs to town. Chettie's family takes up a whole row. On the way in she told me that she spent the entire morning ironing her brothers' shirts.

After the vows, Assunta crosses to an alcove with a smaller marble version of the main altar and a statue of the Blessed Mother on a gold pedestal behind it. Assunta places her bouquet at the foot of the statue. She stands for a moment as the organ plays "Ave Maria." Upon the first notes, a man's voice rings out over the congregation from the choir loft. The voice is so clear and beautiful, I turn to see who is singing. It is Renato Lanzara, whom I have not seen since last November. It's not that I haven't tried. Chettie and I walk by his father's barbershop on Garibaldi in hopes of running into him. And since I started coming to church regularly with Elena, I've looked for him every Sunday, but I've never seen him. Maybe God is punishing me for not having a true spiritual reason for coming to Mass. After all, the priest says God knows everything we're thinking, not just what we do, and coming to Mass with the sole desire of seeing Renato would probably not sit well with the Creator.

Renato is as I remembered him, but as he sings, he takes on a grand stature. Maybe it's the golden midmorning light that pours through the belfry and fills the choir loft, or maybe it's the timbre of his voice as he sings, but I cannot take my eyes off him. Elena nudges me, reminding me to turn back around. Before I do, Chettie winks at me from her pew.

It seems like hours later that Assunta and Alessandro recess down the aisle to the back of the church. When they reach the top of the steps, they turn to each other and kiss. The most exciting part of weddings at Our Lady of Mount Carmel is the parade led by the bride and groom to Pinto's Hall. It's spectacular to see the Rosetans in their finery, the women in their pastel dresses and plumed hats, and the men in their elegant suits, as they process to the reception.

Chettie, dressed in a white eyelet shift with a smart straw hat, meets up with me as I follow the wedding party down the street. "That was a beautiful wedding. One of the best I've seen."

"Think so?" I am hoping everyone in town agrees since we worked so hard on the details.

"The flowers, Assunta's dress, everything was perfect," Chettie says. "Now the fun begins. Have you ever been to Pinto's Hall for a football reception?"

I shake my head that I haven't.

"When you walk in, you tell them if you want ham or roast beef at the door, and they throw you a wrapped sandwich. It's tradition. Watch."

There are two boys with baskets by the door. Chettie says, "Ham, please." A boy tosses her the ham sandwich.

"I'll have ham too," I tell the boy. He tosses me a sandwich wrapped in waxy white paper.

Alessandro leads his new bride onto the dance floor as the band plays "Oh Marie," and they begin to dance. There is a keg of beer for the grown-ups at the end of a long table on the far side of the room, and a keg of soda for the kids on another. The church sodality ladies have crisscrossed white streamers over the low ceiling and hung silver bells in the center. Round tables with white tablecloths anchor either side of the dance floor. The centerpiece for each table is a pyramid of Mama's wedding cookies. Delicate *crustelli* dusted with powdered sugar, coconut balls, and fig squares are piled high on silver trays. Mama snapped the stems off fresh daisies and dotted them among the cookies.

MAMA'S WEDDING COOKIES

1/4 pound unsalted butter

1/4 pound unsalted margarine

1 cup sugar

3 large eggs

1 teaspoon almond extract

1/2 cup milk

31/4–31/2 cups flour

pinch of salt

5 teaspoons baking powder

Cream together the butter, margarine, sugar, and eggs. Add the almond extract and milk. Then add the flour, salt, and baking powder and mix well. Keep hands wet and shape the mixture into 1-inch rounds, high in the center. Bake at 350 degrees for 13 minutes or until lightly browned.

FROSTING

1/2 box powdered sugar

2 tablespoons unsalted butter

milk—just enough to wet the powdered sugar

1 teaspoon almond flavoring

shredded coconut for dusting

Mix well and ice the cookies. Dip the iced cookies in coconut.

As the crowd filters in, they catch their sandwiches from the boys with the baskets and place them on tables, marking their seats for after the dance. Papa takes Mama's hand and leads her onto the dance floor, where he embraces her in his arms and twirls her under the bells. They look happy, but maybe they're just relieved. Assunta has married a good man, and even though it was arranged, you get the feeling they might have chosen each other even if the parents hadn't done the work for them. Assunta is tender with Alessandro, showing a side we've never seen. I hope her sweet nature lasts.

"Nella, right?" a man says from behind me.

I spin on my heel to find myself looking into the face of Renato Lanzara, who seems even more handsome than he did at Delabole farm. He wears a black suit with a dove-gray vestment. His tie is black-and-white-striped silk, which shimmers against his snow-white shirt. He *is* a sheik, or as Chettie calls a very handsome man, a heartbreaker.

"Hello. I'm afraid I don't know your name," I lie, noticing that the golden light in the choir loft seems to follow him around the ordinary world. He doesn't need to know that not only do I know his name, but that I write it everywhere. I've written it with a rock in the mud pit of the pigsty, on the chalkboard in Miss Ciliberti's empty classroom before I wash it down after school, and even in my school ledger until every inch of paper is covered with *Renato Lanzara*, the most musical name I have ever heard.

"I'm Renato."

"Nice to meet you again. You sang beautifully."

"I'm a little rusty."

"It doesn't sound like it to me. Papa has Amedeo Bassi records, and you sound better than he does."

"Thank you." Renato seems impressed that I know about the great Italian tenor. "I'm out of practice because I haven't been in church for a few months."

"Really." Of course, I already know this. I've suffered through catechism, special classes to receive Holy Communion and confirmation, just in hopes of seeing him. "Why haven't you been in church?"

"I went to Italy."

For all the Roseto gossip Chettie repeats, you would think she would have known this little tidbit. "Why did you go?" I ask.

"To study. And to visit my father's village and write about it."

"You're writing?"

"Poetry."

Of course he's a poet! Look at him. He is a romantic, like Keats and Shelley and my favorite, Robert Browning. How many times did I make Miss Stoddard tell the love story of Robert Browning and Elizabeth Barrett? How Robert insisted Elizabeth leave her oppressive father, elope with him, and go to Italy. I wonder if Renato has found his Elizabeth Barrett, and if he hasn't, would he wait for me? I want to tell him that I turned fifteen in January, but that still sounds too young for a man who goes to college and travels the world.

"I should probably be dancing," he says, surveying the girls around the dance floor. Every girl in the place is giving him the eye. "Do you like to dance?" he asks without looking at me.

"I'd rather talk," I tell him honestly.

"Talk?" He laughs and turns to look at me. The way he smiles makes me nervous. I *am* too young, too unsophisticated, and not nearly pretty enough to be talking to the handsomest man in the room. I breathe deeply for courage.

"I'd like to hear more about you," I tell him. "After all, I just learned your name," I lie again. I'm not sure, but it seems that Renato squirms a little. I've made him uncomfortable and I didn't mean to. I have no experience with boys, so I don't know what to say, what not to say, or how to act. Chettie tells me things about boys, but I don't know if they're true, not really. I certainly don't know them from experience. I know that I'm not a coquette. I'm not a modern girl either, or a flapper. And if I go by what I've seen with my sister Assunta, when it comes to a man, a woman should completely change her behavior to woo him. I don't know if that's a good idea. Something tells me it's not. Won't the old Assunta eventually come out and frighten the new husband? And then what?

"What do you want to know?" Renato looks at me with amusement, his composure regained.

My confidence flags, but then curiosity prevails. There are things I want to know. "You go to college."

"I graduate in June."

"I can't wait to go to college. What is it like?"

"Well, college is very hard. You have to study all the time. Or at least I did."

"I don't mind studying. I'll do whatever it takes to become a teacher. I think that teaching a child how to read is the most noble profession there is. Better than a nurse or a housewife. Better than any other job."

"There aren't a lot of girls in college, you know."

"That's their problem." I wave my hand, indicating the girls hovering around the dance floor. He laughs again. "What's it like to live at school, where everyone has the same ambition? What's it like to be around people who think like you?"

Renato smiles. "You may have just said the very thing that I liked best about being away at school. I liked the people I met and how they loved to learn as much as I did. But there's a problem with it. When you come home, you don't fit anywhere."

"That can't be true!"

"Look around. We're quarry miners and farmers and butchers and bakers and factory workers. There's not much of a need for a poet around here."

"You're wrong. Just because we work outside with our hands doesn't mean that we don't dream. We need words to describe our deepest feelings and music to lift us out of the quiet and into a place of inspiration. The Italian people have always found art in the mundane. My mother can milk a cow, but she also makes lace. It's as perfect and delicate as a spiderweb. See?" I show Renato the hem of my skirt. "And

Papa, he plows the field, but he also listens to the opera, and believe me, he understands music with the passion and knowingness of an educated person."

Renato doesn't say a word, he just stares at me.

"I shouldn't ramble on so," I apologize.

"No, no, that's all right," he says, but he looks peevish.

He must think I'm stupid. I'm a flippant farm girl who gets crushes on men far too old for her and then blathers on at them about art while standing in a silly pink dress with juvenile sleeves. This sophisticated man can see right through me. The only true knowledge I have comes from books, not experience. I am outclassed by Renato Lanzara, and now I know it for sure.

Luckily, I see Chettie across the room and walk toward her without saying "excuse me" or "good-bye" to Renato. Why bother? He's more than done with the know-it-all girl from Delabole. But then I feel a hand on my arm. Suddenly, I am not walking to my friend; I'm in the arms of Renato Lanzara, who spins me around the dance floor like the old mop I practice with in Papa's barn. I do my best to keep up, but he is very quick, and I'm new at this. As we whirl around, I catch the faces of Chettie, Elena, and Mrs. Ricci in a blur, who smile at me as though I am dancing well. I know I'm not, though; I am moving through the music, but I don't belong in it. I'm only fifteen and I couldn't even talk my mother into dolman sleeves. I have no business on this dance floor with the most handsome man in the room! How I wish I were twenty-one.

"Thank you," he says as the music stops, depositing me in

the same spot he found me. He disappears into the crowd like a vapor.

"Oh my gosh!" Chettie pulls me aside. "You danced with him! You're the first girl he talked to out of everybody. And the Calzetti girls are here from Martins Creek. The men always go to them first." Chettie looks over at them, and there they are, five sophisticated sisters in cloche hats, split tunic dresses, and shiny stockings, one more alluring than the next. "But not Renato. He went for you!" Chettie is more excited than I am after the first dance of my life. "What did he say? You were talking a long time."

"He talked about college . . . and poetry."

"Poetry?" Chettie sighs. This is better than anything she's read in *Modern Screen*.

"Yes. He writes poetry:

> " '*Never the time and the place*
> '*And the loved one all together!*
> '*This path—how soft to pace!*
> '*This May—what magic weather.*' "

"He wrote that?" Chettie claps her hands together.

"No, Robert Browning. But it's how I feel."

The music swells again and the dance floor fills. I look through the crowd for Renato, but he is gone. I'm not surprised. I don't think it's in my destiny for him to stay, only to come into my life to stir me up and go. Never the time and the place and Renato Lanzara altogether. Not for me, anyway.

*

"The curtains are fine, but I really want a valance. I'll arrange to have some brocade sent over from Delgrosso's." Assunta steps back from the bay window of her living room, surveying my work. Just as she wished, Alessandro bought half a house on Dewey Street, and even negotiated the side with the shade tree. And just as she ordered, I come by and help with the housework. Assunta has made the transition from our farm to town without a hitch. It helps that Alessandro has set up accounts to import nuts and candy with the biggest stores in Allentown, Bethlehem, and Easton. He is making a good living, and Assunta is finding ways to spend the money. She has a mahogany dining table and matching chairs with velvet seats. Room by room, she is turning her home into a showplace.

I am looking forward to the summer passing quickly. I'm hoping Papa makes enough money with his new contract to send me on the trolley from the farm to school, so I don't have to stay with Assunta and Alessandro during the school year. I hate housework and chores, and here, that's all I do, day in and day out. Assunta spends all her time thinking up chores for me to do. She has the cleanest house on Dewey Street.

As soon as Alessandro arrived, Assunta quit her job at the mill, so she has lots of time to worry about things like which way the teacup handles go in the dish hutch. Little bits of Assunta's mean, old ways creep through once in a while, and when her temper flares, Alessandro looks confused. Assunta turns to me. "I'm going to start supper. Nella, take down the laundry on the line in the back."

I grab the deep wicker basket on the back porch and go down the steps to the yard. The clothesline is stretched from tree to tree, almost like a curtain separating the garden from the house. I pull down the stiff white cotton sheets, dried by the hot sun. Alessandro looks up from the garden.

"You need help?" he asks.

"No. This is women's work," I joke.

"Are you going to the farm tonight?"

"I hope so." Quickly I realize I might have hurt his feelings. Alessandro does his best to make me feel at home here, and not like the maid I am. "Just to check on Mama, see if she needs help with the girls. And I want to see the new machinery Papa had delivered." I hope this covers my rudeness.

"My wife is working you too hard."

"It's not so bad," I tell him, but really, what I want to say is that there is no pleasing her and I'll bet every day he wishes he had married one of those quiet girls from his Italian village instead of Assunta the Bossy American.

"In Italy, there is a tradition of a maiden aunt who helps the married sister. Did you know that?"

"I didn't." If Allessandro is trying to cheer me up, it's not working.

"Yes, and the married sister becomes dependent upon the help." He points to the house with the hoe. "I told my wife not to get too comfortable handing chores over to you, because the day will come when you leave us."

"Don't worry about that. College is three years away."

"Ah, yes. You want to go to school," Alessandro remembers.

"Oh, I am *going* to college," I say loudly to him, the old black cat that lies on the stone fence by the garden, and anyone else within earshot on Dewey Street.

"*Bene. Bene.* I believe you." Alessandro laughs. "You are too young to be a maiden aunt, and I think you are meant to be married." He smiles.

"We'll see." I shrug.

"No, you're very agreeable. That goes a long way with a man."

I doubt very much there will be any man who means as much to me as my books, but Alessandro is not going to understand that. Besides, the man I love is too old for me and he'll have a wife before I'm old enough to be one, so what's the use of that? "The Castellucas aren't known for being agreeable," I joke.

"Your family is very loud. It took me time to understand that." Alessandro smiles. "I come from such gentle people."

"So all this is a big shock to you, isn't it?"

"When you love someone, you overlook a lot of things." He says quietly.

"Alessandro?" Assunta appears on the porch. Her tone has the old sharp edge to it.

Alessandro looks up and rests his hoe, wiping his forehead with a red bandanna. "Yes?"

"When you're done there, can you come and move some

furniture? Now that the curtains are up, I see a new way to arrange the chairs so they get the afternoon light. Perfect for reading." Assunta smiles and goes back into the kitchen.

"This is a small house, and yet there is always something to do," Alessandro says with a sigh.

He goes back to his work as I unclip the pillowcases from the line. Assunta has both of us working from sun-up to night-fall. Alessandro will soon realize that there is no pleasing his queen, but I am not going to be the person to point this out to him. He looks at me and shakes his head. Perhaps he already knows.

Papa's contract with the Hellertown stores has been a blessing. He is converting the barn to accommodate a small engine that provides power to the automatic milk tubes so we don't have to do the milking ourselves. Still, Papa has to hook up and run the machines, and he believes it's as much work as the old-fashioned way. But that's Papa, he always thinks the old ways are better, that homemade is always tastier than store-bought, and that anyone who gets in a fancy car and drives fast will miss the views you get when you hitch a wagon to a horse and take your time. Papa likes a slow pace. But he's also ambitious. He knows if he buys a few more cows, he can increase his output for the stores, so without Mama's consent, he has gone back into the quarry to make some extra money. Papa wants two Holstein cows he saw at the market in Allentown.

I put the fresh peach pie Assunta made in the pantry for

supper. She ran out of things for me to do, so she let me go home early. I didn't mind the walk back to the farm; it gives me time to think. I never tire of being alone, and I've learned to savor the long walk from the farm to town and back again. Papa lets me walk by myself as long as it is still day outside. I rarely see anyone coming or going, so I don't know why he worries.

The house is quiet so I grab the last empty tin bucket on the shelf and head out to the field behind our barn. This is perfect weather for berry picking, and when I found the house empty, I knew exactly where Mama and the girls would be.

There was a lot of rain this spring so the ground is loaded with strawberries. There are no trees, and the hot sun on the open field makes for lots of juicy, sweet berries. Mama dug some rows among the bushes, but only so we'd have a place to kneel when we pick them. Mama let the plants grow wild in low, tangled thickets, and everywhere there are clusters of strawberries so red, they're practically magenta, and some are as big as eggs.

Roma takes a bite of one. "Don't eat too many. You'll get sick," I warn her.

"Mama, can we make Papa a strawberry shortcake?" Roma ignores me.

"I don't see why not. Providing there are some left after you're done eating." Mama deposits all the berries from her apron into the bucket.

"Mama, tell us the story of you and Papa," I urge her. The

sun is hot and there are many berries to pick and we need a good story to pass the time.

"Oh, that old story?" Mama complains, but I can tell she's pleased.

"Please," I beg. Of all the stories Mama tells of Italy, their love story is my favorite.

"All right. Papa came to Rimini to fish with his brothers. It was a beautiful day. The ocean was blue and calm, and the sun was hot. Just like today. My father had a small sailboat, but he rented them a canoe, because he wasn't sure they knew what they were doing. But all went well, and they caught many fish, so that night my papa invited all the brothers to supper. Now, my papa was very good at counting. And he saw that your father was one of seven brothers, and Papa had seven daughters. He liked the way the young men behaved on his boat and thought, Surely one of my daughters will like one of these young men. So Mama prepared the barn."

"I love the part about the barn," I tell Elena.

"It's so romantic." Elena sits down on the ground near Mama.

"Well, my mama made supper with the fish. The Castelluca boys had wonderful manners. They were respectful and kind and didn't shove food onto their knives and into their mouths. Mama was impressed that they were so refined. So she invited them to the barn, where she hung lanterns and made a circle with the hay. In the center she put two wooden chairs."

"Why two?" Roma asks.

"Because fate would bring two of us together. Mama arranged us by age, boy-girl, boy-girl, and so on around the circle. Mama was hopeful that my eldest sister—"

"Assunta," Elena and I say in unison.

"—yes, Assunta would find one of the Castelluca boys pleasing, because as the eldest, she must marry first."

"That's so silly. What if you have an eldest who doesn't want to marry?" Elena asks as she empties Dianna's apronful of strawberries into the bucket.

"Every girl wants to marry. Anyway, Papa's eldest brother, Enrico, liked Assunta, but she did not like him. So that left the chairs in the center open for most of the evening. But I was talking with your papa, just friendly, and as Mama was about to put the lanterns out and send everyone home, your father asked me to sit in the chair next to him."

"In the center?"

"And we were married the next week."

"Was Zia Assunta angry?"

"Do you see any letters from my sister Assunta?"

"No," Elena admits.

"She's still angry." Mama sighs. "And still unmarried. Now let's gather these berries. We need to put up the jam."

Elena collects the buckets as I pick a nettle out of my thumb. My hands are stained from the red juice, and even though the afternoon sun is setting on my back, I feel a shiver. My hands look as though there is blood on them. I try not to take this as an omen, but I can't help it. I've always been superstitious and shared my fears with Elena. She looks at my hands and then me, knowing what I am thinking. "Come on, we'll wash up in the springhouse."

We follow Mama and the little ones back down the path to the farmhouse. Assunta and Alessandro pull up in his old Ford with the rumble seat. Assunta is screaming and comes running toward us. "It's Papa! Papa has been hurt! Come!" But Mama is frozen in place. She cannot move. She always said something terrible would happen to Papa in the quarry, and now the news she has always dreaded has come. "*Vieni,* Mama, *vieni!*" Assunta looks at me desperately. I take one arm and she the other and we lift Mama into the car. The girls pile onto the rumble seat and Alessandro steps on the gas.

"Please don't let him die," I say to myself. "Not my papa."

As Alessandro drives us to the hospital, miles from the farm, I see so many new things. Since our family has always had to ride the trolley or walk to Roseto, I see there are lots of small villages beyond our town that I never knew existed. As we pass storefronts and homes with porches that sit on the edges of the sidewalks, I notice that the people don't look Italian. Johnny Bulls, I realize.

Mama has not said a word. She stares straight ahead, but it doesn't look like she's praying. Dianna and Roma hold hands and stay quiet. Elena has tears running down her face, but makes no sound as she cries. Assunta is angry. And me, I'm just numb.

Alessandro turns onto a wide road, which is evidently the main street in a town called Easton. Suddenly the world looks like it does in books. There are sprawling homes set back off the road with green lawns and screened-in porches. Shiny convertible cars sit in garages the size of our barn, and nicer too, with painted doors and small windows. So this is Easton, I think as I look around. This is where the quarry owners live. What a fancy place for Papa to be.

Alessandro parks the car outside the hospital, an enormous gray stone building with pristine white columns in the front. Assunta helps Mama out and we rush into the main entrance. Once inside, we look for help. Assunta points to a nurse behind a large desk. We go to her. Mama tries to speak: "*Mio marito ha avuto un incidente . . .*" Elena and I look at each other. Why is Mama speaking Italian? She knows English as well as we do.

Assunta looks at Mama. "Mama, speak English."

I look at the nurse, a pretty lady with blond hair and a gold cross around her neck. She wears a small gold bar on her white uniform that says L. ANDERSON, R.N. She looks at Mama and then at each one of us. Suddenly, I see in her eyes an expression of such disdain, I am ashamed. She looks at us as though we are animals. She takes a step back and looks down at her notebook.

"We were picking strawberries." I apologize for our appearance. "We own a farm in Delabole. My father's name is Salvatore Castelluca. He was working in the quarry in Pen Argyl. We understand there was an accident."

"There was an accident. An explosion. Your father is in intensive care. That's all I can tell you at this point," she says without looking up from her chart. "I'll tell the doctor you're here." She turns to go.

"Miss Anderson?" She turns back and looks at me, surprised. "Please take Mama with you. Her name is Celeste Castelluca. She wants to see my father. Please."

Mama's eyes fill with tears and she begins to cry. Even the nurse, who has a heart of ice and a pinched mouth that forms a small red o, finally softens. "All right. Mrs. Castellini—"

"Castelluca," I correct her.

"Come with me."

Mama follows the nurse through the doors.

"Girls, come," I tell my sisters, except for Assunta, who stays with Alessandro. As I glance back at them, I see that even they are not dressed for town. Assunta probably had him moving furniture again, as he is in shirtsleeves and doesn't have a hat on. Assunta is wearing an apron. We do look like a bunch of farmers.

I push open the door of the ladies' room. Elena picks up Dianna and places her on one sink, and I pick up Roma and place her on the other. There are no *moppeens* or rags, only soap and water, but we cup our hands under the faucet and rub them full of soap. We wash down our sisters, hands first, and let them rinse under the warm stream of water, then we take my apron and soap the edges and wipe their faces until they are shiny and clean. Then we scrub ourselves.

"Papa would not want to see us dirty," Elena tells the girls. "And you've been very good." She gives them each a hug.

"Give me your aprons," I instruct them. The girls lift them off and hand them to me. Their work jumpers underneath are not so bad. They're shabby, of course, just brown shifts made from an old dress of Mama's, but so what, we were working in the ground. I smooth my sisters' skirts and fix their hair. Without a comb, it's not easy. Then I take our four aprons and fold them into a small square, tying them with the sashes into a small knot. "Now remember, sit quietly," I tell them. Elena takes Dianna's hand and I take Roma's and we go back out into the waiting room. We sit down next to Alessandro and Assunta.

Suddenly the swinging doors that Mama and the nurse went through open wide. Chettie has her arms around her mother, almost holding her up. I run to them but Mrs. Ricci looks through me as though I'm not there. "Mrs. Ricci? It's me, Nella." I look at Chettie. Her face, which I have never seen frowning or sad, seems to break into a thousand pieces as she weeps.

"What happened, Chettie?" Chettie shakes her head and I know. Her father is dead. I can't believe Carlo Ricci—who was so kind to me when I was afraid—is gone.

"Who is watching the children?" I ask her softly.

"Mrs. . . ." she begins to sob. ". . . Mrs. . . . Mrs. Spadoni. Lavinia. We took the trolley."

"I will take you home. Come," Alessandro says, standing behind me.

"Thank you," I say to my brother-in-law, who for the first time since he married my sister feels like real family. He puts his arms around Chettie and her mother. "Come," he says again.

"Oh *Jesu, Jesu*," Mrs. Ricci moans softly.

"Come on, Mama." Chettie holds her mother's waist tightly. I am sure if Chettie let go, her mother would fall to the ground. Alessandro opens the door and walks them out. My heart is so broken for my friend that for a moment I almost forget about my own troubles. Roma puts her hand in mine.

"Is our papa going to die too?" she asks.

"Just pray," I tell her, kissing her on her head. But I am telling her to do something I cannot do myself. I don't know if I believe it even helps, or if God is listening; in fact, I doubt it. If He were, why would He abandon the Ricci family? They are good people, and I know the depth of their goodness, because they have always treated me like one of their own.

"Mama!" Assunta rushes to Mama, who walks slowly through the swinging doors. "How is he?"

Elena helps Mama sit down. "He's going to be all right . . ." she begins. We hug her and then one another. "But not for a while."

"What happened?" I ask softly.

"Papa, Mr. Ricci, and two other men were in the quarry when dynamite exploded nearby. Mr. Ricci was closer to it than Papa. Papa's leg was hurt."

"And the other two men?"

"They got out all right. Papa got hurt trying to save Mr. Ricci." Mama cries. "The doctor doesn't know how well Papa will heal, it's early yet."

"He'll be fine, Mama. I know it," I reassure her. But we are all thinking the same thing: How can we run the farm without Papa? How can we deliver the milk he has promised to the stores? Without Papa, we are lost.

"I prayed," Roma tells Mama.

"Keep praying. All of you. We must."

"Mama . . . Mr. Ricci . . ." Assunta begins.

"I know. I know." Mama puts her hand up. "I don't know what they will do. All those children."

The sun comes up over the barn so brightly it seems to set the cornfield ablaze in yellow light. Even the old fence around the cowshed sparkles as though it is gold-leafed like the Communion railing at Our Lady of Mount Carmel. I have always loved the summertime, but this year it is a burden. With Papa still in the hospital, we have been consumed with all the work that must be done. No wading in the creek, no climbing trees, and no making ice cream in the old vat; there is no time to play, only to work.

The front field that goes from our house over the hill and down to Delabole Road is covered in white daisies. To make Mama feel better, we gather bunches each day and fill every old crock in the house with them. Flowers always seem to cheer her up. Alessandro and Assunta have moved out to the farm for the month that Papa will be in Easton Hospital. I don't know what we would have done if Alessandro did not have a car. He takes Mama to and from the hospital three times a week, and often on Friday nights she sleeps in the chair in Papa's hospital room to keep him company.

The doctor explained that the explosion shattered Papa's right leg. He will have to wear a brace until the bones heal, and that could be many months. Papa will not be able to work the farm until next spring. Alessandro has kept the farm going with all of our help. Sometimes I think he does a better job with the Hellertown contract than Papa, because he thinks of modern ways to economize. For example, Alessandro figured out a way to put a cooling tank in the springhouse. He arranged for the truck to come from the market in late afternoon, to take advantage of a second milking. He still needs Papa's knowledge, though. When the equipment fails, Alessandro drives to Easton Hospital to ask Papa how to fix it.

"Can we wade in the creek?" Roma asks as she pours water into Moxie's trough in the barn.

"It's so hot out." Dianna fans herself.

"Go ahead, but don't stay out all afternoon," I remind them.

"Just holler for us," Roma yells over her shoulder as she races Dianna to the creek.

I follow them outside and watch them run. I pick up my book bag and go out to the old elm to do some reading. Miss Ciliberti gave me a reading list for the summer. I will begin the tenth grade in a few weeks, but with all that has been going on, I haven't had a chance to read everything on the list. I did finish *Oliver Twist*, but I am having a hard time with *Julius Caesar*. I much prefer the sonnets of Shakespeare; the plays are more difficult for me. As soon as I settle in to read the play, I hear the honking of Alessandro's horn.

Alessandro pulls up in front of the gate and jumps out of his car. "I have good news, Nella. Papa is coming home."

"Come in the house. You must tell Mama." I open the gate and we walk up to the porch. "Thank you for all you've done for us. We couldn't have made it this summer without you."

"You are my family now." Alessandro smiles.

"Let me look at you," Mama says as we line up for inspection before we climb into Alessandro's car to go to Easton Hospital. "I want Papa to see us at our very best." Mama has put her hair up and wears her navy blue dress. I am the last to climb into the car; before I get into the rumble seat, I hug her. She smells of lavender cologne that her sisters sent from Italy; she only wears it on special occasions.

Assunta gets in last and sits next to her husband. This summer has been very hard on her. She thought for sure her farm days were over when she moved into Roseto. And although she has been crabby from time to time, for the most part, she has been patient.

"Mama, will we be able to go to the Big Time?" Dianna wants to know. Beginning this weekend Our Lady of Mount Carmel will be holding a weeklong celebration in honor of the Blessed Mother. It has earned the nickname "the Big Time" because there's no greater celebration in Roseto.

There is a carnival, tents filled with Italian delicacies lining Garibaldi Avenue on both sides, a clambake at the American Legion, a cakewalk in front of Tony's Café, and games of chance. Of course, the booths pay rent to the church; any profits they make selling their wares, they can keep.

On Sunday there will be a solemn procession that begins with a rosary and the service of the Blessed Sacrament. This year, for the first time, there will be a queen, a lucky girl chosen from all the girls in Roseto, who will crown the statue of the Blessed Mother before the statue is carried down the street, followed by the priest and the people as they say the rosary.

"We'll see, honey. It depends how Papa is feeling," Mama tells her.

"Mama, I think for certain the girls will be attending the Big Time," Alessandro says with a grin.

"Really?" Roma's eyes widen.

"Someone has to help me in my stand."

"You have a stand?" Dianna is thrilled.

"Well, I'm not just a farmer." Alessandro laughs. "Remember, I sell nuts and candy, and everyone loves *torrone*, yes?"

The girls giggle. "Yes!" *Torrone* is a great delicacy, a white nougat candy made with sugar and nuts. At the carnival, it is sold by weight; the customer asks for a hunk and it is cut off a slab the size of a boulder.

"His family shipped the candy over from Italy. My living room is filled with it. We've got *torrone*, and chickpeas on strings, and red, white, and green ribbon candy," Assunta says.

"Like the Italian flag!" Elena laughs.

"Wait until you see the stuff! If we sell it all we'll make a good profit. Alessandro wants us all to work in the stand." Assunta adds, "I hope you all will help."

"Absolutely," I promise her. After a summer working on the farm, I would love to go to town. There hasn't been any time. I've wanted to catch up with Chettie, though I've heard her family is doing all right. It turns out that Chettie's relatives in Philadelphia sent help, so at least they can stay in the house on Dewey Street. I am looking forward to September and getting back to school. I've missed Chettie terribly this summer.

"What are you thinking about?" Elena asks as we make the turn onto Easton Road to pick Papa up at the hospital.

"How the summer is almost gone."

"It's almost time for you to go back to school."

"I can't wait."

"I'll miss you. When you go to school, it seems like you don't have much time for me. You have all your friends there," Elena says.

"I'm sorry. I don't mean to make you feel left out." I wish I could explain to Elena what it is like to be with people who aren't family. Life on the farm is so claustrophobic sometimes. It takes so long for news to reach us; and when I'm in town, there is an energy that crackles under the surface of everything, fueling my ambition. From the hum of the sewing machines when I visited Assunta at the factory, to the bells on the delivery trucks, to the shops busy with patrons, right down to the hometown newspaper, *Stella di Roseto*, there's motion, and excitement, and a sense of possibility. "Maybe you can stay with Assunta once in a while," I say. "We both will! And we can do things in town."

Elena shakes her head sadly. "Mama needs me. And now, with Papa, she needs me even more."

Alessandro parks the car close to the hospital entrance. One by one he helps us out of the old jalopy, extending his hand until all of the Castelluca girls, including his wife, are standing on the sidewalk. For one awkward moment, we all look to Mama. We haven't seen Papa in a month; only Alessandro and Mama have come by regularly, and although Mama has given us detailed reports on Papa's progress, we are afraid he won't be the same. We follow Mama into the hospital. She goes right up to the nurse's station. Miss Anderson, the same nurse who looked down on us a few weeks ago, is behind the desk. What luck that she will see us all again in our finest clothes.

"Miss Anderson?" Mama says to her.

The nurse turns and surveys us. This time she looks at us with approval. "Good afternoon."

"We've come to collect Mr. Castelluca."

"He's all ready to go," she tells us with a smile. We follow her through the doors to Papa's room. The little ones enter first, followed by Elena and me, then Assunta, Alessandro, and finally Mama. Roma and Dianna run to Papa, who, dressed in a good shirt and trousers, stands up to greet them. He is shaky, but he finds his footing. He is much thinner, and his hair is now mostly white. The accident must have been a worse trauma than we knew. Papa has a crutch in his right arm. His leg is in a brace from ankle to thigh. Ribbons of leather buckled to a steel rod hold Papa's leg in place. We gather around him, hugging and kissing him.

Papa looks at Alessandro. "This is why it's best to have daughters."

CHAPTER FOUR

*S*ome Rosetans are superstitious, so if the Big Time celebration has good weather, this portends a prosperous
year to all those who pray to the Blessed Lady. The opening
night of the festivities is balmy, with a full moon so close,
you'd swear you could touch it from the top of the Ferris
wheel. The night sky is a clear, deep blue, a velvety backdrop
for the twinkling lights that line the booths down either side
of Garibaldi Avenue. There is much to do: games, rides,
trinkets for sale, and Italian delicacies to sample like pizza
fritta, puffs of hot dough doused in sugar.

The Bersaglieri Band of New York City, in their red
plumed hats, march up the steps of the church and into
formation. As they begin to play, the crowd at their feet grows.

People seem to pour out onto the church plaza from every-where—from the side streets, the parking lots, and off the trolley.

"We should do well tonight," I tell Alessandro. I hope he makes lots and lots of money and that there's not a crumb of *torrone* left.

"I hope so." He smiles.

There is no way to thank Alessandro for his help to our family. I doubt Papa will ever be able to do the work he once did. Alessandro has taken over all of Papa's chores, including the most difficult job, plowing the field to collect the hay for the winter. Papa has always done the work with the horses and an old-fashioned plow, and used to be able to break an acre a day during harvesttime. Alessandro figured he could triple that with modern equipment, and went to the bank to borrow money to buy a tractor. Alessandro got the loan and bought a used Allis Chalmers tractor from 1918 from a farmer in nearby Flicksville.

We're happy to be able to reciprocate in a small way for all Alessandro has done by helping him out in his booth. Assunta made us white cotton pinafores with an embroidered *P* on them, so everyone would know that we were working for Pagano's Importing: Dried Fruit, Nuts & Candy Inc.

"Do you think there's too much on the sign?" Alessandro asks as he hacks off a slice of *torrone* for a customer.

I look up at the red, white, and green sign that says PAGANO'S in swirly gold letters. "Nope. I think it looks very professional." Our booth has the best spot on Garibaldi.

We're right across from the church steps at the top of the hill. No one will miss us.

The fire company sells delectable sausage and pepper sandwiches next door to us. We watch as the men work tirelessly over the open grills, basting the peppers and onions in olive oil, turning the sausage until it grills to a crispy brown, then taking a sheet of waxed paper, slicing a crusty roll open, filling it with the delicious mixture, and handing off the finished product to the customer. People come from miles around for the sausage and pepper sandwiches, and if the line outside their booth is any indication, they will run out of sausage before they run out of customers.

"There's the queen." Elena points to a pretty girl who walks through the crowd in a simple white linen chemise.

"That's Michelina de Franco," I tell her. "She graduated from Columbus School in June." Surely she was the prettiest girl in school, with her blond bob and soft blue eyes. The boys called her Venus de Milo because she's a classic beauty. I think she looks a lot like the screen star Mae Murray, with her porcelain skin and Cupid's-bow mouth. Michelina is also graceful and moves through the crowd with ease. She deserves to be the first queen of the Roseto Big Time.

"You know how she won, don't you?" Assunta says quietly.

"She's the most beautiful girl in Roseto?"

"No. She sold the most tickets. That's how you win. You go door-to-door and raise money for the church and whoever sells the most tickets is the queen."

"Hmm," I think aloud. "Industriousness is more important than sheer beauty. That's my kind of contest."

"I don't know what's interesting about it. It's a racket. A greedy parish priest looking to stuff the coffers shouldn't determine who's queen," Assunta huffs.

Assunta is jealous of everybody. Michelina because she's lovely, Father Impeciato because he's powerful, and probably the Columbia Fire Company of the sausage and pepper stand because they have the longest line of customers. She'll never be happy. Alessandro looks at me and winks. He knows. "Why don't you girls take a break and go take a ride on the Ferris wheel?"

"We don't have tickets," Roma says sadly.

Alessandro fishes four yellow tickets out of his shirt pocket. "Now you do. You've been working hard all afternoon. Go."

"Thank you!" Elena says, gathering up Roma and Dianna. She lifts the plank across the side of the stand and we file out. Assunta shoots her husband a dirty look, but before she can call us back to work, we are a part of the crowd, moving toward the line at the Ferris wheel.

"Assunta is in a nasty mood," I say.

"She has good reason," Elena replies.

"Don't make excuses for her. Since the day she got married, she's been hiding her true personality. It's as though she put a lid on a boiling pot of water and sat on it; now, after a few months of hiding it, the steam is about to blow."

"She's going to have a baby," Elena says quietly.

"She is?" I am ashamed of my fresh mouth.

"I heard her tell Mama." Elena motions for me to lower my voice so the little ones won't hear what we're talking about.

"Why hasn't she told us?"

"She's having a lot of pain and isn't sure the baby will grow."

"Why is she working? She's been on her feet all day in the stand in the hot sun. That can't be good for her."

"They need the money," Elena says as she steers us through the crowd. "She wants to keep the house on Dewey Street, and they have a mortgage, and since Alessandro spent the summer helping us on the farm, they are behind."

"Why didn't she tell us so we could help?"

"When has Assunta ever asked anyone for help?"

Elena holds Dianna's hand and Dianna holds Roma's as they get in the line to take a ride on the Ferris wheel. I follow them, looking around for Chettie. She hadn't made it to the candy stand, but maybe I'll run into her. I know she loves the rides.

The line for the Ferris wheel moves quickly. The carney who runs it pulls the large lever crank and stops the ride, depositing a couple out onto the ramp. He motions to Roma and Dianna, who run up the ramp and sit down in the swinging seat.

"This one's too short without an adult." He points at Roma.

"I'll go with them." Elena goes up the ramp. She puts Roma in the middle and then sits down with her arms around her. I motion to them to go ahead without me: there's no room for a fourth person in the seat. Dianna and Roma hold hands as the carney snaps the bar shut.

"What about you?" Dianna shouts as the seat jerks up and over my head. I wave and smile at my sisters.

"Are you gonna go alone?" the carney asks me.

I climb up the ramp and sit alone in the seat. The carney goes to close the bar. I look at the line of ticket holders and see Renato Lanzara, smiling at me. I wave to him. "Wait a second," I tell the carney. I can feel my cheeks flush a little as Renato comes up the ramp and joins me in the seat.

"I can't fly over Roseto alone," I tell him. The carney snaps the bar shut across us and pulls the giant lever, the Ferris wheel jerks, and we move up. I pat my hair, which Elena braided neatly. Then I remember the pinafore over my blouse and skirt. Why am I always wearing something childish when I see Renato? Why can't I be prepared for once?

"Something wrong?" he asks.

I look at him. He is crisp and neat in a white shirt and beige linen trousers. His suspenders are striped red, white, and green, an homage to the Italian celebration, I'm sure. He is tanned, *bronzato*, Mama calls it. "I always look so silly when I see you."

"What are you talking about?"

"This pinafore. It's childish."

"I like it."

"You're just being nice."

"No, really. I like it. What's the P stand for?"

"Pagano. My brother-in-law's candy company. We're next to the sausage and peppers." When I say this, I realize I must smell like them too. This is horrible. Nothing that ever happens to me in real life is like I imagine it. If I'd known I would be meeting Renato for a Ferris wheel ride, I would have worn a simple linen chemise, just like Michelina de Franco, and borrowed some of Mama's lavender cologne instead of smelling like Roseto's favorite sandwich.

"Sausage and pepper sandwiches are my favorite."

"It's a good thing." I smooth my pinafore over my skirt. The ride begins to whirl around. I get butterflies in my stomach, so I grip the safety bar.

"Are you afraid?" Renato wants to know.

"Well, I don't have wings, so if something goes wrong . . ."

Renato puts his arm around me; my insides begin to shake, and I know it's not the ride, but the joy of being so close to him. As we whirl around, I can see my sisters' feet overhead as we spin. I'm so glad they can't see Renato and me. This isn't a very good example for the little ones. I'm with a boy and haven't asked Papa's permission. But I don't care: this is for me, and I don't think in my whole life I have ever been this happy. Suddenly the Ferris wheel lurches to a stop. We're suspended high in the air, the rooftops on Garibaldi Avenue look like stars below us in the moonlight as the hill descends into darkness. I'm a little afraid of the height, but more sad that the ride is half over.

"Look, you can see my sister's roof on Dewey Street from here." I point.

"How's your father?" Renato asks. "He was so gracious to me when I came out for the hog killing."

"We're lucky. He's walking much better." Thoughts of Papa remind me to take Renato's hand from around my shoulder and place it on his lap. I really shouldn't be so close to a man without permission.

"The farm life is very hard. I don't know if I could do it."

The way Renato says this sounds condescending, so I am glad I just took his arm away. There is a part of me that understands how he feels. I would never have chosen to be born into a family of farmers. I wish my papa were a barber or a brick mason or a grocer. But Papa loves the land and his animals and my mother and a life away from the noise of town. He was raised on a farm in Foggia, and the land is what he knows. How can I explain this to an educated man? So instead of trying, I caustically reassure him, "I'm sure you'll never have to, so don't worry about it."

Renato feels the chill of my comment. "I didn't mean to offend you."

"But you did, though I don't hold it against you. See, I'm not a farmer either. I never liked the quiet and the chores as much as I should have. I did them, I still do them, but as soon as I could read and saw what life was like for other people in other places, I began to judge what I came from. And you know, that's not good. Because I can't help what I am or where I come from."

"You should never apologize for what you are."

"I'm not." I look out beyond the sparkling lights of Roseto

and off into the inky black beyond the Blue Mountains. As much as I'm intimidated by Renato and his life experience, I'm equally inspired by it, so I always tell him what's on my mind. I never feel like I have anything to lose. "I have a question for you." I turn to face him.

The carney hollers up from the ground, "Folks, we're stuck. Stay calm and don't swing in the seats. We'll get 'er cranked up shortly."

I take the news from the carney below as an omen. I'm meant to spend a few extra moments with Renato. "Why do you disappear?"

"What do you mean?" he asks innocently.

"It seems like I see you, and then months go by before I see you again. Do I do something to offend you?"

"No. Not at all," Renato says quickly.

"What is it then?"

"You're too young for me, Nella."

"I'm fifteen now."

"I'm twenty-two. Now, you don't seem fifteen—"

"Well, you seem every day of twenty-two."

"—but you are fifteen. And it's not right for me to court someone your age."

"Because we haven't been properly introduced? Because you haven't spoken with Papa and asked his permission?" I am so sorry that I pointed out these things to him. Not only am I too young, but I know he would never compromise my reputation.

"It's just the way it is," he says simply.

"You seem to pick up and go out of town for months on end."

"I went to Italy."

"No, I know that. I mean other times. The rest of the time." I don't want Renato to think that I've been monitoring his comings and goings, but I have. When I would come into town to help Assunta, I would ask around casually about Renato. He is a mystery man of sorts, no one seems to know what he does or where he goes. "Do you have a sweetheart?"

"Some."

"More than one?"

"I'm a young man." He shrugs.

"Not that young. My papa was married at twenty."

He laughs again. "Does it bother you that I see lots of girls?"

"Why should it bother me?" I bury my hands in the pockets of my pinafore.

"I don't know."

"Of course you're going to have girlfriends. Why wouldn't you?" I look over the side of our seat, and my stomach flips. I won't look down again, I decide.

"You're very bold and you're very honest," Renato says without judgment.

"And you're honest with me, which I appreciate. You're right. I'm probably too young for you. But I wish I wasn't." How I wish I hadn't said that. I sound like a silly girl for sure.

Renato reaches into my pocket and takes my hand. "That is something that will change."

The way he looks at me makes me blush. He knows I won't always be fifteen, and so do I. "That's what Mama says. You can't believe where your youth goes. How fast it slips away. It's sugar in the rain."

"Your mama is right."

"So that's why you put your arm around me," I say aloud. "Because you put your arm around all the girls."

"Not all the girls."

"Some?"

"A few."

"Good for you." I look at him and smile. "Why shouldn't you?"

He looks at me quizzically. "Usually I get slapped if I don't make a girl believe she is the only one."

"It's always better to accept the truth." I look away.

"You don't compete with other girls?"

"For a boy?"

"For anything."

"What good would that do? There is always someone more beautiful, more accomplished, and then someone backward, less intelligent. Why would I compare myself to anyone else?"

"All girls do."

"Not me. That's a waste of time. I have a sister who has spent her life complaining because she feels she never gets what she wants. She's a true malcontent. She always thinks there's somebody out there who has it better than she does. She can never say to another girl, 'That's a pretty dress you're wearing,' because she's worried that her own dress isn't pretty enough."

"That's how girls are. At least the ones I know."

"Well, that's too bad," I tell him.

Renato looks out over Roseto and smiles. "You're a rare one, Nella."

"Well, sometimes I'd like to be more like everybody else. But I can't. I think about things too much, and that's not good. Being thoughtful is a curse."

"Not if you value your intellect."

"I do. I just wish I had . . . whimsy. That's it. Whimsy. The ability to dance through life instead of trudging like a farmer."

"Leave whimsy to the giggly girls. You don't need it. You have brains and beauty, a rare combination."

"Why do you think I'm beautiful?" I'm not playing the coquette. I really want to know what Renato Lanzara finds beautiful.

"Let's see." Renato takes my face in his hands and looks at me clinically. "You have a good nose. It's straight. And the freckles from the sun . . ."

"My mother won't let me use powder, but the minute she does, I'm covering them," I promise.

"Don't ever cover them. They're you." He moves my face to a different angle. "Your eyes I like best because they change color in the light. Now they're dark brown, but in bright sunlight, they have a lot of green in them. Emerald green."

We sit quietly. This is one part of being alone with a man that Chettie never mentioned. The silence. The in-between-the-words time, when no talking is necessary. I watch the movement of the crowd below. There are no empty spaces in the streets. From this angle, it seems people are shoulder to shoulder, which will make Father Impeciato very happy, as the church will raise lots of money.

Suspended there in the soft summer night, I suddenly wish the Ferris wheel would start again so this ride would end. I don't want to be near him anymore, it's too hard. I don't want to fall for Renato any more deeply than this girlish crush I have on him. He will never be mine. Something inside tells me so. I also know that I've met my match with him, but that doesn't mean I'll get what I long for. There are many women in his circle, and I'm just a kid to him. That's the extent of it. I have gotten all the good stuff I can out of our spontaneous rendezvous. He told me I was beautiful, something no one has ever told me before, and it is not going to get any better than that. Now I know a little more about him, and really, that is all I ever hoped for from Renato Lanzara.

"Nella?"

I look at him. He puts one arm around me and, with the other, takes my hand. He leans over and kisses my nose. I try to say something, but I can't. If I were a proper girl, I would tell him to stop. I always thought I was a proper girl, but I guess you can't know that until you are faced with a kiss from a man you're not courting. Now I know for sure I'm not a proper girl. He smiles at me, then he kisses my cheek. He gives me several small kisses on my mouth. I want to say something, but cannot. I just feel the soft presses of his lips against mine. The kisses are more tender than I ever imagined them, and certainly more welcome. Why don't I tell him to stop?

"All right, folks. We're startin' 'er up," the carney says from below. My first kiss is over too fast. I sit back in the seat, which swings precariously back and forth as the wheel starts to turn again. I put my hand on my lips and look away. The full moon, round and silver like a vanity mirror, is so close I can practically see my reflection in it. If only I could stay in midair forever, my feet far from the ground and my heart beating so loudly all of Roseto must be able to hear it.

"You cannot tell me the first-kiss story enough," Chettie whispers as we follow the parishioners down Garibaldi Avenue, saying the rosary. The Sunday solemn procession has commenced. We follow Michelina de Franco, who leads the procession in a white gown and cape. She's crowned the statue of the Blessed Lady with a tiara made with the gemstones donated by all the ladies of the town. Father Impeciato went door-to-door collecting jewelry, old rings, precious stones, and gold from parishioners in order to commission the crown. A jeweler in New York City took the jewels and gold and turned them into the spectacular tiara.

The statue is being carried on a board by six men in black suits and sashes. The Knights of Columbus, in their regal white-plumed hats and swords, follow her, creating an honor guard. Michelina's court, which includes her sisters and senior girls from Columbus School, follow behind carrying baskets of deep red roses.

Father Impeciato walks alongside the statue, turning to observe the sea of penitents who follow behind with their rosaries threaded through their fingers. There seem to be hundreds of us. Evidently many people need the help of the Blessed Mother to intercede for them in heaven. I am praying for Papa to heal. The Roseto Coronet Band provides a somber drumbeat as we walk.

Chettie leans close to me. "That is the most magnificent kiss I have ever heard of. Gloria Swanson's never been kissed like that. Never in midair!"

"I'll never see him again," I tell her. I know we shouldn't be talking about kisses when we're praying, but that kiss was more real to me than any prayer I've ever said.

"Sure you will. He lives on Garibaldi, for crying out loud."

"No, no, I'll never see him again because I'll never walk down this street again." As we pass the Lanzara Barbershop, I refuse to look.

"He's not there. But his father is," Chettie whispers.

"What about his mother?"

"His mother died many years ago. Didn't he tell you?" Chettie looks over her shoulder. "Okay, we're past the house now."

I take a deep breath and exhale slowly.

"Nella, you didn't do anything wrong. He kissed *you*, don't forget that. You should walk down Garibaldi with pride.

Besides, you have to walk down this street when you start back to school. It's where the trolley stops."

"I'll go down Chestnut instead."

"That's silly. Remember what he said: you're young, but that will change. He practically promised to wait for you!"

This is where Chettie, with her big heart, lacks common sense. Renato told me plainly that there are lots of girls in his life. He can choose whomever he wants. Why would a man so handsome and smart wait for *me*? I am more of an expert on boys than Chettie now. I could teach her a thing or two.

Sister Bernarda, in her black Salesian habit with the veil to her waist and white wimple, gives us a warning look. I rub my rosary beads and pray along with the group: "Hail Mary, full of grace . . ." I let my mind wander while my lips move through the familiar prayer. I feel like such a phony. I don't believe indulgences do one bit of good. Does God really want us to offer up our suffering to prove our love for Him? There is enough suffering without playacting it for God. What are all these people doing? Why are they walking and praying in the hot sun? Do they think their prayers have any chance of being answered? Do they really believe that the requests they write on slips of paper and give to the queen of the Big Time to put in a box and offer up later at Mass will have any impact in heaven? I am amazed at their tenacity, for I have not one ounce of it. I can't believe that Chettie can still pray after all she has been through. Not only does she pray out of duty, she prays out of a desire for good to come to everyone. I think she would have a better chance shooting skeet and hitting the bull's-eye blindfolded at the archery booth than having God answer her prayers. Is there any chance at all that God is listening?

As I walk Chettie home to Dewey Street after the procession, our feet ache.

"I should have prayed for shoes that didn't rub," I say.

Chettie laughs. "Next time."

"Do you ever have a feeling of doom?" I ask her. The moment it comes out of my mouth, I regret saying it. After all, she lost her father in a horrible quarry disaster; of course she knows tragedy.

"I never have one before something happens, if that's what you mean. Why, do you?"

"Yes. All the time."

"About what? Renato?"

"Everything."

"You're just afraid, that's all. You really like him and you want him to like you, so you're telling yourself something terrible will happen so you won't get hurt. But my mother says there is no way to get through life without getting hurt."

"Now *there's* something to pray for: not getting hurt."

"Like Sister Theresa said, 'Life is a vale of tears,'" Chettie says sadly. "I wish Papa would come back. But he won't. We still have to live."

"I know."

"Even with all the bad things, something beautiful can happen. You got kissed! I can't wait for my first kiss."

"Anthony Marucci?"

"Too shy, with me anyway. If I wait for him to kiss me, I'll have white hair."

"He might surprise you," I say.

"Nella, there's something I have to tell you." Chettie stops in front of her house and turns to me. The August sun is beating down hard on us, and I wish it were like the old days when we were girls and Mrs. Ricci would make us lemonade and we'd sit out under the porch awning and tell stories. "I'm not going back to school."

"*What?*"

"I have to go to work."

"I thought your uncle in Philadelphia was helping you!"

"It's not enough, and my mother is afraid we're too much of a burden on him. They're taking me at the blouse factory. They have a lot of openings there."

"But Chettie, you want to be a nurse."

"We need the money now, Nella."

"But your education . . ."

"I can't think about that right now."

"There has to be another way."

"There isn't," Chettie says. "But it's all right. I'm sure it won't be so bad." She turns and goes slowly up the steps.

I walk to the trolley stop. Alessandro gave me money for the trolley back to Delabole if I promised to say a rosary for his and Assunta's baby. They finally told us the happy news this morning after Mass.

By the time I arrive at the farm, I'm tired from the long procession, and the news from Chettie depresses me.

As I lift the latch on the gate at the end of our lane, I see Alessandro's car parked by the barn. I wish Chettie weren't the oldest in her family. How lucky we are that Assunta has married a nice man who helps us. It's as if Papa finally got the son he wanted so badly.

I go to the house, following the sound of voices. I hear a lot of murmuring between Alessandro and Papa, probably another discussion about the equipment on the farm. I hear Papa say, "You must go," just as I open the screen door and slip into the house.

"What's wrong?" I ask when everyone turns to look at me. Assunta leans back on the settee while Papa sits on a straight-backed chair from the kitchen, his leg with the brace strapped tightly to it extended in front of him. Mama stands and paces. Alessandro leans against the doorframe, holding what looks like a letter.

"How was the procession?" Papa asks.

"I prayed for everyone."

"We need it." Papa looks at Alessandro.

I turn to my brother-in-law. "Did you get bad news?"

"Alessandro has to go home to Italy. His father is very ill," Assunta says quietly.

"I will not go," he tells her. "You are not feeling well. My place is with my wife."

"If it were my papa, I would go," Assunta tells her husband. "You must go."

"We have the farm to worry about," Alessandro says, looking at Papa.

My heart sinks at this news. Alessandro can't go back to Italy! What will we do? It takes a month to get there, a month to get back; even if he stays a short while, even a couple of weeks, it will be winter by the time he returns, and who will run the farm until then? Papa stands up slowly. "My leg is getting better every day."

"But it's not completely healed," Mama argues.

"Celeste." Papa makes a motion to Mama to stop nagging. "Alessandro has his own family back home. Let him go. We'll have to make do."

"I'm going to work in the blouse factory," Elena says, looking at me.

Instantly, I calculate Elena's absence in terms of chores around the farm. "I can do the milking before I go to school in the morning," I say. "And when I get home at night, I can feed the horses and tend to the chickens."

"We need more help than that, Nella."

"Anything, Papa. I can plow, I can harvest, I can take care of the hogs and the cows. I'll do whatever you need."

"To keep the contract with the stores, you'll have to go to work, too," Papa says sadly.

"But Papa . . . " I feel a lump form in the pit of my stomach. "I have school."

"It wouldn't be for long. You could go back in a year." Papa goes on to explain how it would be no problem for me to take a year off and then return to high school, as though it were done every day. I know if I leave Columbus School now, it is unlikely that I will return.

"No one goes back, Papa."

"Sure they do. You skipped eighth grade right into the ninth."

"It's different now. It's high school. They have rules."

"I will talk to the teacher."

"Fine, Papa," I tell him. Papa has made his mind up and there is no changing it. I feel my eyes sting with tears, hot tears of self-pity, and I don't want anyone to see them. I slip out the front door and head toward the barn, where I can be alone. I barely make it there before I kneel down and start to cry. I'm never going to be a teacher. My dream is gone, and all because of this stupid farm. How I wish Papa would sell it! Sell it and we'll move to town and make a living like everyone else. The extra money Papa used to make in the quarry is gone forever, and we've relied for too many months on Alessandro's generosity. If I were a man, no one would tell me what to do with my life. I can't give up my dream—I won't!

CHAPTER FIVE

*T*he doors of Our Lady of Mount Carmel are locked at midnight and reopened in time for daily Mass at 7 A.M. For all the hours the church is open, we sinners are welcome to stop by and lessen our burdens.

As I climb the steps and pull the church door open, I fish out six pennies from my apron pocket. There is an old lady sitting in the back row muttering the rosary as I pass. I kneel and cross myself at the main altar (but only because there is someone watching) and then open the Communion railing and go into the alcove where the Blessed Mother statue resides for the rest of the year when she is not being carried down Garibaldi Avenue with an elaborate crown on her head for the Big Time celebration.

I kneel before her and begin. I don't recite the Hail Mary or the Litany of the Saints, but my own prayer. "Blessed Lady, my life has taken a terrible turn. I only wanted to be a teacher to help children, not out of my own selfish needs. Okay, maybe that's not entirely true. I like to read and I'm proud of being smart. But now I can't go to school. I'm lighting these candles to beg you to change my father's mind. I need to go to Columbus School and then I need to go to college. Please help me." I push the pennies through the slot, one at a time, until all six have clunked to the bottom of the brass box. I want God to hear exactly how much money I am sacrificing for this indulgence.

I light six candles at the feet of the Blessed Mother, hoping that she hears me. At least she will see these candles and know that I am serious. That is, *if* she is listening. I am so desperate to go back to school that I am inventing faith to get me what I want. Maybe I am being punished for my doubts, but I can't help them. It seems whenever we get a little bit ahead, something terrible happens and we have to start all over again. Yes, we have been blessed with Alessandro, and yes, I suppose I'm lucky that Miss Stoddard thought I was smart enough to continue on in school, but these gifts have been yanked away at the whims of fate. If six pennies and six candles will help my cause, I can only pray that they will bring me the results I want.

The old lady kneels next to me. She makes the sign of the cross and gathers her rosary beads in one hand. She wears a black lace mantilla; her hair is artfully arranged underneath the veil like a cluster of white roses. I quickly make the sign of the cross and get up to leave.

"Why six?" she whispers.

I kneel back down and look at the blazing row of candles at the feet of the statue. "I had six pennies."

"Light a seventh candle."

I look at the old lady as if she's crazy. "I don't have another penny," I tell her as I get up.

"No, you must light a seventh. It's a mystical number."

I smile politely and then decide to be honest. "If it's so mystical, then why did God send me in here with six pennies?"

The lady does not smile; she keeps her eyes on the Blessed Lady and fishes in her pocket, dropping a penny into the box. "Light the candle and pray for what you need," she says.

I light the candle. "Thank you."

"Don't forget Saint Anthony in your prayers. He's never failed me."

The windows on either side of the aisle are propped open, but there is no breeze. I make my way quickly to the back of the church, pushing the door open. I run right into Father Impeciato.

"Miss Castelluca." Father Impeciato regains his footing.

"I'm sorry, Father."

"You're always in a rush. I have looked for you after Sunday Mass, but as soon as we sing the recessional, you're gone."

"I have a lot of chores at home." What business is it of Father Impeciato's where I'm going? He wouldn't understand milking cows and cleaning the barn.

"I need your help."

"I just put all the money I had in the candle box."

He smiles. "No, no, not financial help. I would like you to start the Society of Mary here at Our Lady of Mount Carmel."

"I've never heard of it."

"It's an organization for young women to honor the Blessed Mother. It would be a great privilege for you to serve our church in this way."

"Then I should be honest with you, Father. You shouldn't hold me up as an example for other girls."

"And why not?"

"I don't know what I really believe." Father Impeciato looks at me quizzically, and I try to help him understand what I am saying. "If anything, I struggle with every word you say every Sunday."

"You do?"

"I don't understand all the terrible things that happen in the world. My friend Chettie lost her father, and we may lose our farm because my father's leg isn't healing like it should. I don't know if the Blessed Mother would want me to start anything on her behalf."

"That's where your faith comes in."

"Well, I try, I guess. I come in here and I pray. I go to Mass. Maybe my family is being punished because I'm the only one who comes, but that's because there is so much work to do on the farm. And God doesn't send help directly, in the way of money, if you know what I mean. But I'm sincere when I ask

God for help, and I never get any indication back that He has heard me."

"God isn't a magician."

"I don't expect tricks, Father. But I do expect some sort of protection."

"God protects you."

"How do you know that, Father?"

"Because God loves all His children."

Instead of arguing with him, I change the subject. "So the Society of Mary . . ."

"There isn't any organization for our young women. And I believe you're a leader. Your teachers tell me that you're excellent in school and helpful to them. I would help you establish the group, of course. You would help the church in many ways. There is much to be done. For example, the choir needs their music set out each Sunday before Mass . . ." Father Impeciato drones on about all the chores that need tending to, like ironing the altar linens, and how we would be responsible for the May crowning of the statue, and as he goes on and on, I close my eyes in the afternoon sun and remember Renato singing on Assunta's wedding day and decide that that is reason enough to help out. There's an even bigger reason to say yes to Father Impeciato's request. If I organize the Society of Mary, there will be no question in the minds of the Roseto girls that I am at last a genuine part of them and this church. We are farmers, and while this has never been anything to be ashamed of, it makes us different and separate. We aren't automatically included in Roseto

122 / ADRIANA TRIGIANI

life, but if I do a good job for Father Impeciato, I can change that.

"I'll do it, Father."

"Thank you, Miss Castelluca. God will reward you for your kindness."

Assunta invited Elena and me to stay the night at her house before our first day of work at Roseto Manufacturing Company on Front Street. Alessandro left for Philadelphia by train yesterday to take the ship to Italy. He should be back by the first of the year, in plenty of time for the baby's birth in mid-January.

"How did you sleep?" I ask Assunta as she heats milk in a pan on her stove.

"Not well. How about you?"

Elena and I shared a bed in the spare room. She tossed and turned all night, as she does whenever she is about to start something new. She's nervous about our new jobs at the factory. "I slept fine."

The milk foams up in the pan. Assunta removes it from the stove and gently pours it into three bowls. She lifts the small espresso pot off the stove and splashes a bit in each of the bowls of hot milk. She spoons sugar into each and stirs them. She motions for me to sit at the table, handing me one of the bowls of *gabagule*. "Here," she says, giving me the heel of the bread from last night's dinner. "The butter is on the table." I break the crusty bread and spread soft butter on it, then dip it into the bowl, taking a bite of the buttery bread and sweet milk together.

"It's good. Thank you," I say. "And thank you for letting us stay over."

"No one should have to walk three miles on their first day of work," she says without looking at me. "I remember when I worked there, and it wasn't easy."

Assunta forgets that she's talking about the very same day that I walked to school for the first time. I never minded the walk when I knew I was going to school. "The training wasn't so bad at the factory. Elmira Clements seemed nice."

"Be careful. She's a Johnny Bull," Assunta warns. "She puts on a smile, but she's watching every move you make. She spies on everyone for the boss. My friend Donata took two black buttons from work one day, two buttons! And she was fired."

"I won't take anything," I promise.

Elena comes down the stairs dressed for work. She is wearing a gingham jumper with deep pockets and has put her hair up in a topknot. "Is this okay?" she asks, sitting next to me at the table.

"You look fine," I tell her.

Assunta gives Elena her bowl of milk and bread. We eat our breakfast in silence. Assunta is blue because Alessandro is gone, Elena would rather be working on the farm, and I've given up school. This is not a good year for the Castelluca girls.

As Elena and I make the turn onto Front Street, we can hear the whirl of the sewing machines through the open windows of the Roseto Manufacturing Company. There is also the loud whoosh of the steam presses that come from the finishing department, but unlike at school or church, there is not the sound of a single human voice in the din. At 7 A.M. the factory is up and running. The new workers start a half hour later than the regulars, so as not to disrupt productivity.

On the other side of the street, I see some students on their way to Columbus School. My heart is heavy in my chest. I wish I could turn and follow them. I can't think about what I am missing when the bell rings at school. I would have sworn the day I set foot in the Columbus School that I would have graduated on time with honors. Mama and Papa promise I will go back to school as soon as we're on our feet again, but I think they are dreaming.

"Nella!" Chettie waves at us from the factory entrance. We join her in line to punch the clock. "Elmira has us starting in the cutting room."

"What about me?" Elena asks.

"You're in pressing," Chettie says.

"The hottest month of the year and I'm working the steam press."

"I'll do the pressing," I say. "You go with Chettie to the cutting room."

"No, no, they won't let you switch," Chettie, who has one week's experience already, explains.

"I'll talk to Miss Clements. I'm sure she won't care," I say, but I hear Chettie muttering, "She won't like it. She doesn't like change," as I walk away.

The main room of the factory is wide and deep, filled with rows of sewing machines anchored by low wooden work-tables. The operators sit on low-backed metal chairs on wheels, which allow them to move between the bins and the machines while staying seated.

At the end of each row is a metal bin, also on wheels. A thick gray haze of dust hangs over the machines. Small filaments of fabric fill the air, visible in the glow of the bright lightbulbs hanging from the ceiling on long cords. It looks as though more machines were crowded in after the lights were hung, as some of the workers squint to examine their stitch work.

The women glance up when I pass, but only for a second or two. They go right back to pumping the pedal that pushes the needle in and out of the fabric. Their experienced hands guide the fabric through the threader and bobbin in even strokes, pulling it out the other end with a yank, and moving the garment along to the next girl, who sews a different portion. I take a deep breath and instantly regret it. My nose fills with fabric fibers and I sneeze loudly. I fish for my handkerchief. Someone hands me a clean, pressed, faded red bandanna. "Thank you," I say as I blow my nose.

"You'll get used to the dust," a man's voice replies.

"Thank you." I fold the bandanna back into a square and hand it to him.

"No, no, you keep it." He smiles. Mama would like this young man's good manners. He's about eighteen. His dark Italian eyes seem to pierce me; he has a Barese nose, long and straight, but large. His full lips are bow-shaped, which complements the deep cleft in his chin. His hair is parted neatly, but a black lock falls on his forehead in the heat. He reminds me of the men in the pictures my father has saved from his village in Italy. He looks like any marble miner from Roseto Valfortore, posing in a group picture at the mouth of the quarry. As he walks away, I see he is tall and walks with confidence. How odd to find that kind of confidence in a factory.

"Miss Castelluca?" Elmira Clements smiles through pursed lips. She would be a pretty woman if she weren't so tense, I decide. She has a short brown bob, wavy on the ends, and wears a shirtwaist dress of blue and white ticking and black leather lace-up shoes with a stacked heel. She's slim, but she has thick ankles and big hands. She is definitely Welsh, with her round face, tiny nose, and small mouth. She's probably twenty-five, but looks older. "You're supposed to be in the cutting room," she tells me.

"May I switch with my sister Elena?"

"We assign the jobs lottery-style. You lucked out getting in the cutting room. Are you sure you want to switch to pressing? No one wants pressing."

"I'll take it," I say, attempting a reassuring smile at the same time. I don't want her to think I'm a troublemaker. And, as far as I'm concerned, all these jobs are horrible because they keep me from being in school, so put me in the worst department, I don't care. I follow Miss Clements to the pressing department. I look around at my coworkers, all of them men.

I try to distinguish one from the other, but they all wear denim aprons and caps on their heads. "Here." One of them hands me an apron. I quickly tie it on over my jumpsuit. Now I'm glad I wore pants. This is going to be hard work, with a lot of lifting. "I'm Federico," says the man. He is far older than me, and I would feel disrespectful calling him by his first name.

"Mr. Federico?"

"Federico Albanese. No need to call me 'mister' in here, we're all in the same boat." He smiles.

"Just because we're working doesn't mean we should forget our manners, Mr. Albanese. My papa would be very disappointed if I was rude."

He smiles and shakes his head. Mr. Albanese shows me my workstation, a deep bin filled with bundles of finished blouses. I untie the first bundle and put the blouse on the mannequin, a torso without arms on an adjustable steel pole. Mr. Albanese adjusts the pole to my height. "Press the facing first, sleeves next. Then finishing takes it for hanging, bagging, and shipping." He hands me a tube that emits hot steam. He shows me how not to scorch or dampen the fabric; if I hold the tube at the right angle, the steam takes the wrinkles right out of the garment. But the tube is unwieldy, and the first time I hold it, I lose control and get a blast of steam that burns a red splotch on my arm. "Careful," Mr. Albanese says. "You'll get the hang of it."

Mr. Albanese watches as I smooth the next blouse onto the mannequin. "Faster," he says pleasantly. Soon I am in the rhythm of the work, and I'm able to pick up speed as I master the hose. When the lunch bell rings, the hum of the machinery instantly stops, and the workers gets up en masse and leave their stations, midstitch. I want to finish the blouse I'm working on. "Don't," Mr. Albanese says. "Take your lunch. Always take the break time."

How strange, I'm thinking as I follow the crowd outside. When I worked in school, the extra hours counted the most. Factory life is the exact opposite: Do exactly what is expected of you between the bells and nothing more.

I take my lunch bucket from the cubbyhole marked with my name and head out into the open field dotted with maple trees behind the factory. I see Chettie and Elena eating their lunch in the shade and join them. "You have fifteen minutes," Chettie tells me, gulping down water.

"I feel badly that you got stuck in pressing." Elena looks up at me. "I should have taken the assignment."

"The cutting room is no cakewalk." Chettie sits behind Elena, and makes a motion that Elena is not handling the work very well.

"What happened to your arm?" Elena looks at my burn.

"The steam hose has a mind of its own." I shrug. I decide I'm not going to be like Elena. If I have to do this work, I am not going to complain, I will endure it. I'm hoping my first paycheck will make up for the despair I feel. "What's it like in the cutting room?"

"I can't stop sneezing." Elena takes a bite of her sandwich.

"The sneezing stops after a couple of days," Chettie says. "You get used to it."

The talk of sneezing reminds me of the polite young man. "One of the workers gave me his bandanna."

"What does he look like?"

I look around the field filled with workers, but I can't find him. "I don't see him. He has black hair."

Chettie laughs. "That's every Italian in Roseto. You'll have to describe him better than that."

"Okay, he had a dignified look. That's the only way I can say it. A dimpled chin."

"Franco!" Chettie exclaims with a laugh. "Franco Zollerano! He's a machinist. Very smart."

"Oh yeah. Very smart people wind up working here," I tell her sarcastically.

"That's uncalled for. We're working here."

"You know I don't mean us."

"I can tell you this after one week: You better change your attitude, because people can read your true feelings. We work closely together here and not much is hidden. So if you want to stay on the job and make your money, you'd better wise up."

Chettie has never chided me before, and I know she's right. There is nothing worse than a snob. I remember when Nurse Anderson looked down on us in Easton Hospital. "I'm sorry," I say. "I just don't want to be here."

"Like *I* do?" She stands up and shakes the crumbs from her skirt.

"We're . . ." I begin to make her laugh but she stops me cold.

"There's no 'we,' Nella. I don't have a father anymore. And I have five children under me that need raising. Mama hasn't gotten over Papa, and it doesn't look like she will anytime soon. She spends most of her days in bed crying. This is all on me. So if you want to complain or stand around acting like you're better than the people that have to work in places like this, that's your business. But I don't want to be your friend under those circumstances."

My eyes begin to burn with tears. After all, this is my best friend, who used to be gay and laugh and run and make jokes. That girl is gone, and for no good reason except her papa was trying to make a little extra money to take care of his children. "Please, Chettie. Don't hate me. I'm just scared."

Elena stands up and gives me a hug. "It's all my fault. I'm complaining too much, and it's rubbing off on you."

"No, it's nobody's fault. Except maybe God's. God got us into this mess."

"It's not God," Chettie says quietly.

"Oh really? We've been abandoned, girls. Totally abandoned."

The bell goes off, and the field empties out as quickly as the factory did. Soon the whirl and hum of the machines is in full force and we are back at work.

By four o'clock, with one ten-minute break since lunch, we stand in line to punch out. I feel the first day of factory work in every bone of my body.

"You did well," Mr. Albanese tells me.

"I tried." I smile.

"You'll get better. Soon you'll do double the bundles you're doing now."

I want to turn and tell Mr. Albanese he'll never see double bundles from me. I worked so fast that I couldn't count how many blouses I pressed. How could I possibly go faster?

Assunta receives a letter each week from Alessandro, who returned home to find his father far more ill than he anticipated. His brothers are taking good care of the family farm, but Alessandro feels guilty leaving them to do all the work.

"His place is with me," Assunta insists. She has assembled an Advent wreath, a circle of evergreens with three purple candles and one pink one nestled among the green. We will say a prayer and light one candle a week before dinner until all four are lit on Christmas Eve.

I try to cheer her up. "He'll be home before you know it." Mama says that when a woman is expecting a baby, she needs protection. This is the worst time for Alessandro to be gone. Assunta needs his strength. Elena and I stay with her every night now and it seems to help soothe her nerves.

"Have you thought about names for the baby yet?" I ask.

"Celestina for a girl. And Alessandro for a boy."

"Mama will be so happy you're naming the baby after her."

"I hope it's a boy. Just like his father." Assunta rubs her round belly. "Everyone worried that Alessandro would not be a good man, now look. He saved our family."

"Just goes to show you: you can marry from the other side."

Assunta, who never laughs at my jokes, chuckles a little. What a strange friendship we have, so defined by her moods and needs. And it's odd, because Assunta cannot see that she is the center of the universe. In her view, she is serving everyone else, sacrificing for us, when in fact we are all trying to please her.

Elena comes up from the basement with fresh linens. "This is the last batch of new sheets for the baby." She goes up the front stairs.

"Nella?" I hear an unfamiliar note of fear in Assunta's voice. When I look up, she begins to cry.

"What's wrong?"

"He's not coming back." She cries for a few moments and then stops. "I have a feeling something terrible is going to happen to him. I just know he won't ever come back. I'll never see him again."

"Assunta, listen to me. You're just overwhelmed, that's all. He loves you, he's coming back to be with you and the baby. Whenever you get these feelings, please try to tell yourself that he loves you. Because I've seen it. It's true. You don't have anything to worry about."

"Really?" She looks at me, for the first time in my life, as though I am a real friend.

"I promise you that he is coming home and he loves you more than anything in the world."

She nods. "I believe you."

*

I have learned how to be a good factory worker. Mr. Albanese has taught me all the tricks: Take your lunch and break time, and while you're working, do your job. No chitchat. And when you punch your time card and walk out, leave the problems there. You can always fix a mistake the next day. Therefore, I don't give the blouse mill a second thought after I punch the clock.

We are getting a lot of snow this December, and the pressing job that was terrible in the heat is comforting in the cold. As we get closer to Christmas, Elena and I are looking forward to having Papa, Mama, Roma, and Dianna come into town to stay at Assunta's. We'll all go to Mass together, and then have a breakfast that includes *biscotti* from Marcella's.

"Wake up, Nella!" Elena says excitedly.

I roll over in the bed and bury my face in the pillow. It can't be time to get up and go to work.

"Come, it's Assunta! She's having the baby!"

I sit bolt upright in bed. "The baby isn't due for another month," I tell her.

"She got the pains and her water broke. Come on."

I get out of bed and jump into my work trousers. "I'll go get Mrs. Avanzato," I tell Elena, grabbing my coat. Every baby in Roseto is born at home with the help of a midwife. Mrs. Avanzato's schedule is as well planned as the baker's.

"Hurry." Elena runs down the hall to Assunta's room. As I race down the front stairs, I can hear Assunta screaming. I fly down Dewey Street and over to Chestnut and bang on Mrs. Avanzato's door. Her husband answers. He yells for his wife, a small woman around seventy, who throws a coat on over her nightgown and comes with me.

"The baby is early. No good. No good," she says.

"It's not that early," I tell her, though I am thinking the same thing. We walk quickly back to Assunta's house.

"Elena! Mrs. Avanzato is here!" I take her coat and show her up the stairs to Assunta's room. Assunta is writhing in pain on the bed. Elena has prepared the bed as Mama instructed us, with clean sheets layered underneath Assunta. Fresh towels and a pan of water sit close by. Mrs. Avanzato goes to Assunta and comforts her, encouraging her to gently roll onto her back.

Mrs. Avanzato whispers to Assunta supportively. She lets Assunta lean against her as she moans.

"Should we go and get Mama?" Elena whispers.

"There isn't time," Mrs. Avanzato tells us.

"The baby is coming soon?" I ask.

Mrs. Avanzato seems impatient. "I need your help here. Both of you stay."

Assunta moans and grabs Mrs. Avanzato, pulling her down toward the bed. This is much worse than Mama said it would be. She carefully explained the signs of labor and the birthing process to Elena and me because we have never seen a baby born. It was Assunta who helped with the births of Dianna and Roma; of course, Mama had a midwife too.

Watching Assunta in labor is not like watching our calves born in the barn. That seems like nature; this is watching my sister in torment. An hour passes as Assunta wails.

The midwife places her hands on Assunta's stomach and presses gently.

"Assunta, it is time to push," Mrs. Avanzato tells her.

"I can't," Assunta moans, her eyes closed, but tears running down her face.

"You can do it. Push!" the midwife coaches gently.

"Come on, Assunta! You're so close!" I squeeze her hand.

"You can do it!" Elena says encouragingly.

Assunta pushes, and soon the baby's head appears. Mrs. Avanzato catches the baby as it slithers out. There is blood everywhere. I unfold more sheets and tuck them around my sister. Elena cuts the long blue cord connecting mother to child as Mrs. Avanzato instructs her. Assunta passes out.

"It's a girl," Elena says. We are all so relieved the pain is over for our sister. The baby begins to cry. We smile at one another, happy the baby is safe. I go to Assunta and wipe her brow. But my sister is still. She's not moving, and her chest barely rises with each new breath. "Something is wrong," I say. I take Assunta's hand and squeeze it; she does not squeeze back.

"Mrs. Avanzato!"

She pushes me aside and puts her hands on Assunta. "Go get the doctor! Right away! Dr. Latini," she tells me.

As I run down the hallway and out the door for the second time that night, I can hear the wails of my niece. I run down

Garibaldi to Dr. Latini's house. His wife comes to the door and quickly calls for her husband. As we wait, I realize I forgot my coat, but I haven't felt the cold at all until this moment. Dr. Latini grabs his bag and follows me back to Dewey Street. When we reach Assunta's room, Mrs. Avanzato is holding her hand. When she looks up at Dr. Latini, she shakes her head sadly. Dr. Latini walks over to the bed and checks Assunta's pulse. I follow right behind him, terrified by Assunta's awful stillness. When he lifts her eyelids, I see that her brown eyes don't flicker, and the deep groove between them is relaxed. "She's gone," he says quietly. Elena, who holds the baby, shakes in fear. Mrs. Avanzato takes our niece from her.

I throw myself on Dr. Latini. "What do you mean, she's gone?"

"Calm down," he says gently, putting his arms around me. "Stay calm."

"What happened?" I begin to sob.

"She hemorrhaged," he says gently. "This happens sometimes. I'm very sorry."

"But why . . . how . . ." I plead with him.

"There is nothing that could have been done. Now, please, tend to the baby." Elena and I look at each other, and then our niece, unable to believe what has happened in a few seconds. Our sister is dead. How is this possible?

Dr. Latini takes one of the clean, folded sheets from the side table and covers my sister. He shows us out of the room. We take Mrs. Avanzato and the new baby down to the nursery. "She needs to eat. Go and get Carmella Menecola. She has milk," the midwife tells us.

Once again, I go out into the night, but now it is turning to morning. The cold yellow sun comes up over the Blue Mountains, helping me find my way to Jewel Street, where Carmella is fixing breakfast for her husband, who works in the cutting room of Roseto Manufacturing. She puts her arms around me when she sees me; my tears have frozen on my face. "My . . . my sister died . . . in childbirth . . . Assunta." My sobs become heaves. This is really happening. My niece doesn't have a mother and I've lost my sister, my complicated sister, for whom everything was a struggle.

"Okay, don't worry. I'm coming with you." Carmella grabs her coat and scarf. By the time we reach Dewey Street, the undertaker, John Fiori, with another man to help, has arrived to take Assunta away.

"Dr. Latini sent for me . . ." Mr. Fiori says impatiently. Elena lets them into the house.

I fall to the ground, unable to comprehend this terrible thing. Elena comes outside and helps me up. "You've got to stop. We have a baby to take care of."

My sister Elena, who has always seemed frail and vulnerable, suddenly has a steely resolve. She puts her arm around my waist and helps me up the porch steps. "I sent for Mama and Papa," she tells me. "Mr. Avanzato drove out to the farm to get them." When we get to the baby's nursery, Carmella holds the infant against her breast. The baby devours the milk.

"She's hungry," Mrs. Avanzato says impatiently. "Come, let Carmella feed her." Carmella looks up at us and smiles.

Mrs. Avanzato leads us out into the hallway. She takes Elena's hand and then mine. "Listen to me. It does the baby no good to be around your tears."

"But Assunta . . ."

Mrs. Avanzato is old. Her hair is white, and in her pale blue eyes, she has the look of a woman who has seen many things in her lifetime and lacks patience with those of us who have not. I can see that she is struggling to find the right words for us. Something tells me she has been here before. "You may cry for your sister. But not around the baby. Understood?" We nod that we understand. "I will get you a cup and dropper to feed her. Carmella can help for a day or two, but she has her own baby to feed."

"Maybe there's another lady who can—"

Mrs. Avanzato stops Elena. "Yes, I will ask." She wraps her scarf tightly around her head and goes. Elena and I hear the murmurs of Mr. Fiori and his helper at the end of the hallway.

"Don't look," Elena warns me.

But I can't help it. I can't believe this terrible turn of fate, and must see it for myself. Elena turns away, and I watch as the undertaker and his man carry Assunta, wrapped in white muslin, down the stairs. Assunta looks so small, like the morning glories Mama covers in muslin in the autumn to keep the frost away. I wonder if the baby knows her mother is gone forever.

*

The night after Assunta died is the biggest snowstorm that anyone in Roseto can remember. Mama wants to hold her wake at the farm, but Father Impeciato advises that we cancel the viewing and just have a funeral Mass in church. Everyone within walking distance braves the blizzard, so Assunta has a full church.

Mama hasn't shed a tear. It is Papa who is destroyed, though Elena thinks that Mama is in shock. We open Alessandro's most recent letter to Assunta, which gave his itinerary for his trip home to Roseto. We consider sending Alessandro a telegram on the ship, but decide against it. The news of Assunta's passing would be too devastating coming in a letter, so it is decided that Papa will meet him in Philadelphia and tell him in person, hopefully allowing Alessandro time to adjust to the shock of it before he meets his daughter for the first time.

We call the little one Bambina. I tell Mama that Assunta wanted to name her Celestina, but Mama won't hear of it. She thinks Alessandro should name his daughter, so we wait for him to make a final decision.

I have gone back to work in the factory, and Elena stays home with the baby. Elena is a good substitute mother. Somehow we've all been less worried about Papa and the farm with a new baby in the house. We hope once Alessandro comes home, everything will get better, so Elena's salary is a sacrifice we can make for now.

The baby is very cranky and sleeps in spurts. Elena feeds

her with a cup and dropper when the wet nurse is not available. Carmella has a sister, Beatrice, who was weaning her son, and she has come to feed the baby twice a day. Beatrice is not good-tempered like Carmella, and considers her charity to us a real sacrifice. Elena doesn't think that Beatrice gives Bambina much milk anyway. The baby seems more satisfied with the cow's milk that Elena gives her.

"What is that?" I ask Elena as she warms milk for the baby.

"It's some rice powder." Elena stirs the mixture. "You know, cereal."

"Can the baby take that?"

"She loves it. Just a little bit, though."

I take off my work shoes and socks and put them by the fireplace to dry. I stretch out on the floor near the warmth. "How did this happen, Elena?"

"Are you talking about Assunta?"

"All of it." I roll over on my side and look into the flames as they crackle on the dry wood.

"I don't know. We have to thank God the baby survived."

"I know."

"I can't imagine the world without her in it." Elena sits down in the rocker as she holds the baby. "What do you think will happen when Alessandro comes back? Do you think he'll let me take care of the baby?"

"Somebody has to."

"I really want to." She kisses the baby tenderly.

"You must tell him that." I sit up and watch Elena rock the baby. "He's going to be so devastated." I imagine Papa telling

Alessandro the news and close my eyes, as it is too painful to think about.

"Doesn't it all seem like a dream?" Elena says softly. "She was gone in a moment."

"And you know, all my life I wanted her to go." At long last, I say my innermost thought aloud.

"Don't say that," Elena says quietly.

"No, I did. No sense lying about it now. But then, when I came here to help her with the chores, I started to see her in a different way. I saw how she loved her husband and her home, and how she just wanted everything to be nice. It was hard for her all those years on the farm, working outside, doing chores that men should do. She hated it, and yet she did what she was told. Maybe she didn't have a sweet disposition, but she always did her duty."

"Yes, she did." Elena holds the baby close.

"When she died, I felt like I saw her for the first time. Assunta's face in repose was so gentle. She was beautiful, and I never saw her that way. Why is it that I learn everything too late?" I roll onto my back and look at the ceiling.

"You're only fifteen."

"Almost sixteen. Mama had Assunta when she was sixteen."

"So maybe you're not wise yet. You're other things." Elena looks at the baby. "She's just like her."

"What do you mean?"

"The baby. She's just like Assunta. She struggles with everything."

"You can tell already?"

"Mama says that people come to be as they are the day they're born."

"Is that true?"

"We'll have to wait and see, I guess."

The creak of the rocker and the crackle of the fire are all we hear. This house has become home to us, despite all the sadness. Maybe the place where you feel that you're building something is home. There is a knock at the front door. I get up to answer it.

"I'm sorry to bother you," says the small man who stands in the doorway. He has short gray hair and a white mustache. And I recognize his deep blue eyes. Renato has them too. I've seen Mr. Lanzara from a distance at Mass, and when I pass his barbershop on Garibaldi, but we've never formally been introduced. "You're Nella?" he asks.

"Yes, sir. Please come in."

"No, no, I don't want to bother you at suppertime. I am simply acting as a mailman for my son, Renato. I have a letter from him for you."

"Thank you." Mr. Lanzara hands me a pale blue envelope, just like the ones Mama gets from her family.

"Renato is with my sister in Connecticut," he explains. "I send him the newsletter from church each week, and he saw the announcement about your sister."

"Thank you." I force the words out, though I am nearly speechless with surprise.

Mr. Lanzara graciously says good-bye and goes. I look

down at my bare feet and sigh. I'm never at my best when meeting Lanzaras, it seems. I take the letter back into the living room and sit down by the fire. Elena has taken the baby upstairs, so I have a moment alone. I open the back flap of the pale envelope carefully.

Carissima Nella,

I am sorry to hear the terrible news about your sister Assunta. Papa wrote that you have a new niece, which must give you great joy amidst your grief. Please tell your father and mother that I am praying for them, as I am for you and your sisters, and the new baby. I can tell you that it is very hard to grow up without a mother. My heart breaks for your niece, because she will be searching her whole life for the love that has been denied her. I still have many moments in the day when I long for my mother, for her affection and advice. This need does not lessen with age. But aunts and uncles and grandparents can help fill the void. The baby will need a close circle around her, and I know you will be an invaluable part of that circle. I wish I could be there to be of some help to you. I trust you are working hard in school. Don't forget what I told you on the Ferris wheel, for I meant it with all my heart.

Your Renato

I reread the last line of the letter over and over again. So little has changed for him since last summer. But for me, nothing will be the same.

*

Mr. Albanese was right: I'm pressing double the bundles I did when I began. I don't like the work any more than I did on the first day, but I do take pride in mastering my job. I have stayed after work to learn how to operate a new machine. Elmira has been pleased with my progress, and soon I'll be a collar setter, considered to be one of the hardest jobs in the factory. And I often pick up a little extra money doing piece-work.

Each worker is paid by the bundle. We get a penny per bundle, if we complete our task perfectly. If a girl is fast and diligent, she can earn a nice paycheck. The best machine operators have a second language with their machines; the foot pedals and the knee pedals are extensions of their bodies. The best workers never talk, stop, or stretch. They keep their eye on the needle and stitch and pull, stitch and pull, until their bin is empty.

Our factory operates on an assembly line. The fabric is draped, measured, and cut according to a pattern on the cutting table in a workroom attached to the main floor. In the cutting process, large bolts of fabric are unwound off a giant wheel and layered back and forth, making a multilayered base. The pattern, made of sheer parchment, is laid on the fabric and pinned to the top layer. Every inch of the fabric is used. On the cutting table, it almost looks like a map has been laid on top of the fabric. Then an overhead blade cuts each layer of fabric according to the pattern. These shapes become the parts of a blouse: the front, the back, the sleeves, the collar, the facing. These pieces are bundled by the dozen and tagged, then delivered to the bins, where the machine operator sews the pieces together. The more she sews, the more she makes.

These bundles are passed along through the factory, with each worker performing a particular task until all the pieces are sewn together and become a blouse.

"Nella, Mr. Jenkins wants to see you in his office." Elmira checks her clipboard.

"What for, if I may ask?"

She shrugs. "I don't know everything that goes on around here."

Liar, I think as I make my way to the front office. A bookkeeper with a short blond bob types as I tell her why I'm stopping in. All the girls who work in the factory have cut their hair into the latest style, not because we're out boozing it up with the flappers over in Easton come Saturday night, but because it's easier to operate a machine without a pompadour or braids to get in the way. "You can go in." The bookkeeper motions.

Mr. Jenkins is a tall, slim man with a trace of a Welsh accent. He seems to like the Italians, though. The workers think Mr. Jenkins is a good boss, but I've never met an employee who's had any real affection for the person he or she works for—it's a job, and it's always obvious who stands to gain the most in the exchange.

"Miss Castelluca?" He looks up from his work. He has a thin face with a weary expression and clear brown eyes. "I'm losing a forelady."

"Who?" I am surprised.

"Miss Clements. She's getting married."

"But why is she quitting?" I ask.

Mr. Jenkins gives me a puzzled look. "Her husband won't let her work. So, I need a smart girl in her place. I understand you just turned sixteen."

"Yes, sir."

"That's awfully young for a forelady." He taps his pencil on the desk and looks out the window. "But I don't have anybody else. We've all been watching you and you're the obvious heir apparent."

I don't mean to, but I laugh. "Heir apparent" is such a strange term to use for an uneducated farm girl and not a blood relative to the factory owners.

"Something funny?" Mr. Jenkins looks over his glasses.

"Just a little, sir. If I were your heir, I don't think I would be running the steam hose in the pressing department." Everyone knows Jenkins's children live in a nice house over the New Jersey state line and attend fancy boarding schools.

He smiles. "No, you wouldn't. Not that it would hurt any of my children to work. But that's not how it is anymore. Not like when I was a boy."

I imagine Mr. Jenkins working in a factory. I don't quite believe it. He is too refined to come from common laborers, and his soft hands give him away. "How much are you going to pay me as forelady?"

He seems surprised that I asked. "Twenty cents an hour.

And a bonus of one penny per bundle that you produce in your department."

"Why only twenty cents an hour? Miss Clements makes thirty-five."

"How do you know that?"

"She saved exactly enough for her wedding reception at Pinto's Hall by working for two months. She told me, and I did the math."

"You're an odd duck, Miss Castelluca." He stands up, but I know that is only a ploy to make me back down from the salary figure I named. He said it himself, he needs me, and if he needs me, I know he'll pay. "Very direct."

"I know, sir. I am also smart and fast, and I've figured out how to get better production off the floor or you wouldn't be talking to me."

"How? By giving all your coworkers a raise?" He laughs nervously.

"Eventually. But first, I believe you need to reconfigure the machines. See, you have a mix of single, double, overlock, and blind-stitch machines on the floor. But you don't have them in the order they are used in."

"That's because operators handle more than one machine."

"But they shouldn't. Use your fastest girls on collar settings and cuffs. The way you have it now, the best girls are sewing fronts and backs. Too easy. It only makes sense to give the fastest girls the hardest work. They'll figure out how to do it better."

Jenkins's eyes narrow. "Okay, thirty-five cents an hour. And a penny a bundle."

"A penny a bundle unless I hit one thousand bundles a week, then anything over a thousand, a nickel a bundle," I reply.

He laughs again. "You're crazy!"

"Do we have a deal?" I ask him. I used to watch Papa negotiate with the stores when he sold his milk and butter, and he would rather drive home with a carriage full of product then undersell himself. He used to say, "Better we drink the milk and eat the butter ourselves than give it away."

"You drive a hard bargain, Miss Castelluca."

"I have to. I have a family to support and a new niece. I can't monkey around. Every other week there's another blouse mill going up in Roseto. I know what I'm worth. Do we have a deal?"

Mr. Jenkins shakes his head ruefully but says, "We have a deal."

I leave Mr. Jenkins's office, and as soon as I do, I begin to shake. It's cold and drafty in the entry area, but it's not the temperature. I'm shaking from fear. I could have lost my job in there, but I came away with a raise. Wait until I tell Elena. Papa and Mama will be so proud.

Franco Zollerano comes from the factory with a group of machinists. They look at me, then bid Franco good-bye and go outside. He smiles at me.

"Are you ever going to return my handkerchief?" he asks as he wipes his hands on a rag.

"Who sees you?" I tease him back. Now that I've gotten a promotion, I'm a first-class smart aleck.

He smiles. "I'm around."

"Not that I can ever tell."

"You're keeping tabs on me?" He looks at the floor and then drinks me in from the tip of my shoes to the top of my head.

I am not going to let him intimidate me. "No, if I were keeping tabs on you, I would make it my business to know where you go."

"Good point." He laughs, and I see nice white teeth. The front teeth overlap a bit, but it's charming. "I work at all Jenkins's mills. So I'm over in Jersey quite a bit. That's maybe why you've missed me."

"No one said anything about missing you."

"You will, though." Franco stuffs the rag into the back pocket of his coveralls and folds his arms across his chest. "I'm Franco Zollerano. I don't think we've ever been formally introduced."

"We haven't. I'm Nella Castelluca." I extend my hand; he does not take it. He shows me the grease on them instead. His hands are big, too big for a man who must deal with intricate machines. "You're a machinist."

"Yep. And you?"

"Pressing. Then collar setting. But I just made forelady."

He throws his head back and laughs. "You're a kid."

"Mr. Jenkins doesn't think so."

"He must have gotten you cheap."

."No, he didn't. Of course, I knew what to ask for." Why am I getting into a discussion about my pay with a machinist? What does he know about running a factory?

"Well, good then. Congratulations." Franco turns to go.

"Hey," I call after him.

He looks at me.

"You don't like management?"

"Good guess." Franco pushes the door open and goes outside. As it closes, a cold draft of air hits me hard and I shiver. I feel badly that I bragged about my new job. I sounded impudent. But there is something about this man that makes me want to one-up him. I don't like his cocky attitude, not one bit.

Elena has prepared the house and baby for Alessandro's homecoming. She has cooked a pot of sauce, baked bread, and made a cream pie. She has scrubbed the house from top to bottom, changed, washed, and pressed all the linens, and chopped plenty of firewood for the weekend. Mama, Papa, Roma, and Dianna will stay in town with us. Mama is very nervous about this homecoming.

"Mama, why do you think Alessandro would reject his own daughter?" I ask her as we set the table.

"Men don't take to babies, especially girls, without the mother's coaxing."

"Even Papa?"

"He kept his distance until Assunta was nearly one year old. Then he realized what he was missing, and when the rest of you came along, he held you from the start. That's why I worry about Alessandro. After all, he can't take care of the baby himself."

"I will take care of her. Always," Elena promises. "If he doesn't want her, she can come with us on the farm."

"A child should be with her father."

"Only if he loves her," Elena says quietly.

"They're here!" Roma says from her perch in the front window. Papa walks with a permanent limp since his accident, so Alessandro helps him navigate the icy sidewalk. Dianna opens the door for them. Mama, Roma, and I go to Alessandro. He embraces us. "Where is she?" Alessandro asks softly. He takes off his hat and coat. We can see his face is pale, and his eyes are red from crying. Papa wipes his eyes with a handkerchief. "Elena?" Mama calls out.

Elena comes from the kitchen with a pink bundle. Alessandro opens his arms, and Elena hands him the baby. She fusses with the blanket. Alessandro looks down at her; her pink face and black hair are like his own. His eyes fill with tears. "*Bella*." He kisses her.

"Thank you for taking such good care of her," Alessandro says to Elena. He kisses the baby tenderly. Mama need not worry: Alessandro will be as good a father to his daughter as he was a husband.

"She needs a name." A tear slides down Elena's cheek.

"I think she should be named for her mother . . ." Alessandro begins to cry, and the baby coos as if to comfort him. He stops his tears and looks at the baby intently. The baby looks back at him, as if she is waiting for him to say something. "Yes, she should be called Assunta."

For the first time since my sister died, my mother lets out a low, painful moan of despair. Papa holds Mama tightly and she begins to sob. Her loss is now real. Until Bambina had a name, her own daughter was not really gone. Alessandro holds his baby close. "She's here," Alessandro whispers. "This is my wife. Her eyes."

Mama turns away. "Mama, don't cry," Alessandro says. He walks over to her and puts the baby in her arms. Mama kisses Assunta. Alessandro puts his arms around his daughter and her grandmother.

CHAPTER SIX

Many years ago, before Father Impeciato took over Our Lady of Mount Carmel, there was a priest, Father Pasquale DeNisco, who turned Roseto from a quarry camp into a beautiful village. He died in 1911, one year before Roseto became incorporated as a borough, but the impact of his leadership is everywhere. He knew the Italians needed to learn English, so he taught language classes, and then instructed them on how to become U.S. citizens. He organized a branch of the American Federation of Labor as the blouse mills cropped up all over town. Father DeNisco organized Roseto's first sport teams, the Roseto Coronet Band, the Philodramatic Club, and the first volunteer fire company.

Each June, Father DeNisco gave a cash prize of ten dollars in gold to the family who planted the prettiest flower gardens. The prize is long gone, but the habit of growing glorious flowers has remained with the people. As I walk to work down Dewey Street, the lilac bushes, orange trumpet vines climbing trellises, and hanging baskets dripping with fragrant white flox are a testament to his legacy.

Elena made me a new summer work dress, a sleeveless sky-blue sheath with a matching smock over it. The smock has a white collar and satin bow, very chic. Elena sewed two deep pockets on the front, which are useful for the endless supply of tags and pins that I need all day.

Last week my workers produced over a thousand bundles. I got a nickel for each bundle over a thousand. It will probably be the money I am most proud of earning in my entire life. It was the money Jenkins thought I would never make, so the moment was that much sweeter when I marched into his office and showed him the tags from the overrun.

When I took over from Elmira Clements, with Chettie's advice, I learned how the workers felt about conditions at Roseto Manufacturing, and slowly I've begun to make some improvements. Mr. Jenkins's chief concern is profit, of course, but I have learned that if the workers are happy, production naturally increases. It's my job to make conditions better.

Once I reorganized the machines, the work output increased. When I was a machine operator, it was hard to see the stitching in the overhead light, so I had lamps installed over each machine. This made a tremendous difference in the quality of the work. I made the sewing machine tables adjustable so they are comfortable for everyone, from the most petite to the tallest girl in the shop. I ordered special work gloves that go to the elbow for the workers in the steam area. My arm will always have a scar from the accident I had on my first day. I want my employees to be safe.

In a couple of months, I will mark my one-year anniversary working here, and my six-month anniversary as forelady. As the weeks have gone by, I've thought about school less and less. Sometimes I feel a pang over what I'm missing, and sad about not becoming a teacher. I wonder what it would be like to teach a classroom of children eager to learn, but I use those skills when I'm teaching the girls a new operation in the mill. My work life is gratifying; I never think about whether I like what I'm doing or not, I just concentrate on doing it well. I am at my best when I have a purpose. The goal of taking care of my family is met every week when I pick up my paycheck. That feels good.

Alessandro helps Papa out on the farm, while Elena and I stay in town with the baby. Our brother-in-law makes it into town three nights a week. There's always talk about selling the house on Dewey Street and moving us back to the farm. But the house in town makes my work life so much easier, and my salary is too important to jeopardize with a three-mile walk in bad weather that might make me miss the start bell. Another reason to hold on to the house is that Dianna will come into town next year to attend Columbus School.

My younger sisters will not have to work at the blouse mill as Assunta, Elena, and I have. Financially, our family is doing better now, so there is no need to sacrifice their educations for the extra income they could bring in. I know a lot of that has to do with how hard I work and save. The more effort I put in at work, the easier it is on Mama and Papa. I used to put my ambition in books; now I put it in productivity at the mill.

Bright and early Monday morning, Chettie meets me on the street and we walk to the factory. "Anthony Marucci has gotten off the dime and asked me out. He's going to take me to the show this Saturday in Easton. Wanna come?"

"I don't think so. Who wants a third wheel on a date?"

"We could get someone to go with you."

"No thanks."

"Come on. Anthony has lots of friends. Franco Zollerano thinks you're cute."

"No, thank you. That guy is so full of himself."

"That's just the way fellas are," Chettie replies. She always thinks the best of people. "He's just trying to impress you."

"Boys. You can keep them. What a waste of time."

Chettie gives me a knowing look. "Well, I heard one of the girls talking in line about Renato. His father says he's coming home today."

News of Renato's return sends a rush through me. I wonder why he didn't mention a visit home in his last letter. Maybe he wanted to surprise me. I haven't seen him since the Ferris wheel ride, but we've been writing back and forth since he sent me that beautiful letter about Assunta.

Chettie gets in line to punch her time card while I go into the office to sign in. Jenkins has a new policy with the fore-ladies and foremen: he wants us to sign in and give a brief description of the job at hand that day with projections of output. I always try to beat the figures I put down on the sheet; it's a little game I play with myself.

Today the truck comes from New York to pick up our shipment. I will stay late and oversee the load-in. Mr. Jenkins used to stay for the truck, but no longer. He trusts me to count every blouse for the buyer.

When the final bell rings, the factory empties in seconds. I reposition the large fans in front of the windows. I've found that the fans facing out helps keep down the haze from the filaments somewhat. In the heat, it's harder to control, but if I position them this way at night, the factory is cooler in the morning. I lower the lights in the main factory room and go to check the cutting room.

I am surprised to see Franco working late. He seems to slip in and out, of course, since machinists go from factory to factory fixing equipment. Days go by without an appearance at Roseto Manufacturing. Sometimes I find myself looking for him, and then I remember Renato. No one can compare with Renato, especially not a machinist with a smart remark.

Franco has taken apart the spreader. It sits in small pieces on the cutting table while he works.

"What happened?" I ask him.

"The wheel isn't working properly. I'm replacing it."

I start to go. "Well, good luck."

"I like your dress," he says, looking me over.

I fold my arms across my chest. "Thank you. My sister made it. The last thing I want to do when I go home is sew."

"That's one of the hazards of working in a blouse factory."

"I guess. But I bet I wouldn't feel that way about cream puffs if I worked at Marcella's bakery."

"Probably not." He laughs.

Franco lifts the blade off the spreader, pulling out the gears. I don't know how he gets his big hands around those tiny joints and screws. The top half of his coveralls dangles around his waist. He wears a sleeveless undershirt, and I can't help but notice how broad his shoulders are, and how defined the muscles in his arms. He is built beautifully; maybe it's his height, or the perfect proportions of his face and shoulders. He could almost be a sheik, I think to myself.

"Do you need something?" he asks, looking up.

"No. No. I was just watching your . . . work." I don't want Franco to think I'm looking at his body. What kind of girl does that? Not a girl who goes to Mass every Sunday, I'm certain.

"Why won't you go to the movies with me?"

I'm surprised he would bring up my rejection, so I try to joke my way out of it. "You haven't asked."

"Chettie asked for me."

"That's not the way to invite me."

"Miss Castelluca, would you do me the honor of attending the picture show with me this Saturday night?"

"No."

Franco laughs. "Well, even your own technique didn't work. Are you sweet on someone already?"

"You could say that."

"But I see you around town. Alone. It doesn't look like you have a fella."

"I do have a . . . well, he's older and . . . you know what? I don't want to discuss it."

"Sounds like an excuse."

"I assure you, it's not an excuse."

"I'm older," he offers.

"Not as much."

"Oh, so he's a lot older. Why would you want an older man? You'd have a lot more fun with me."

I put my hands on my hips. I can't believe this guy. "You think a lot of yourself, don't you?"

"When it comes to you, yeah."

"Well, I don't know if you're familiar with the term 'unrequited love'?"

"Who said anything about love?" Franco smiles.

"It isn't love exactly," I backpedal quickly. "It's when a person likes someone who doesn't return the same feeling."

"You don't like me as much as I like you, is that what you're saying?"

"Yes."

"That's not what I think." Franco comes from behind the cutting table and walks toward me. I take a step back.

"You have no business thinking about me like that." I tilt

my head just like Jean Harlow. She knows how to throw off unwelcome suitors, and thanks to her, so do I.

Franco takes another step toward me. I take a step back, thinking I'm in the open doorway, but actually, I bump against the wall. He blocks the door with his arm and leans in toward me. "Someday you're going to love me."

He is so close, I put my hands against his chest and push him away. He doesn't resist. He steps back. "Your confidence does not appeal to me, Mr. Zollerano," I say.

"It will."

I make a quick exit, grab my notebook, and go outside where the finishing department loads the blouses onto the truck, each tagged by size and in an overlay of white tissue paper. I walk between the racks of blouses and catch my breath. When I feel calm, I peek out of the racks and look for Franco. He's gone. I'm relieved. I go to the soda machine and get a bottle of orange soda from the bin. I snap off the cap and swig.

"Can I have a sip?" Renato Lanzara says from the doorway. "I heard you were working late. Congratulations, Forelady." Renato walks over to me, takes me in his arms, and kisses me on the cheek. "I saw Chettie over at Joe Mamesce's. She told me all about it. She also said you were looking for me."

"No, she didn't!" I'm going to give it to Chettie when I see her. Or maybe not. I don't care if Renato knows how I feel. He feels the same! He must like me very much. As soon as he arrived home, he must have dropped off his suitcase, gone looking for me, and didn't stop until he found me.

"Oh yeah, she said you missed me every single day and she had to hold you while you cried buckets."

"I never cried, not once!" Oh, how I wish I could tell him how much I think about him. I hope he thinks about me half as much!

"That's not what I heard," Renato teases. He gives me a small package wrapped in striped paper with a bow. "Open it."

I hold the package gently, savoring the moment. Renato brought me a present. I must be his girl. I don't even want to open it; it's enough that he thought to bring me a package tied with a ribbon.

"Go ahead." He smiles.

I tear into the package. It's a silk handkerchief with my initials embroidered along the scalloped edge. "It's lovely. Thank you." I look at Renato and wonder how it can be possible for someone to be gone for months and then return as if he had never left. Our connection is that immediate. "Oh, and I suppose you cried for me?" I tease him back.

"Every day." Then, just as he did on the Ferris wheel, he leans over and kisses me. I've tried to forget about his kiss, figuring it was never to happen again, and here it is. I hear a floorboard creak. Renato and I look toward the sound.

"Excuse me." Franco looks at me with a stony expression and turns to walk back out the door. Instead of being embarrassed, I am glad he saw Renato kiss me. Now he can see for himself who truly owns my heart. The whole town can see! Renato Lanzara is home, and he has chosen me.

*

Chettie and Anthony Marucci sit in the front seat of his freshly scrubbed Ford roadster, which smells of linseed and fresh wax, while Renato and I sit in the backseat. This is Anthony's chariot, and he's really spiffed her up.

I asked Papa if I could go to the movies, and he said yes. I didn't describe it as a double date, because if I had, I'm sure the answer would have been no. Since I've been working, I don't ask Papa's permission so much anymore. If I were still in school, I know things would be different. I would still be living on the farm and walking to town each day. But since I give most of my paycheck from the mill to Papa, I'm not a kid anymore, so I try not to act like one.

"I loved the picture," Chettie swoons.

"Greta Garbo is so beautiful," I sigh.

"You know, Garbo and John Gilbert are in love in real life too. I read about it in *Photoplay. Flesh and the Devil* should be a big hit." Chettie turns around and looks at me.

"She's the flesh, he's the devil," Anthony says to Renato in the rearview mirror.

"It looked very authentic to me," I tell him.

Renato laughs.

"What's so funny?" I ask him. Sometimes when Renato laughs at something I say, it makes me feel like a kid.

"Have you seen that many love stories to compare it to?"

"I saw *The Sheik, The Son of the Sheik,* and *Blood and Sand,* every picture Rudolph Valentino ever made. And I got very blue when he died this year, and so young. So, yes, if you're asking if I'm an expert on motion-picture love stories, I am. A little."

Chettie can hear a defensive tone in my voice, so she quickly changes the subject. "So, Renato, do you know what you're going to do?" she asks. "Where you're going to work now that you've graduated and traveled?"

"Pop heard they need a literature teacher at Columbus School . . ."

"That would be wonderful," Chettie says.

". . . but I'm not sure about teaching."

The conversation hits a lull. Anthony is probably thinking about his job in construction, and Chettie is thinking about how her life changed when her father died and she was forced to work in the mill, and me, when I hear the word "teach," I get very blue. If only it were me who had the college degree when there was an opening at Columbus School.

"Teaching is a great profession," Renato explains. "I just don't know if it's for me."

"Maybe you'll have the chance to find out," I say, forcing a smile. It seems that the people with passion never get the thing they're after. Circumstances seem to play out against people like Chettie and me, who know what we truly want. And then there's Renato, who has the luxury of time and choice. I wonder if he knows how lucky he is.

Baby Assunta is a fighter. She has overcome colic and is starting to gain weight. She is a pretty baby, with soft brown eyes and lots of thick black hair. Elena is madly in love with her, and the baby responds to her as though Elena is her mother. Elena keeps Alessandro's home running beautifully; she cooks, cleans, and does the laundry. It's as though Elena has found her perfect place in the world. I have never seen her so happy.

I take the trolley out to the farm every Sunday after Mass to visit Mama and Papa. I feel insincere when I go to church because I'm not really sure why I'm there. My machine operators love to see me at Our Lady of Mount Carmel on Sundays, but I have yet to feel an epiphany. I hope the clouds will part and the angels will sing and I'll be filled with the faith I long to possess. Father Impeciato expects the president of the Society of Mary to set a good example, so I never miss Mass, despite my doubts.

The walk from the trolley stop to the farm is less than half a mile. Papa has put paving stones down on the old dirt road to the farmhouse to make it easier for the milk trucks to get through. The barn is almost completely mechanical now, and Alessandro recently purchased another milk cow, bringing the herd up to fifteen. Papa oversees the work, but without Alessandro, I doubt the farm could continue.

As I open the old gate at the end of the lane, the farmhouse seems smaller, and the fields surrounding it seem less rambling than they used to. The Queen Anne's lace that grows in white starry bunches is sparse this year. Even the field where the cows graze seems like a mere patch of land, when it used to look like acres. The world I come from is so small, after life in town, I wonder if I could ever be happy here again.

Mama and Papa are sitting on the porch. Mama is mending and Papa is reading the paper. I give them each a kiss.

"How's the baby?" Mama asks.

"She's over the colic."

"We'll come in to see her this week."

"How's the dairy business, Pop?"

He looks up and smiles. "We're holding our own, thank you."

"Alessandro's in the barn if you want to take a look." Mama breaks a thread between her teeth.

"Sure." On my way to the barn, I peek into the springhouse, which looks to be in need of repairs. "Alessandro?" I call out as I go into the barn.

"Up here," he says from the loft. I climb the ladder to join him.

"What are you doing?"

"The flashing on the roof was ruined over the winter. I'm replacing it," he says without putting down his hammer. He yanks a rotten plank of wood off the roof. "Water damage. Nothing is worse. I did the same job on my father's house in Italy."

"How is he?"

"Much better."

"You didn't get into town this week."

"Too much to do here. How's my baby?"

"Good."

"Still with the colic?"

"Nope. Elena said she's cured."

"And how is Elena?"

"She's good."

There's an awkward silence as Alessandro stops yanking nails and looks at me intently.

"Nella, I want to talk to you about something." Alessandro sounds serious.

"Sure. Anything." The lines in Alessandro's face have deepened since he came to America. He's out in the field all day, and there are the worry creases that weren't there before Assunta died.

"I love Elena," he says quietly.

"I love her too—"

"Not like a brother," he interrupts.

"You're in love with Elena?" I say it out loud, but I can barely comprehend what he is saying. This is my sister Assunta's husband. How could he love another Castelluca girl? It doesn't seem right.

"I've done nothing about it. But I think maybe she loves me too."

Elena has never discussed Alessandro with me, and the thought of the two of them falling in love after all that has happened is too strange to be real. And so soon! It hasn't been a year since Assunta died. Did we do the right thing letting Elena take care of the baby? Maybe Mama should have taken over. I am stunned, somehow feeling betrayed for Assunta.

It's as if Alessandro has read my mind. He sits down next to me and says, "There was nothing between us when Assunta was alive."

"I know that."

"But it's very odd, Nella. I don't see Elena in the same way I used to, when she was my sister-in-law. I can't even remember that time. It's as if it all washed away."

"You forgot all about Assunta?"

"No, no. I will never forget her. No, and she is the mother of my daughter. I still love her. But Elena has saved me. She kept my home together all these months."

"I know. She's a good girl." I say this less for his benefit than to remind myself of Elena's excellent character.

"I would not have wished for this, believe me. But I see Elena with my daughter and my heart fills with so much joy I can't describe it."

"What are you going to do?"

"I wanted to talk to you first. Even though you are younger, you have always been the leader. Elena looks up to you. Your parents respect your opinion. You understand your family better than anyone. I seek your advice on this."

"I don't know what to say." And I don't. I feel blindsided. I never imagined my brother-in-law would fall in love with my sister. Anyone who sees Elena with the baby is moved by the love that she has for her. It's beyond being an aunt; Elena is a mother to the baby in every way. But is she in love with Alessandro? I remember moments now when Elena looked at Alessandro with such affection. I saw them in the yard one day with the baby on a blanket taking sun, and they were laughing and playing with her. At night when Elena's cleaning up the dishes, Alessandro sits and talks with her. They seem to be such good friends, I shouldn't be surprised that those feelings have turned to love. "You must wait, Alessandro."

"I shouldn't abandon the idea altogether?" Alessandro asks.

"No, of course not. You love Elena. I know that. But my mother and father would be insulted if a year had not gone by. They are still grieving my sister. It would seem disrespectful for you to tell them your feelings now. In time, I think it will be fine, but now it's too soon."

"What about Elena?"

"What you say to her is between the two of you. I don't have anything to say about that."

"I will wait then." Alessandro seems relieved that he has unburdened his feelings to me. But now I have a heavy heart. I'm not sure Papa and Mama will approve of this, and in light of Alessandro's feelings, our living situation in town is inappropriate. The Roseto grapevine will be electrified with this news when Alessandro makes his intentions known.

Every spare moment of the summer, when I'm not working, I spend with Renato. The girls in the mill nod at us appreciatively when he comes to have lunch with me in the field. I love the looks we get when we walk down Garibaldi after supper. His father makes me feel a part of town life, inviting me to sit on their porch and have espresso. And Renato seems to know every back road in the county. He takes me up to the Poconos to walk in the woods, we canoe on the Delaware, and we even go to Philadelphia on the train to visit the zoo.

"I brought you a present." Renato lifts a satchel out of his father's car, parked on the shore of Minsi Lake on the outskirts of Roseto. "You don't have to go to college to read all the great books," Renato begins. "Many intellectuals believe self-education is as valid as any degree from a university."

The brown ducks make lazy Ss as they swim across the smooth surface of the lake. I dip my toe in the water. The summer sun is so hot today, the lake is like a bath. "Do we know any intellectuals who could verify this?"

"Very funny." Renato pulls me down to the ground and onto his lap. He wraps his arms around me. "There are those who would say I am an intellectual." He kisses me before turning his attention back to his satchel of books.

"We will begin with Dante's *Inferno*, then we will read *The Confessions of Saint Augustine* and the Greeks: plays by Euripides, Aeschylus, and Socrates."

"I don't like plays."

"How can that be? You like the picture show."

"That's different. They're silent."

"You should get used to words. Not just that sappy organ music they use to underscore the scenes." Renato leans over and kisses me again, this time on the nose. "What happened to the farm girl who was hungry for knowledge?"

"She got a job in a mill," I tell him wryly. "And she's tired after a ten-hour workday."

Renato opens Dante's *Inferno*. "You'll like this one. It's about faith."

"You think I'll get some if I read it?"

"Maybe."

"You really believe in the power of books, don't you?"

"Whatever it is that you're feeling, whatever it is you have a question about, whatever it is that you long to know, there is some book, somewhere, with the key. You just have to search for it." Renato opens the book and gives it to me.

"I used to want to learn everything. But life is so complicated now."

"So simplify. Who said that?"

"Who said what?"

"Simplicity, simplicity, simplicity."

"Henry David Thoreau in *Walden*."

"Correct." Renato could be a teacher. He certainly sounds like one.

"And Thoreau also said, 'Beware all enterprises that require new clothes,' and I think of that every time the truck leaves the Roseto mill with a shipment."

Renato laughs. I bury my face in his shoulder. "You are so much more than a forelady at the Roseto Manufacturing Company," he says.

"That's true. I'm also your girl." I lift my head onto his shoulder. "But you'll leave someday, won't you?" Renato squeezes me closer but does not answer. "Okay, if you won't answer that, I will. I plan on leaving you long before you leave me. I've learned to head off a problem by addressing it first. That's a rule in the mill handed down from forelady to forelady since the first blouse was made."

Renato laughs, and there is no sweeter sound in the world to me. I wonder if he knows that every time I make a joke, a little piece of my heart breaks off. It's just self-defense. It seems whenever we get close, he leaves. From the first time I saw Renato, he seemed to swoop in, mesmerize me, and then leave without an explanation. When I'm with him and we're happy and anything seems possible is the time when I'm most afraid of losing him. I have a feeling of dread that I cannot shake, even here in the sun on this clear summer day.

By August, the heat has made the mill unbearable. We've added more fans, but all they seem to do is push the hot air around in suffocating gusts. The combination of heat from the machines and the temperature outside makes for terrible work conditions in the mill. If I owned this factory, I wouldn't operate it in this heat.

My girls try to maintain their usual pace, but they cannot. We are falling behind. I sit down at a machine to help the girls set cuffs. The blouse we are working on for this shipment is complicated. There are darts, a fluted hem, and a wide collar with a satin facing. We're struggling with the complexity of the design, and the heat makes it worse.

I push the cuffs through the threader. "Miss Castelluca?" I look up at Mr. Jenkins. "We're behind."

"That's why I'm pitching in. You should too. We're short a body in pressing," I tell him.

As quickly as Mr. Jenkins turns to go to pressing, the mill fills with black smoke. It happens so fast that by the time I stand up, I cannot see where it is coming from. The whirl of the machines stops, replaced with cries for help and the sound of metal work chairs overturning. Smoke seems to be coming from the cutting room. The workers try to run for the exit.

"Ladies! Get down! Crawl!" I drop to my knees. "Follow me! To the back!" There is an emergency door out back where we load the truck. I push it open, then yell to the men to help the girls file out. Some girls have gone out the front, but most of them are stuck in their stations. In the din, workers have run and pushed the metal bins on wheels into the center aisle, crowding it, trapping the girls at their machines.

"Nella, get out of there!" Chettie yells from outside. She must have escaped out the front doors. I ignore her and go back into the mill. I hear the sounds of the fire truck on its way. I trip on what I think is a bolt of fabric, but it's not, it's Mr. Albanese. He has taken in too much smoke. "Help! Someone, over here, help!"

A man lifts me up by the waist and carries me to the open door, depositing me on the truck ramp. I look out in the field and begin to count heads. A lot of the girls have gotten out or been rescued by now, but some were overtaken by the smoke. Franco emerges down the ramp with Mr. Albanese. "Get him the tank!" Franco yells to the fire captain. "He's not breathing." Franco goes back in and returns carrying three more workers, one by one, to safety.

As the fire department douses the blaze, the smoke subsides enough that we can see what is happening. There must have been an electrical fire. Most of the wires in the mill were rigged quickly to accommodate more machines. We must have overloaded the system with the latest additions, and the fans to keep the air moving.

As I make the rounds through the girls, the gravity of what has happened begins to settle in, and some of the girls weep. I organize the girls by department to see who is missing. It appears that everyone got out.

I see Franco doubled over by the ramp, gasping for air. I go to him. "Come away from the building, Franco," I tell him, putting my arm around his waist and leading him to the field. "Let me get you some water."

By now word has spread of the fire, and many Rosetans have arrived with buckets of cold water and cups to drink with. I dip into a bucket and give Franco a cup of water, which he guzzles. "What happened, Franco? Could you tell?"

"Too much power. The heat. The circuits blew. It started in the wall."

I watch as the firemen finish their work. The smoke has subsided, revealing the charred walls and the dank smell of burnt silk and cotton. It's frightening how fast it happened. Some days I could smell the electrical wires overloading with power, and we'd turn some of the fans off, but the building, with its old wooden frame and oiled floors, was bound to go up like a tinderbox. I see Mr. Jenkins standing with the fire chief, and I go to them.

"Is everyone all right?" Mr. Jenkins asks me.

"I think so. Our regulars are all accounted for, department by department."

From this vantage point, I can see the damage to the structure more clearly. One side of the building is gone, and the rest ruined by smoke. I hear the muffled cries of the girls in the field, and I know some are crying because they were frightened, but most are devastated because their jobs are gone.

Chettie and I walk home to Dewey Street at nightfall.

"It's not like I even ever liked that mill," Chettie says, breaking a long silence between us.

"I know."

"But when it's gone . . ."

"I know."

"What are we going to do?" Chettie asks. There's no fear or self-pity in her voice. By now we are so used to dealing with bad breaks, we almost expect them.

"Jenkins will find another building."

"Do you think so?"

"Absolutely." I give Chettie a hug before she climbs her porch steps. "Jenkins won't want to miss making money for long. Don't worry."

When I reach Alessandro's house, I climb the porch steps slowly. Elena meets me in the doorway.

"Are you all right? I've been so worried about you and Chettie, and everyone."

"This was a very bad day. But I'm okay. No one was seriously hurt."

"Lavinia Spadoni said the factory is ruined."

"We won't be returning to that building, that's for sure."

"Nella, I have more bad news."

"Is something wrong with the baby?" I ask, my pulse racing.

"No, no, Assunta's fine. It's Renato's father. He died this afternoon."

"I just saw him last night!" I can't believe what I'm hearing. Today we almost lost workers in the fire, but a couple of streets away, Renato was enduring a much greater loss.

"It was a heart attack, Nella. It was very sudden."

Instead of going into the house and washing up, I turn around and walk down Garibaldi Avenue to Renato's home. There is a small crowd on the porch. I greet them and go inside. As always, I'm surprised at how neat and clean the place is. Renato's mother died years ago, and he's an only child, so it's only been the two of them for years, and yet the sparkling copper pots hang neatly in the kitchen, and the green plants flourish in the front windows. I hear Renato in the kitchen, so I follow his voice. He is standing by the sink with Father Impeciato. "Excuse me," I say to them. "Renato, I'm so sorry."

Renato embraces me. "I heard about the mill."

"It was horrible." I begin to cry. Finally, with his strong arms around me, the sadness and loss of the day overwhelm me. "I feel so silly crying when your papa—"

"I was with him." Renato's eyes fill with tears. "I was able to say good-bye. I thank God for that."

For Nicola Lanzara's funeral, Our Lady of Mount Carmel was filled to capacity. Renato delivered a eulogy that was so moving, even those who were not close to his father in life felt closer to him after hearing the inspiring words. I sat with Renato through the wake and at the funeral, and I hope I was of some comfort to him.

Renato said good-bye to his cousins from Philadelphia on the porch as I cleaned up the last of the dishes and glasses, taking them into the kitchen. The neighbors were all helpful with the dinner, and Renato was a gentleman throughout, tending to his guests as though they were invited to a feast, not a funeral.

"Don't do another thing," Renato says as he comes into the kitchen.

"I want to," I tell him. I go to him and put my arms around him. He has cried here and there throughout the day, but as I hold him, he weeps. The harder he weeps, the closer I hold him. I hope that wherever Mr. Lanzara is, he knows that I will take good care of his son.

"I miss him already," Renato says through his tears. "I loved him so much."

"I know you did. And he knew it."

"No, no, I never said it."

"He knew."

"I wish I had told him."

"Renato, he *knew*."

"When Mama died, he never brought another woman around. One time I asked him why, and he said, 'Out of respect for you. That was your mother. How could I bring another woman in here to replace her?' "

"He was a good man," I say softly.

"Now I'm all alone." Renato lets go of me and turns away, reaching in his pocket for his handkerchief.

"You are not alone. You have me," I say. "Renato. Look at me."

But he can't.

"I'll be okay," he says and leaves the kitchen. I have a terrible moment of not knowing what to do. Does he want me to stay? Or should I go home and give him some privacy? I long to hold him and comfort him, but he has pushed me away. He is so complex, and so often I don't understand him. I feel inadequate, and yet I know he needs me. I go into the front parlor, but he isn't there. I open the door gently and look out, but he's not on the porch either. I turn and look up the narrow staircase to the second floor and see a light on in a room at the top of the stairs. "Renato?" I say quietly as I climb the stairs. He doesn't answer. I follow the light to the bedroom and push the door open. Renato is sitting on the end of his bed with his head in his hands. He sobs, much like

Papa did when Assunta died. It is from the gut, the place of deepest feeling. I cannot bear to see him suffering like this, and if I could, I would take on his pain so he would have it no longer. I climb across the bed and wrap myself around him. He doesn't push me away. "I love you," I tell him softly. He turns and faces me, taking me in his arms. "Let me love you." He shakes his head no, but he doesn't mean it. I kiss him tenderly on his face until the tears stop. His heart is pounding, and I kiss him until his breathing softens and he is calm. Then he kisses me tenderly, and in an instant, I want to give him everything I have. I would give him the world, I would give him his father back, I would make it so that he would never cry again. He unbuttons my dress; all the while I think, He must never be alone. He must have me all the days of his life. I think about Father Impeciato and the banns of marriage, and the rings, and the vows, and none of it, not one single element of it, matters to me in this moment. I love Renato Lanzara, I have from the first moment I saw him. I only wish I had more of myself to give; somehow my heart does not seem big enough to hold what I feel for him. He owns me, my first, last, and true love.

Mr. Jenkins takes me on a tour of the new home of Roseto Manufacturing Company. We have moved to the end of Garibaldi Avenue, in an old box factory. Jenkins brought in a team of men from Jersey who salvaged some of the machines, bins, and supplies from the fire. Whatever was lost will be replaced with equipment from his other factories. The workers need not have worried that they would lose their jobs; Mr. Jenkins had the new mill up and running within a week.

A few of the girls did go to the competition (in the past couple years three more blouse mills have opened in our town), but for the most part, our roster will return intact. Only Mr. Albanese, who was a year from retirement, will not return. He told me his close brush with death helped him realize that time waits for no one, and while he still feels good, he wants to take it easy.

"How's Renato doing?" Chettie asks as she helps me set up the workstations.

"Not so good," I admit. Renato has been distant in the weeks since his father died. I've tried repeatedly to draw him out, but he sinks more deeply into some dark place inside. When I hold him now, it's not because I want to make love, I only want to help him heal. He rejects me, though, and then later apologizes. I don't know how to handle him. "Chet . . ." I say, breaking down. "I don't know what I'm going to do."

"What do you mean?" she asks.

"I've tried everything. Even leaving him alone. When I try to reach out to him, he pushes me away."

"It's like he's blaming you because his father died," she says. "I know something about that. When my father died I hated anyone who still had a father. It's hard to understand why, out of all the people in the world, your father has to die."

"And it's even worse for him. His mother is gone too. He's all alone in the world, except for me."

"Just be present for him. That's all you can do. Sit there. And when he's ready, he'll talk."

After work, I walk home on Garibaldi Avenue. I'm going to stop in and see if Renato wants to come over to Alessandro's for dinner. As I climb the steps, I notice that the shades are drawn and the curtains are closed in the front parlor. I go to the front door and knock. There's no response. I try the door, but it's locked. Then my eye catches something. I see an envelope wedged in the door. I pull it out. My hands begin to shake when I see the familiar writing on the outside of the envelope. It is addressed to me. I breathe deeply and sit down on the milk box.

Dear Nella,

I hesitate to leave you this letter, because it is my hope that you will remember me and think of me at my best. I'm sorry, but I have to leave you and my home that I love because it is the only way for me to find my purpose. I know you will blame yourself, but I write this letter so you will not. I treasure what we had but it was not right. I took advantage of you when I was afraid, and that is not fair to you. I want you to be happy and to find peace. I am not the man who can give it to you. I will think of you always with affection.

Your Renato

I inhale, realizing that I have held my breath the entire time I was reading. I stand up and hold the wall to steady myself. I don't know how I will make the hill home to Dewey Street, but I have to, so I will. I stuff the letter into my pocket, and later, when I find a match, I will burn it.

CHAPTER SEVEN

*E*very Christmas Eve, Papa would go out to the woods on the outskirts of Delabole farm and cut down a tree. Mama baked gingerbread cookies, which we iced, then hung on the tree with satin ribbons. There was a cookie with each of our names on it, which we ate on Christmas morning. Tiny candles were nestled in foil cups, attached to the branches, and we'd light them as soon as the sun went down. There was caroling, and midnight Mass, and presents that we made for one another. The holiday was always the happiest time for our family, but not anymore.

This year, it seems everyone in the Castelluca family is sad for a different reason. Mama and Papa miss Assunta, I'm sad without Renato, and my younger sisters can see that the farm life they loved is not going to last forever. Alessandro wants to focus on importing and open a shop in town, and without his help Papa won't be able to keep the farm going. Alessandro has asked Mama and Papa to move into town, and they are considering it.

Elena has put up a tree in the front window on Dewey Street. She has invited the family for Christmas dinner. I place cloth napkins next to the dishes on the table. "Nella?" Elena gives me a pair of candlesticks to place on the table. "I want to talk to you about Alessandro."

"About how he feels about you?"

Elena inhales quickly. I look at her.

"How did you know? You couldn't tell, could you?" Elena puts her hand to her face, embarrassed.

"No, of course not. He told me about his feelings months ago."

"What did you say to him?"

"I told him to wait until a year had passed. And now it's been a year."

"He has asked me to marry him. What do you think?"

"I think . . . he's a very good man. Do you love him?"

"Very much. It's only when I think about our sister that I hesitate."

"Elena," I say, taking her hand into mine. "She would want her daughter raised by a good woman."

"Thank you, Nella."

"And she would want her daughter to have a proper upbringing."

"You know, people talk. I hear things. There have been comments about me."

"Who cares what people think?"

"I do. I'm raising a baby, and I care how she will be treated. I don't want her to be ashamed of my choices."

"Have you talked to Mama and Papa?" I ask.

"Not yet. I'm afraid to. I'm afraid they'll think it's disrespectful to Assunta."

"I think you'll be surprised. Mama and Papa want you to be happy. And they love Alessandro. You haven't done anything wrong."

Elena's voice breaks. "I know. But I wish . . ."

"What do you wish?"

"That I would have met him first. That he would have loved me first. That the baby was ours. I know it's not a perfect world, but why did it happen this way? When Assunta was alive, I was always in her shadow. And I have this terrible feeling that it's my fate to stay there."

"It's not your fate to be second. You didn't plan this. It happened. And as for the petty gossips, I have a little experience with that myself. Ignore it. There will soon be another story burning up and down Garibaldi Avenue, long after your wedding corsage has wilted. There's always something new to talk about."

"Will you be my maid of honor?" she asks, clearly relieved to know that I don't judge her or Alessandro for their decision to marry.

"I would love to."

*

Father Impeciato marries Alessandro Pagano to Elena Teresa Castelluca on December 31, 1926. Assunta Pagano chatters through the entire service. Even on Elena's wedding day, her niece hogs the spotlight. Mama is happy for Elena, but Papa has not said a word. It's not that he disapproves, it's that this marriage will always remind him of the daughter he lost, and a year later, he still cannot accept it.

Roma and Dianna move in with Elena and Alessandro for the winter. It is much easier for them to walk to school, and they are a great help with the baby. But the quarters are getting tight here; with three bedrooms, there is no extra room. I decide to move back out to the farm. I don't mind taking the trolley in the morning, and with my salary, I can afford to do it. And Mama is glad to have me back home.

"It's so lonely here when you're all in town," she says. "I love having you back home."

"I like it too." I give her a hug. "I'm going to bed. It's supposed to snow tonight." I look out the window at the pasture. The full moon casts a hazy silver glow on the field, which looks like a lake blue in the darkness. I can see the white flakes begin their tangled descent to the cold ground. Dizzy snowflakes usually mean a blizzard.

"More snow?" Mama complains. She misses the warmth of Italy. She has never liked these cold Pennsylvania winters, and she longs for the warm beaches of her Adriatic Sea.

I climb the stairs to the room I used to share with my sisters. Mama has left it intact. As I get undressed, I think about how my life is going backward. I am becoming the maiden aunt, even though I never planned to be. I hang my dress on the same hook I hung my pantalets and apron on when I was small. It's so odd to be in this old farmhouse without my sisters. Now I know what it would have been like to be an only child, and I don't think I would have liked it.

Every night before I go to sleep, I reread the letter Renato left me, hoping to find some new meaning in the words. It's been months, and I hate myself for reading it over and over again. Each time I read it, I promise myself that tomorrow will be the day that I throw it in the fire once and for all, but something always holds me back.

I pray to Saint Anthony to help me find myself. He's the saint of lost items, and though my self-confidence is slightly more valuable than a set of keys, he seems to be the right saint for my troubles. There has been no word of Renato's whereabouts. I guess he went back to Italy; he always said it was the place he felt most comfortable and inspired. He sold his family home to his cousins, and when Chettie inquired, they said they had no idea where he had gone.

I'm sure Renato is happily in the arms of another girl now. She is educated and beautiful and has no responsibilities except to please him. Chettie thinks I should find a new beau. But I don't want one. No one will ever compare with Renato.

News of a movie house opening in Roseto has everyone excited. Nestled among the houses on Chestnut Street, it can only seat a hundred people per show, but it doesn't matter. We no longer have to go all the way to Easton to see the serials.

The first showing will be *The Scarlet Letter*, starring Lillian Gish. She is my favorite actress, because her troubles on-screen seem so real. There are two shorts with Buster Keaton, and I can't wait to see them. I need to laugh.

With the opening of the new mill, Mr. Jenkins has more work for us than ever. And I like the new mill better than the old one. When we open the windows, there are trees right outside, not like the open field we were in before. And the cross-ventilation keeps the gray haze from the fabric to a minimum. During the winter, the girls take lunch at their machines. This isn't ideal, but it's too cold outside, and the shipping area in the new building can't accommodate everyone. When the girls take lunch, I don't. This is when I go through the bin and count the tickets on the bundles. One day, when I reach the pressing department, there's a small cardboard bakery box on a shelf where I place the finished tickets. It has my name on it. I open the box, and there's a single cream puff inside.

"Thanks, Chettie," I tell her as I pass her station a few minutes later.

"For what?" she asks.

"The cream puff."

"What cream puff?" She looks baffled.

"This one." I hold up the box. "It's sweet of you."

"I didn't leave it for you."

"Well, then, who did?"

"I don't know." Chettie smiles. "You must have a secret admirer."

I take the box by the string and go into the office. I pour a cup of coffee out of my thermos and sit down to enjoy the cream puff. No matter who it's from, I love a pastry from Marcella's.

"Mama, I am not going."

"Please, Nella. Beatrice Zollerano is expecting the entire family for dinner."

"I know what you're up to. You're trying to make a match with me and Franco. I don't want any part of it."

"I am not trying to make a match!" Mama puts her hands on her hips. "It is very important for Elena to socialize with the other families in Roseto now that she's married to Alessandro."

"So let them go to dinner."

"Franco wants you to come."

"Ma, I know he wants me to come to family dinner. He's invited me out several times. I always say no."

"But why? He's so handsome."

"Because, Mama, I . . . that is . . ."

"Ay. He's gone! Renato is gone. He's not coming back. Beatrice has invited the entire family. It will look terrible if you don't come."

I give in, not only because Mama is persistent, but because I think she's right. If Elena and Alessandro befriend the families on Garibaldi, they will be a part of things. I would hate to see little Assunta ostracized because her father and aunt married. So, Mama, Papa, and I take the trolley into town, stopping at Elena's so the whole family can walk to the Zolleranos' together.

Mama looks us over before our walk to Garibaldi. Roma looks sweet in her velvet jumper, Dianna has on a wool skirt and a crisp white blouse; even baby Assunta has a bow in her hair. Alessandro and Papa wear their suits, while Elena and I have put on our best dresses.

When we arrive, Mama knocks on the Zolleranos' door. Mrs. Zollerano, in a plain black shift and a pearl brooch, answers the door. "Come in, please. Welcome." She's around Mama's age, but her black hair has more white in it. She's very tiny, with a trim waist and small hands and feet. Mr. Zollerano—who Papa knows from the Marconi Club, where they play cards—takes our coats, while Papa makes all the introductions.

Franco comes from the kitchen carrying a tray of bitters in small rainbow-colored glasses. He offers my father the first glass, then proceeds around the room serving all of us. He wears a blue serge suit with a crisp white shirt and gray silk tie. When he serves the little ones soda, he looks like a giant next to them.

"Thank you for coming," he says when he reaches me. As he does in the factory, he takes me in from head to toe. To make a point, I follow along, examining my dress and shoes just as he does. He catches himself. "I'm sorry. You look beautiful."

"Thank you." I take a drink from the tray.

When Mrs. Zollerano calls us to dinner, she seats us as we enter the dining room. Franco is the middle of three sons. The eldest, Giacomo, is recently married to a nice girl from West Bangor named Maria. Mrs. Zollerano seats them across from each other. She asks me to sit next to Giacomo and puts Franco next to me. (Just as I predicted, I am the Plan B of Mama's Plan A evening.)

The youngest son, Alberto, is ten years old and knows Roma and Dianna from school. Mrs. Zollerano seats them together. She fills the rest of us in around the edges, with Papa opposite the head of the table from Mr. Zollerano. Mama is next to Papa. Alberto says grace before we take our seats. Franco pulls my chair out for me.

The conversation at dinner is much livelier than I had expected. Papa and Mr. Zollerano talk about Italy. Papa talks about what Roseto is like on the other side, while Mr. Zollerano talks about his hometown of Biccari, a few miles from Papa's. The kids laugh at the funny stories of goats and chickens living in the same house as people.

The meal is a feast of polenta and chicken. Mrs. Zollerano made the chicken in a thick tomato sauce with a touch of cinnamon. She serves the polenta as a base, then smothers it in tender chicken and sauce. She follows the meal with a salad and cheese board. For dessert, she has made cream puffs.

"I think I solved a mystery," I say quietly to Franco.

"What mystery?"

"Someone leaves me cream puffs at the mill. Would you know anything about that?"

"Nope. You must have a secret admirer." He smiles.

"You call that a secret?" I roll my eyes. Franco laughs.

Elena and I insist on helping Mrs. Zollerano clean up after the dinner, while the men go into the living room to smoke.

"I always wanted daughters, now I know why!" Mrs. Zollerano laughs.

"We have five girls at the ready whenever you need us."

"I may take you up on that," she says. "Franco tells me that you're the forelady at the factory. How can that be? You're so young."

"I don't know. I'm very lucky. The boss noticed that I was fast and figured things out quickly. I was supposed to be in school, but then things happened and, well, I guess I've just made the best of things."

"That's too bad about school, though."

"I used to feel that way, but now I accept it. When you're part of a family, they come first."

"Yes, sometimes life gets in the way of what we want to do. Often young people take a long time to understand that. You're better off learning it now, even if it is a hard lesson."

Mrs. Zollerano is amazed at how quickly Elena and I can clean up the dishes, but there aren't that many more than we used every night in Delabole. Mrs. Zollerano has nice things: a full set of china and simple silverware that look as though they were handed down to her. The decor of the house is very Rosetan. Flowery red chintz slipcovers adorn the couch, and the furniture is mostly mahogany. There is a hutch full of dishes, with teacups hanging on small gold hooks. Mrs. Zollerano has artfully placed the dinnerware on the open shelves. As in all homes in Roseto, the front parlor leads to a long hallway that connects to the kitchen in the back of the house. There is usually a sunporch off the kitchen, for sitting in the summer and storage in the winter.

Baby Assunta is asleep on a blanket in the front room. The conversation and laughter of the men lulled her to sleep. Alberto, Roma, and Dianna play a board game and seem to get along beautifully.

When it's time to go home (we're all staying on Dewey Street since it's such a late night), Franco offers to walk with us.

"There's no need to," I tell him with a smile. "We know the way."

"No, no, I insist," he says, pulling on his coat.

Elena bundles up the baby, while I help my sisters with their coats and hats. The air is fresh, though cold. Roma and Dianna run ahead.

"Thank you for a lovely evening," Elena tells Franco.

"Thank you for helping Ma clean up. She never has kitchen help with boys around."

"So she said. Once in a while, help her with the pots and pans," I tease.

As we walk up Garibaldi, we pass what used to be Renato's house. There is a lamp on in the front room. Even though his cousins bought the house, seeing the light on reminds me of what I have lost. I don't say anything the rest of the way home, leaving Elena and Franco to chat. When we reach the house, the girls run inside. Elena kisses Franco on the cheek and joins them.

"You have a wonderful family," Franco says.

"So do you. And please thank your mother for making such delicious cream puffs for dessert tonight. They're better than Marcella's."

"I will." Franco smiles. "I was wondering . . ."

"You're not going to ask me out again, are you?"

"Are you going to say no again?" he asks.

"Probably."

"Why don't I ask anyway, and you give me the first answer that pops into your head. Would you like to go to a show sometime?"

"I don't know," I tell him.

"What's to know? We go to the show, I buy you popcorn, we laugh at the story, or you cry, depending on what's showing."

When I don't reply, Franco shakes his head and slowly walks down the steps. At the bottom, he looks up at me. "You still love him?"

The question stops me cold. I might have been thinking of Renato all the way home, but I'm smart enough to pretend I don't know what Franco's talking about. "Love who?"

"Lanzara."

I am taken aback at how forthright Franco is, and a little unglued at how astute. "Can you tell?"

"Yeah. I guess I was hoping you were over him."

Franco says this with such a cavalier tone that it infuriates me. "I'm not over him. I will never be over him."

"Never?" Franco seems surprised.

"You obviously have never really truly loved someone, because if you had, you would understand that love isn't something you get over like a head cold, or grow out of like an old pair of shoes. If you really fall in love, it becomes a part of you, and you would as soon cut off your own hand as lose it."

"Jesus." Franco shakes his head. "I had no idea. I saw you two in the factory, but it didn't seem—"

"Didn't seem like what? And how dare you spy on us, anyhow!"

"I wasn't spying on you!" He grows defensive. "You shouldn't have been kissing in the middle of the cutting room! That's a nice way for a forelady to act."

"What would you know about being in charge?" I practically shout.

"Hey, don't take it out on me. I didn't leave you. He did."

The words sting because they're true. I take a deep breath. "I'm sorry, Franco. I shouldn't have said that, but you'd be angry too if everything you ever wanted was out of reach. Not just the big things, even the little things." I am sorry that I have revealed even this much of myself to him. I turn to go inside. This conversation is over.

"You think I get everything I want?" he says quietly. "I was hoping to get a kiss tonight, to tell you the truth, and it doesn't look like that's going to happen."

I put my hands on my hips and look down on him. "Not in a million years." I turn to go into the house and have my hand on the knob. As I'm about to push the door open, Franco comes up the steps, pulls me away from the door, and takes me in his arms and kisses me. This is no soft, gentle Renato kiss. This is a hungry kiss, and I am shocked by the intensity of his feelings. There is not only passion, there is determination in this kiss. I can't believe he has the temerity to take me on. He lets go of me and goes back down the steps.

"That will never happen again," I call after him.

"We'll see," he says as he crosses Dewey Street.

PART TWO

1931–1971

$\mathcal{I}$n a few days, I will turn twenty-one, and although everyone teases me that I will finally be a legal adult, the official rite of passage is lost on me. I've been a forelady since I was sixteen, and in the factory since I was fifteen, so I don't see that I am reaching a major milestone. Rather, it's just more of the same.

Mama and Papa go home to Italy every January now, returning to Pennsylvania at Easter. Papa rented the farm out to some of his cousins from Italy. They pay Papa a stipend for the use of the land, and a percentage of what the contract brings in. Papa is forty-eight years old and Mama is forty-six, and they like making money without having to get up at dawn and work until night. Even though we are in the midst of the Great Depression, somehow our little part of the world is surviving just fine. There is plenty of work in the mills, and because Rosetans traditionally have grown their own food, made their own wine, put up fruit and vegetables for the winter, and kept their own cows and pigs, there is always plenty to eat.

When Mama and Papa come home to Roseto, they have their hands full with grandchildren: Assunta is a feisty six-year-old. Alessandro and Elena have had two more children of their own, a daughter, Aurelia, and a son, Peter. Alessandro bought the other side of his two-family home, so Mama, Papa, and I live next door with a shared porch between us.

I am still unmarried, and I like it just fine. Work is my husband, and I love the rewards it brings, and the satisfaction I feel when I deposit my paycheck into the First National Bank in Bangor.

"You wanted to see me?" I take a seat in Mr. Jenkins's office. I remember how frightened I was the first time I was summoned here. Now, when I look at him, I see an old man behind a cluttered desk in a small closet of an office. He is not the mogul I imagined him to be, he's just a cranky man with business headaches.

"We're switching gears here," he begins. "I've been taking contracts from the Rosenbergs on Long Island all these years, but now we're ready to go from making original designs to knockoffs."

"Whose knockoffs?"

"Hollywood's."

"I don't understand."

"It's very simple. The Rosenbergs are working with a middleman in Hollywood who draws the costumes seen in the latest pictures. He sends the design to Rosenberg, who cuts the pattern from the drawing. The blouses are named for the star who wore them. For example, our first order is a sailor blouse called the Joan Crawford from *Dance, Fools, Dance*. The movie is coming out this fall." Mr. Jenkins slides a drawing across the desk to me.

The sketch is the perfect likeness of Miss Crawford, the strong jaw, the arched eyebrows, the thick lashes. The costume sketch is of her upper torso only, and in the corner, the artist has drawn out the pattern pieces with proportions.

"What do you think?" he asks.

"It's so far-fetched it could work. You mean the customer will go to the movies, see her favorite star in a blouse, go to the department store, and it will be hanging there ready for her to buy?"

"You got it. Edith Head, Adrian, all the big names, all of them are participating. Hell, even Schiaparelli and Chanel are getting in on it. You might say we are mass-producing the Hollywood dream."

"I like the movies as much as anyone, but it sounds like we're creating the trend before the movies even come out."

"That's exactly right. As quickly as Myrna Loy can shake a martini, you have to be able to manufacture what she's wearing. It doesn't help us if the blouse comes out after the fact."

"What if Myrna Loy's in a turkey?"

"We use the name of the actress, not just the film. We're betting that the fans will flock to the stores to look like their favorite movie star regardless of the picture she's in."

Moments after leaving Mr. Jenkins's office, I find Chettie in the finishing department.

"What are you doing June first?" Chettie asks, before I can even mention Mr. Jenkins's new affinity for Myrna Loy.

"I'm busy."

She laughs. "Well, get unbusy. Anthony Marucci has asked me to marry him, and I'm going to. You're the maid of honor!"

"Congratulations!" I give her a big hug. "I'm so happy for you."

"I know you are. Now, don't get blue because you're not getting married too. I'm four months older than you."

"Right, right. I'm getting used to that 'maid' title, though. I'm starting to believe it suits me."

Over lunch I tell Chettie all about the factory's new direction. She thinks it sounds like a swell idea.

As the new designs are sent, there are some new skills to master in the mill. Hollywood styling requires topstitching, beading, embossed pockets, all sorts of fancy details that we have never dealt with. I keep the girls after hours to train them. I ask Jenkins if I can assign three of my best girls to do accent work. He agrees. We should be up to production speed in no time.

Soon the designs are pouring in at the rate new movies come to town: the Carole Lombard, a sleek chiffon tank; the

Constance Bennett, a silk tunic with a satin collar; the Barbara Stanwyck, a cotton pique button-down with vest; and the Ginger Rogers, a kicky white cotton peplum with black piping and a satin belt. I know the designs will sell because the machine operators all want to own them. Before they hit the stores, the Hollywood knockoffs are already a success. I have to hang a notice in the entrance near the time clock: PLEASE REFRAIN FROM TAKING BLOUSE TAGS FEATURING MOVIE STARS FROM THE FINISHING DEPARTMENT. Turns out the girls like to have souvenirs of their favorite stars, and the sizing tags with the beautiful faces of their matinee idols printed in color are sweet remembrances.

Chettie and Anthony are taking me out for my birthday. We're going to the Americus Hotel over on Hamilton Street in Allentown. I have some paperwork to finish before I go home to dress. I am alone, except for a maintenance man, who mops the main floor. I chuckle to myself when I read the production numbers. Since we started making the Hollywood blouses, production has increased by 30 percent. Even though our work is more complicated, there is something about the glamour girls that inspires my workers. Maybe we read *Modern Screen* too much, but it certainly seems like elegance, beauty, and style lift our spirits and help us aspire to be better at what we do.

Franco comes into the office and leaves a work order on the board. "I heard it's your birthday."

"I'm twenty-one. A genuine old lady."

"I'm still older than you are."

"I wouldn't brag about it."

I go back to my work. Franco stands in front of me. "Can I help you with something?" I ask. I hope he's not going to ask me out again; I am tired of turning him down. Sometimes I think he's forgotten about me, and then I'll walk to the finishing department and there will be a cream puff on my clipboard. He doesn't give up.

"I'm seeing a girl in West Bangor."

"Congratulations." I try not to act surprised and go back to my work.

"Nella." I look up at him. "I'm not going to ask you out anymore."

"Um, okay."

"I'd just like you to answer one question. Why wouldn't you see me?"

I never really thought about why I kept saying no, except that it felt like the right thing to do, or maybe rejecting him became a habit. I don't want to hurt Franco's feelings, but I aimed much higher than a machinist when I dreamed of love. Yes, I have a sort of animal attraction to him, but that's all. He would never engage my intellect the way Renato did.

I tap my pencil on my spreadsheet. "I just don't think we'd be a good match."

"We are a good match," he insists.

"There's more to it than kissing," I correct him.

"It's a start."

"Franco, you have a girlfriend, whoever she is, in West Bangor. Why are you asking me about us?"

"Because if you said you'd give us a shot, you know I'd never look at another woman again."

I look down at my papers. I admire his persistence. The truth is, I am lonely on Saturday nights. There are only so many movies to see, and so many card games to play, and so much laundry to do. And while I love babysitting the kids, I wish I had my own home. I've been dating a little, at Chettie's insistence. I went on a few dates with Imero Donatelli, but he was too slick for me. I feel badly that I compare every man to Renato, but the truth is, I want what I had, and it's gone.

"You don't want me, Franco."

"Why don't you let me decide?"

"I'm trying to tell you something. I'm not perfect."

He laughs. "Neither am I. One date. That's all. Just one. Give me a chance."

Unbridled ardor is an element in all my favorite books. Unrequited love is another one. I read about men who give up countries, riches, and power for the love of a good woman. Here's a nice Italian boy who wants to make me happy, and I won't give him a chance. What would it hurt to have dinner with him? Will it kill me to go to one show with him? He's not asking me for much. "Okay, one date."

His face breaks into a wide, boyish grin. "When?"

"I'm going out tonight. Tomorrow night I'm busy. How about next Saturday?"

"Next Saturday it is."

"Oh, and Franco . . ."

"Yeah?"

"I take it we're not going to West Bangor."

"I think I can do better than that."

In the week between my acceptance of Franco's invitation and the moments leading to his picking me up at 137 Dewey Street, I find myself thinking about him from time to time. There are things about him I like. He makes me laugh, and I do find him handsome. But I can't imagine what we'll talk about. Chettie thinks I'm nuts, that a man and a woman can always find something to say to each other.

I dress in Elena's spare bedroom because it has a three-way mirror. Next door, we are furnished with the bare minimum until Mama and Papa decide to move to town permanently. I pull on my stockings slowly, lining up the seams perfectly. I am wearing a blue silk cocktail dress. It has a boat neck, three-quarter-length sleeves, and a bow that anchors over my hips. I saw this dress in Hess Brothers and had to have it. I feel like Constance Bennett, long, cool, and sophisticated. Or at least I'm a good Roseto imitation.

The doorbell rings and I hear Elena answer it. I check the clock. He's right on time. I dab perfume behind my ears. My hair is shiny, cropped into a shorter bob and combed close to my head. It curls just right to the nape of my neck. I wear Elena's earrings; small clusters of rhinestones dangle from my ears. I have on soft pink lipstick, inspired by the sketch of Paulette Goddard on the ticket bearing her likeness at the factory. I want to look pretty, though I'm not sure why. Chettie thinks I like Franco deep down and won't admit it.

"Hello, Franco."

My niece lets out a low whistle when she sees me descending the stairs.

"I agree, Assunta." Franco winks at my niece then helps me into my coat. I pull on my gloves and hat. We say our good nights. Once we're out in the cold night air, I look up at him. "You look handsome," I tell him.

He beams. "You think so?"

"I wouldn't say it if I didn't mean it."

We chat about work as we drive through town. "I thought I'd take you somewhere different," he says as he turns off the main road outside Roseto. The pond at the Roseto Rod and Gun Club is frozen over with a silvery glaze of ice that shimmers in the moonlight like sugar on a cake. Franco parks his Hudson coupe up in a clearing of trees by the edge of the pond. "I'm coming around for you," he says.

"I don't have boots," I tell him when he opens the door. I look down at my Sunday shoes, black satin pumps with a strap and simple rhinestone shoe clips, and pull my feet back into the car.

"I do." He pulls a pair of clean rubber work boots out of the backseat. "Here, I'll help you." Like the prince in *Cinderella*, he removes my shoe and slips the boot over my stocking feet. He does the same with the other foot, but for my money, he lingers too long at my knee. I pull my dress tightly around my calves and smooth my coat over them, pushing his hands away. Franco may have good intentions, but he has a few bad ones as well.

He helps me out of the car. The boots are a few sizes too big, so it's hard to find my footing. I trip and fall against him. He catches me and we laugh.

"Wait here." He goes to the trunk of the car and pulls out a large wicker basket. "We're having a picnic," he says with a smile.

"It's awfully cold for a picnic," I tell him.

"It won't be," he promises.

He takes my hand and leads me to the edge of the pond. His hands are large and have the rough calluses of a workingman. He has been here earlier, and he's already prepared a campfire. He reaches in his pocket for a match. The dry wood ignites into an orange blaze. He unpacks a thick blanket from the basket and invites me to sit on it. He uncorks a jug of wine and pours me a glass, and then one for himself. "We'll eat a little later, okay?"

"Okay." I find this all so curious. I'm on a date with a machinist with a theatrical bent. The curtain has been raised, the orchestra plays; in a moment I expect to see Ruby Keeler tap across the ice followed by a string of chorus girls in red velvet skating costumes. But the only sound here is the spit and crackle of the fire. Even the moon, which has gone behind a cloud, seems to know we don't need it right now.

"I thought I'd read to you." Franco pulls a book from the basket.

"It's a little dark, isn't it?" I regret saying that when I see the look on his face. I need to play along at this romantic scene a little better than that. "I would love for you to read to me," I tell him kindly.

"It's a poem," he says, opening the book on his lap.

"Really, what is it?"

"You'll see." He smiles. And he has a beautiful smile. I can hear Mama's voice reminding me to always check a man's teeth. "Something funny?" he asks.

"I just thought of my mama. Something funny she said once." I look at him. "Go ahead. Please. Read."

I notice this book has been read a lot, because the pages lie flat where the spine has been broken. Franco leans in to read by the firelight as he cradles the book gently in one hand, holding the page with the other, like a scholar who returns to the words time and time again to find new meaning in them. As he reads, I watch the moon as it pushes back through the clouds and through the bare branches of the old birch trees around the pond. I wonder how many lovers have come to this place. Then his deep, soft voice breaks the quiet.

> "When you are old and grey and full of sleep,
> And nodding by the fire, take down this book,
> And slowly read, and dream of the soft look
> Your eyes had once, and of their shadows deep;
>
> How many loved your moments of glad grace,
> And loved your beauty with love false or true,
> But one man loved the pilgrim soul in you,
> And loved the sorrows of your changing face;

And bending down beside the glowing bars,
Murmur, a little sadly, how Love fled
And paced upon the mountains overhead
And hid his face amid a crowd of stars."

"That was beautiful." My voice breaks a little. Renato used to make me read, and when he read aloud it was with the pomposity of a professor. "William Butler Yeats. When did you first read it?"

"I was a boy. And I knew I wanted to feel that way about someone someday."

"Do you feel that way about me?" I say, apparently too loudly, because something rustles in the woods, as if I disturbed it with the timbre of my voice.

"You say whatever is on your mind, don't you?"

My face turns red, but maybe it's the heat from the fire. "I think it's good to . . . ask questions."

"I've never known a girl like you. You just come out with it." Franco closes the book and leans back against an old tree stump. I have somehow offended him, and I didn't mean to. This is a lovely evening, and I know better than to blurt the first thing that pops into my mind. After all, I've seen Joan Crawford, Norma Shearer, and Jean Harlow handle men with ease. They slither and slide and giggle, they don't ask questions; they say very little in a low, throaty voice and most important, they don't assume that the man is smitten. The smitten part always happens at the end of the picture. Here I am, a half hour into this date, and I've already asked him for a declaration of intention.

"Is my honesty a problem?"

He looks at me. "No."

"I'm not a flirt like the girls from West Bangor, or silly like the girls who slouched through school instead of studying. I'm not a beautiful girl who doesn't have to work. I know what I am, and maybe that's why I'm not soft. I never had a chance to be delicate; it wasn't called for on the farm."

"But you are tender. I've seen it."

"I have feelings, if that's what you're talking about."

"I know you have feelings. It's just that you put on this tough act, and I don't know how you want me to take that."

"You don't have to take it at all," I say quietly.

"I want to."

"Why?"

"The first time I saw you, you walked so tall, with confidence. I thought you were older. And then you sneezed. You were so cute."

"I'll remember that when I have a cold."

"Then you let me have it when I said you were too young to be a forelady. I like that you stood up for yourself. I want a girl who pushes me . . . I don't know, who makes me want to do better. Be better."

"You like a challenge?"

"No, I like *you*." He looks at the basket, unsure whether he should serve dinner or not. I help him decide by opening the basket and unpacking the sandwiches.

"The poem talks about love that has lasted a long time."

"A lifetime," Franco corrects me gently. "I believe it's a young man saying it to his young love, and telling her that no matter what comes, no matter how her beauty fades, he will still love her. It's more of a promise than a poem."

"You wouldn't mind me old and wizened?"

"Not at all."

"Why? Are you saying you would take me any way you could get me?"

He doesn't answer. He looks off and thinks about the question, and I see that he thinks deeply. Maybe his process is not profound or cultivated, and he hasn't been to a fancy school (like most of the Roseto boys, he's probably only been through the third grade), but he analyzes things in a way that all sharp minds do. I can see that. He looks at me. "I go on chemistry. You know I have to fix machines all day, and I've learned that even a machine has a personality. There is a way to handle it to get it to work. And people aren't much different. It's a process of figuring out what someone needs and giving it to them."

"That would make you happy?"

"Oh yeah. That *is* happiness. I wouldn't take you any way I could get you. I wouldn't want to be with you unless you loved me. I'm not the kind of guy who wants to be with a girl who doesn't want me. But I also see that you're wrong about me. You think I'm simple."

"I never said that."

"Why else would you hold on to a guy who is gone? The only thing he has that I don't have is an education."

"I don't have one either."

"You don't need one. You could teach professors a thing or two."

"You think so?" I haven't thought about school in a long time. As the months and years go by, I think about it less and less, like it's an old dream, one that when you look back, you don't remember wanting it as much as you thought you did.

"It's so funny. You may not think I'm smart enough for you, but what I admire most about you is your mind. What sixteen-year-old girl gets made forelady in a mill? You're the first, you know."

"You really pay attention."

"When I'm interested. And why not? There's the surface and then there's what's underneath. What's underneath is what is true." Franco unwraps a delicate sandwich and gives it to me. I take a bite.

The fire spits orange sparks out onto the edge of the ice. The flames can see their own reflections before they sputter out against the cold. I bury my glass in a clump of snow, then take Franco's glass and do the same. I take his sandwich from him and wrap it in the cloth napkin, setting it aside. I move over onto his lap and put my arms around his neck.

"I've made my decision," I tell him.

"And?"

"And I want you to keep reading to me."

I bury my face in his neck, remembering when I walked to Roseto Manufacturing Company for my first day of work. I remember knowing that I would never return to school. Just as I let go of that dream, in this cold night, I let go of Renato. I cannot keep my heart locked for the rest of my life, for a man who did not even have the courage to tell me good-bye. It is better to be with someone who cares about me than to pine for someone who does not.

"Can we take things slowly?"

"Whatever you say." Franco kisses me, and this time I am not taken by surprise. This time I'm ready for him.

$\mathcal{F}$ ranco's mother is now the happiest woman in the world, second only to my mother. It isn't because April 1931 is the most glorious ever, so warm that the gardens of Roseto have already burst into full bloom. Mrs. Zollerano is happy because her son Franco is in love. She tells me that she prayed to Saint Theresa every day that I would see the light. My mother is convinced that her prayers to Saint Ann brought us together.

Once I gave in to the idea of being with Franco, I quickly saw the many pluses: he is a good man from a good family on Garibaldi Avenue. My girlhood dreams have not all been lost; fragments of them have become real. I left Delabole farm for the place I longed to be. When I marry Franco, we will live in town. I will have my own home and still be near my family.

There is one problem. As I climb the steps to Our Lady of Mount Carmel, I know that Father Impeciato will have the answer. Between the hours of three o'clock and five o'clock in the afternoon on Saturdays, he hears confession. There is a long line the weeks before Easter, as parishioners have a deadline: all good Catholics must make a full confession before the resurrection. But now Easter is over, and the pews are empty again. I see the red light is on on the priest's side of the confessional, which means Father Impeciato is inside. The curtain is drawn open on the sinner's side. I look around the church, and except for Mrs. Stampone, who changes the altar linens, it is empty. I slip into the booth and pull the curtain.

I make the sign of the cross and say the opening prayer. The last time I was at confession was two weeks ago. The sin I am about to confess is one I have never mentioned in the booth before.

"Father, I am in love with a nice boy, and I need your advice."

"Go ahead," Father Impeciato says.

"There is something in my past that I did that might be a problem. I don't believe what I did was a sin, because if I thought it was, I wouldn't have done it."

"There are many definitions of sin, as you know."

"The catechism is pretty clear on this one, Father."

"Which particular sin do you refer to?"

"Intimate relations. I made love to a boy once five years ago. And he left. I intended to marry him, but that was not to be. Now I'm in love with a different man."

"Any prior indiscretion would not impede you from marriage now—" Father begins.

"I disagree with the word 'indiscretion.' As I said, I wanted to do what I did. I had full knowledge of the consequences, and I did it anyway. Right and wrong is not why I'm here, Father."

"Then why are you here?"

"Must I tell the young man I'm with now that I'm not a virgin?"

There is such a long silence, I wonder if Father Impeciato has gone to sleep or left the booth to stretch his legs. I put my ear up to the screen, and I can hear him breathing, so he must be thinking. As I kneel, I lean back on my calves and relax a little. Apparently this could take awhile. What a strange ritual this is: admitting secrets in a closet to a man who can't see you.

"I do not believe you should tell the young man what happened."

"Really?" This marks the first time I've ever smiled in a confessional. This was the answer I was hoping for.

"What good would come of it? He would surely have a problem with it, any man would. This young man, is he Italian?"

"Yes, Father, and Catholic."

Father breathes a sigh on the other side. Part of his job and mission from the diocese is to woo back the Italian immigrants who converted to Presbyterianism when Roseto was founded years ago. I can tell he doesn't want to come down too hard on me now, for fear I will flee to the pretty little church at the other end of Garibaldi.

"Marriage will be a new beginning for you. Fornication is a sin, make no mistake about it . . ."

I remember Renato and the sad day his father died, and the tenderness between us, and what it meant to me to be close to him. Father Impeciato's words have nothing to do with that day, but I'm smart enough to know that you don't argue with a priest.

". . . but it sounds like you have lived a chaste life since."

"I would say so, Father." I feel no need to confess the nights Franco and I spend at the pond pitching woo. I've never gone as far with Franco as I did that night with Renato, but I don't believe these details are any of Father Impeciato's business.

"Then keep the knowledge to yourself." He launches into the prayer of forgiveness; the Latin tumbles out of him effortlessly, and I listen, but my mind is elsewhere. Talking about Renato, even in these vague terms, makes the memories so clear. Maybe it's the darkness of this booth that helps me see my past clearly. I will always love Renato, and maybe that's a bigger sin toward Franco than the loss of my virginity. But I have flummoxed Father Impeciato enough today.

"Go and sin no more," he says through the screen.

"I'll do my best, Father."

※

"A man wants to marry a virgin because he wants to know his wife has moral character." Chettie takes a bite of panini, a thin sandwich of *prosciutto* and butter between crusts of soft bread.

"A man wants a virgin because he doesn't want the competition. If she knows another man, she might start comparing." I pour each of us a cup of coffee from my thermos. "And what about the moral character of men? Do you ever wonder why it is acceptable for a man to spend the night in Hellertown carrying on and carousing with the local girls, but if we did the same thing with their men, we'd be hussies?"

Chettie shakes her head. "What's the big deal to wait for your wedding night?"

"It seems silly to me."

"What would your parents say?"

"What do you think?" I dip *anisette* toast into my coffee. "I can't talk to them about such things."

"I won't do it because I'm afraid I'd burn in hell. When Anthony tries, I remind him of the black pit with the flames in the window of Our Lady of Mount Carmel and what happens to frisky young men. They fry like pork fat for all eternity."

"Do you think that God knows the day you get married?"

"Of course He does. It's a sacrament."

"Oh, so you think He keeps a log up there and knows the exact moment you get your ring."

"It's a matter of faith, so yes, I think He knows."

"I don't think He knows or cares."

Chettie's eyes widen at such talk. "Cripes, Nella. You aren't a very good Catholic."

"I'm nowhere near as good as you."

"Why do you bother going to church?"

"It's not like I don't believe in right and wrong. And I like the Mass, I like the routine of it, the music, the church when it's filled with gold light through the stained-glass windows. I like the incense and Holy Communion. And it's important. If I'm going to be a forelady and live in Roseto, I have to be part of the church."

"That's true. They like a churchgoer around here."

"They don't need to know that when I kneel in prayer I follow my own heart, or that I trust my own conscience as much as I trust a priest or a bishop."

"When you put it that way it doesn't sound so bad."

"I don't think people should run around blaspheming and fornicating—but there's a difference between that and caring about someone and showing it."

"It's just better if you're married. You're safe then. The man can't leave you," Chettie says with authority.

It's the first thing she's said regarding intimate relations that makes some sense. Only a girl like me who's actually been left by a man would know how true that sentiment is.

I've never told Chettie about what happened with Renato. She was a big help when he left, but I never told her why I was so distraught. I suppose it would have been easier to get over him had we not crossed the line. When we made love, everything changed for me. It wasn't puppy love; it became a sort of devotion. Maybe that's why it has taken five years for me not to feel sick when I think of him.

I wish I could tell Chettie what making love was like. It didn't seem like I had fallen off the earth into an abyss of sin. I even longed to repeat that night, but alas, Renato would not, probably because he already knew he had no intention of marrying me.

". . . you agree, right? It's better if you're married," Chettie persists.

"Whatever you say."

"You and Franco?"

"Not yet."

She exhales a sigh of relief. "Good. Because if Anthony ever found out, I would never make it until June first, believe me. All he'd have to hear is that Zollerano and Castelluca were having at it, and that's all the encouragement he'd need to put the final pressure on me."

"It's right for you to wait for your wedding night. So wait."

"I know you don't want to hear this, but if you're smart, you'll wait too. Italian men are hypocrites. They beg for it, but they really don't want us to do it. If we gave in, they would hold it against us for the rest of our lives."

"Italian men are big babies. They want what they want when they want it."

"Well, Anthony will just have to wait."

I think about my lunch with Chettie as I walk home from work. I decide to take the route up Chestnut Street, because when I walk up Garibaldi, Mrs. Zollerano is waiting on the porch for a chat. Sometimes I'm there the better part of an hour hearing all the Roseto gossip. Tonight I want to soak in a hot bath and go to bed early.

When I climb the steps to Elena's porch, I hear one of the kids crying. I slip into the house and hear Elena comforting Assunta in the kitchen.

"Now, honey, we always told you the truth."

"But I don't have a mommy," Assunta wails.

"You do have a mommy, she's in heaven," Elena promises her.

"Ellie Montagano said that it was wrong for you to marry my papa. She said that it would have killed my mother."

I put down my purse and gloves and go into the kitchen. Elena has her hands on her hips, trying to reason with Assunta. For a moment, they look just like Mama and my sister Assunta arguing in the kitchen at the farm, and I have to remember where I am. "That is nonsense, Assunta." I give her my handkerchief. "Now, stop crying." Little Assunta is so much like her mother, fierce, proud, and never content. I'm sure she fished for the fight with Ellie Montagano.

"Look at me," I say. "Your mama loved you. She was so excited for you to be born. But God decided He needed her in heaven." Once I say this out loud, I realize how ridiculous it sounds. What does God need her up there for anyway? He needs another harp player, third angel from the left? But Assunta looks at me with interest, so I continue. "And back here on earth, you were a tiny thing, and we were afraid you wouldn't make it. Your aunt Elena took care of you from the first moment you were born. Now, would Ellie Montagano have a problem with that?"

"No, I guess not."

"Okay, so here we all were, Aunt Elena, Aunt Roma, Aunt Dianna, your nonna, me—we were all looking out for you. And your papa saw what a good mother Aunt Elena was, even though she did not have any of her own children then. He saw that and loved her for it. Then they got married. And you were there, at the wedding."

"I was just a little girl, right?"

"Right. There is nothing wrong with Aunt Elena taking care of you and your papa and your sister, Aurelia, and your brother. Understood?"

Assunta nods.

I look up at Elena. "And are you going to be okay?" She nods too.

I grab my purse and gloves and go back outside. I remember that the Montaganos live on Cemetery Road, so I head in that direction. As I walk, I begin to fume. Rosetans can be warm and delightful, but at the same time, their rigidity and judgments are sickening. Six-year-old Ellie did not make up this scurrilous gossip, she heard it somewhere. Her mother, Isidora, used to work for me at the mill and is known to carry more stories than *The Saturday Evening Post*. I don't care who she talks about, as long as it's not my family. I knock on the door at 17 Cemetery Road.

"Is your mother home?" I ask a girl with jet-black ringlets.

"Yeah." She chews gum and turns and hollers, "Mama, there's a lady here."

Then the girl runs off, leaving me on the porch. Isidora comes to the door. At the mill, she never struck me as bright and she was never on time, two characteristics that still run up my spine.

"How are you, Nella?" she says, smiling. Isidora is small and round, like a bobbin. "Would you like to come in?"

"No, no, I would not."

This gets her attention. "You seem upset about something."

"My niece Assunta is home crying because of something your daughter said to her."

"I can't imagine it. What?"

"She passed a comment about my sister Elena marrying Alessandro."

"That's terrible," Isidora says.

"I'm glad you think so."

"You know, sometimes Ellie hears things at school. It's too bad that your sister Assunta died the way she did, but people will talk. And Elena and Alessandro did marry rather quickly. There really wasn't a proper period of mourning. I'm sure that's all that was said."

"That was five years ago, and you're still talking about this?" I was aware of the gossip at the time, but disregarded it. There is always a story going around Roseto, and if you're in the middle of it, you hope that it will soon pass. Usually, it does.

"It's just that the children all go to school together. It

comes up. You know, in light of Alessandro and Elena's natural children."

"Look, Isidora. When you worked for me at the mill you had the loosest lips in the lunchroom. I'm sure 'the children' have nothing to do with this vicious gossip, and you can consider this a warning. If I hear another crass comment about my sister coming from anyone in your family, you will have me to deal with. Understood?"

"You're being ridiculous." Her eyes narrow.

"And you hide behind children to spread your nasty stories. If I have something to say, I say it." I turn to go down the steps.

"You Castellucas, who do you think you are? A bunch of farmers," she sneers from behind the screen door. "Big boss lady. Big deal."

I smile; if this is the worst thing she can say about me and mine, that's fine with me. "Remember what I told you," I say without turning around to look at her again. "I mean what I say."

What I will always remember about Anthony and Chettie's wedding day is not the beautiful bride, the handsome groom, or the church festooned in white carnations and yellow daisies on a sunny June morning, but rather the knock-down, drag-out fight that Anthony's aunts had on the steps of Our Lady of Mount Carmel after the service.

Anthony's family is so large, they filled up every seat plus the side aisles and took over the choir loft as well as their side of the church. One of his aunts felt slighted, as she had to sit in the back pew. When her rival sister-in-law came down the aisle at the recessional, having sat in the second row, she made a comment. They had words, which were thankfully lost on the crowd because of the organ music, but once they got outside, the fight escalated. One pushed the other down the stairs, and fists, purses, and feathered hats flew. Chettie did the right thing, ignored them, and proceeded in Anthony's borrowed Cadillac convertible to Pinto's Hall for the reception.

"Didn't the pictures turn out nicely?" Chettie says as she shows them to me over lunch. The cool breezes of autumn have come to Roseto, but the sun is warm. Chettie and I love the fresh air, so we eat outside instead of in the lunchroom that Mr. Jenkins built for the workers.

"They're beautiful. And look, you can't see Aunt Rosa's black eye." I point to the group photo of the Marucci clan.

"Somebody said the fight was good luck. But of course, everything is good luck on a wedding day: rain, sun, left hooks." Chettie grins. "I sure hope so, because I'm gonna need all the luck I can get."

"Why's that?"

"Nella, I'm having a baby."

"Oh my God!" I give Chettie a big hug, knowing this is something she has wanted. It's fast too, as Anthony and she have only been married three months.

"I hoped you and I would have our children together," she says.

"Somebody has to be first," I say. "And I'm glad it's you."

"Do you think Franco will pop the question soon?"

"I don't know. You know I'm not one of those girls who sits around hoping for a diamond. I figure it will happen when it happens."

"Somebody saw him at Steckel's." Chettie raises her eyebrow just as Franco comes down the steps carrying his toolbox.

"What are you girls talking about?" he asks. I still marvel at his height, his strong arms and neck. I could watch him repair equipment for hours.

"You."

"Nella!" Chettie is horrified.

"Really?" Franco throws his toolbox in the back of the truck.

"Somebody saw you at Steckel's. Were you jewelry shopping?" I ask him.

"Nella, I can't believe you!" Chettie is stunned at my candor.

"I was getting my watch fixed." Franco gets into his truck. "I'm going to Jersey. I'll pick you up around seven." He starts the engine, waves to us, and pulls out of the parking lot onto Slate Belt Boulevard.

"What's the matter with you? You'll ruin his surprise!"

"I don't like surprises."

"But what about romance?"

"Oh, there's romance. Don't worry about that."

The bell rings to call us back in from lunch. I watch

Chettie go back to finishing; she'll have the baby, her mother will watch it during the day, and she'll continue to work. For all the girls in Roseto, our mothers are built-in help; and if we're really lucky, the nonnas live with us too, so there's an extra set of hands and eyes to help raise the children. The mill hours are built around the children. We start in the mornings by seven and finish by four, in time to be with the little ones after they've come home from school.

I dream about a home of my own, and as often as not, I imagine a big, rambling Victorian on Garibaldi with lots of furniture and a big kitchen and one tenant: me. I love Franco, but marriage seems like another job on top of the work I do at the mill. I won't be able to hold Franco off forever, but I love these days that are filled with dinner dates, long drives, and endless conversation instead of obligations.

On the way to Easton to see the new Norma Shearer picture, A Free Soul, I tell Franco Chettie's news. He is happy for them, but doesn't say much. I think his reaction is odd. Maybe he's angry with me for talking about him with Chettie, and maybe my mention of Steckel's embarrassed him. He probably was getting his watch fixed.

Franco settles me in my seat in the theater and goes for popcorn. I look around at the couples there for the show and wonder how many of them will marry, and if they do, whether they will be happy. Working at the mill gives me my own money, and I wonder whether I'd be a little more anxious to get married if I didn't have a job. Why don't I crave a wedding day and the title of wife like all the other girls?

Some cannot wait, grabbing the first boy that suits them, and others are destroyed when they're not chosen. I've never seen a happy old maid in Roseto. There is always a bitterness, an undercurrent of anger at getting stuck in the house they grew up in, caring for the older parents and looking out for their nieces and nephews. I'm sure when they look at the children they wonder what might have been. Why don't I? Perhaps my heart never mended from Renato. I compare Franco with him in big ways and in small details. They are very different, but Renato always has the advantage. It's a fact Franco cannot compete with: Renato was my first love.

Franco slides down in the seat next to me and gives me a sack of fresh popcorn smothered in butter, just as I like it. I feel guilty for thinking about Renato when I'm out with Franco, so I give him a kiss on the cheek. He turns to me and kisses me on the lips tenderly. I guess he's not angry at me about teasing him at the mill.

The newsreel shows President Roosevelt and a team of workers from the WPA building a bridge outside Washington, D.C. I know people are suffering, but somehow I feel not only blessed but oddly detached. There is nothing about the Depression that I haven't lived already. During the boom years, we were on the farm struggling, sometimes barely surviving. We were alone then in our despair, and now we are alone in our prosperity.

The story of A Free Soul is dark and complex. Clark Gable plays a gangster. Lionel Barrymore is the lawyer who gets him off a rap. Norma Shearer plays Lionel's daughter, a flapper

230 / ADRIANA TRIGIANI

who falls for Clark Gable. The father, who's a lush, is bereft when his daughter goes for a gangster.

"Get ready. This is the best scene," Franco whispers.

"Have you already seen it?" I whisper back.

He nods that he has. That's odd. He came all the way to Easton to see the show and now he's back? Who did he see it with the first time, and why would he see it again?

Clark Gable is telling Norma Shearer in no uncertain terms that she is his woman; she resists him but then tells him that she loves him and that nothing will keep them apart. Franco reaches to hold my hand. He threads his fingers through mine. Then I feel something cold on my ring finger. He has slid an engagement ring onto my hand! I look down at the emerald-cut diamond and squeal with delight.

"*Shhh*," the patrons behind me say. I lean over and kiss Franco. He puts his arm around me and holds me close. We slide down in the seats and kiss.

"Will you have me?" he whispers.

"Yes, I will," I tell him. I want to build a future, and as I sit here with Franco, I believe he is the man with whom I want to share my life and work.

On the drive home, I sit close to Franco and rub the back of his neck as he drives. I check the ring over his shoulder. It is a beauty, catching the headlights of the cars in the other lanes as they pass. "You know, you didn't really ask me."

"Ask you what?" Franco says innocently.

"Don't get fresh. You didn't ask me to marry you."

"Will you marry me?"

"I don't like your tone."

"Will thou marry me?"

"Better. It sounds like Yeats."

"Thank you. So, when do you want to get married?" Franco asks.

"How about the spring?"

"How about tomorrow? We'll go up to Sailor's Lake and get a justice of the peace to marry us."

"Catholics don't elope," I remind him. "Good Catholics, anyway." As soon as I say it, I realize the irony.

"My aunt Serafina DeMarco eloped."

"She doesn't count. She had to."

"Don't be catty. Let's go see Father Impeciato then." Franco turns off the road.

"This doesn't look like the Our Lady of Mount Carmel rectory." Franco drives into a clearing; there's a red barn lit by lanterns. He pulls up and parks.

"What is this?" I want to know.

"For a girl from Delabole, you ought to know what a barn looks like."

"No, I mean, what are we doing here?"

"Chettie spoiled the ring, I'm not spoiling this." Franco takes me by the hand and into the barn. There's an old man napping on a stool leaning against a horse stall. "Mr. Finkbeiner?" Franco shakes him gently. "Sir?"

Mr. Finkbeiner wakes up. "Oh, Franco. I got the hitch all ready. Come on."

Mr. Finkbeiner leads us out the back of the barn. He has rigged a horse to a wagon filled with hay.

"Ever been on a hay ride?" Franco asks.

"Not since I was thirteen."

Franco helps me up into the driver's seat. He slides in next to me. "See you later," he says to Mr. Finkbeiner.

"You're so romantic," I sigh.

"I got a romantic girl, so I have to stay on my toes." Franco pulls me close. The horse leads the wagon into a deep, black field. He seems to know his way. I remember breaking ground with my father in our cornfield with the plow when I was a girl. There never seemed to be enough hours in the day to finish the work that had to be done. I have that feeling tonight with Franco, the fear that there just isn't enough time. Not even the bliss of this moment will last, even with a diamond from Steckel's to prove it.

"You'll do anything to be alone with me," I tell him, getting my mind off these dark thoughts. "Hire a hay wagon? This has to be a first."

"Do you know how tired I am of dropping you off on Dewey Street? I can't stand it anymore. Then I go home to my room, the room I grew up in, and I feel like I'm in prison. I want you in my bed every night for the rest of my life." Franco stops the horse and leans down and kisses me. He jumps off the seat and comes around to my side. He lifts me off and carries me to the wagon in the back. On the way, he covers my face in kisses. I feel more than possessed, more than a girl in love; I am hungry for him. He sets me down and takes off his jacket, laying it on the fresh hay in the wagon. Then he places me gently on top of it. I pull him close and we laugh. As we roll into the hay, it kicks up like confetti. As we kiss, the moon dances in and out of the clouds as though it is flashing a warning. I ignore it and roll on top of Franco, cradling his face in my hands. "I've loved you since the first time I saw you," he whispers. "Don't ever leave me."

The final sacrament Father Impeciato will perform before his retirement as pastor of Our Lady of Mount Carmel will happen tomorrow morning, March 1, 1932, with the wedding of Antonella Margarita Castelluca and Franco Danielo Zollerano. Elena will stand up for me, as I stood up for her, and Franco's eldest brother will be the best man. Elena made my wedding dress, a two-tiered champagne satin gown with dolman sleeves. The headpiece, a wide band of satin, will be anchored by a plume of stephanotis. Chettie, whose summer baby is starting to show, will direct the wedding.

Something old, a red bandanna handkerchief, given to me on my first day in the mill by Franco, will serve as the garter. I will tie it around my thigh, right above the knee, in a neat bow. Elena gave me a miraculous medal pin of the Blessed Mother for something new, which I will pin to it. Something borrowed will be Chettie's rosary, and something blue will be a single iris among the roses in my bouquet.

Pinto's Hall has been booked, Franco's morning suit has been fitted, and the house that we will rent, in the hope of buying one day, is a brick two-story at 169 Garibaldi Avenue. There is a long, lush lot in the back where I plan to have a garden.

The first thing I did once we set the date was to go down to Marcella's bakery and order our cake. I chose one with ten tiers of yellow cake and white frosting. In honor of our trade, marzipan needles and spools of thread will dance up the sides of the cake.

Alessandro went to Philadelphia to pick up Mama and Papa, who are returning home a few weeks early from their winter sabbatical to Roseto Valfortore. Papa wrote a beautiful letter to me, which I will always cherish. He said that in all things, he trusted my judgment, and I have surely done Mama and him a great honor by choosing Franco. When I showed Franco the letter, he was as moved as I was.

"Come on, come on, let's get started!" Chettie calls from the top of the stairs of the church.

"We're coming!" I call out from Franco's car. He comes around and opens the door, helps me out, and kisses me as he pulls me onto the sidewalk.

"I don't understand why we have to rehearse. How hard is this anyway?" he says as we walk up the steps.

"Father Impeciato likes everything to be perfect."

Chettie and Anthony have prepared a meal following the rehearsal dinner, and both of our families have been invited. When I open the door, Papa meets me. "Pop, you look so good." I give him a big hug. "*Bronzato!*"

"I have a box of presents from the other side. You won't

believe it. Lace, linens, and even a corkscrew. Your Italian relatives are so happy for you."

"I *am* happy, Papa."

Chettie, a veteran of wedding rehearsals, knows exactly where Papa and I should stand in the back of the church. I peek through the doors and can see Father Impeciato at the altar checking his watch. Chettie walks me through the processional, placing Elena a few steps ahead as matron of honor.

There, at the end of the aisle, Franco waits for me. He is tall and handsome and strong, all the things I noticed the very first time I saw him at the mill. It is hard to reconcile the man I thought he was with the man he has become. It's not that Franco Zollerano changed for me, but we have somehow changed each other. He has made me softer and more tolerant, and I hope I have made him more introspective.

"You go to there . . ." Father Impeciato points to the step behind the Communion railing, ". . . and Franco, you join us there." He points again. Franco takes my hand and we face Father Impeciato.

Out of the sacristy, through a door to the right of the altar, comes a priest. With his head bowed, he goes to the tabernacle and places the chalice and paten next to the small golden door. There is something about the priest that is familiar, and while I keep my eyes on Father Impeciato, I am drawn to the figure in the long black cassock with his back turned to us.

Father Impeciato, eager to move the rehearsal along, calls out to the priest, "Father Lanzara?"

I am confused when I first hear the name, and then my heart begins to race. I tighten my grip on Franco's hand. The priest turns around and looks at us. It is the same sandy hair, the strong jaw, the clear blue eyes. It is Renato. My Renato.

Chettie and Elena, as shocked as I am, crowd close to me. Franco looks down at me, utterly confused. Finally, I break the stunned silence. "Renato? You're a priest?"

"Yes, I am." He smiles, and it isn't even a sheepish smile, but rather a cordial one. He genuflects and comes around to the front of the altar. Renato is as handsome as ever. The cassock seems like a costume, and in an instant I feel as though I am playacting through a wedding ceremony and he has taken his cue to come to the stage and rescue me.

Renato extends his hand to Franco. "Congratulations." Then he takes my hand. Without looking in my eyes, he focuses on a point beyond the top of my head and says warmly, "And to you too."

"When did you become a priest?" Chettie blurts.

"In Rome, last spring." He gives a sort of half bow from the waist, as if to say that the pleasantries are over. I look at Chettie and she looks at me. We don't know what to think.

So this is what happened to Renato. He didn't disappear, marry a girl in Allentown, or flee the country. He went to the seminary and entered the priesthood. But why? He was the world's least likely candidate for the priesthood! He loved women and fine clothing and poetry.

"He is my replacement. Your new pastor," Father Impeciato

adds. "The bishop thought the perfect choice would be a native son of Roseto. I quite agreed."

"It's good to see you all again. I won't interrupt your rehearsal any longer," Renato says curtly and goes.

Father Impeciato continues blabbering about our service, what will happen when, when to move to the Blessed Mother statue for the Ave Maria, but all I want to do is run back to the sacristy and talk to Renato. I've been waiting for an explanation from him for five years, and even though I'm about to undertake the most holy of sacraments with Franco, I want to know why Renato left me. Franco feels my attention go, and squeezes my hand to bring me back to the moment. But the moment, our moment, is gone. I am back to the day I pulled Renato's letter from the screen door, when I felt the full force of his rejection after I loved him with the deepest truth. My head spins. Chettie whispers that the rehearsal is almost over. "You need air."

Chettie is right. It will help to get outside. We practice the stately recessional, but I make it back down the aisle in record time. I almost run out of Our Lady of Mount Carmel.

Once we reach the doors, Franco pushes them open. When I get outside, I hold the hand railing for balance.

"That was the goddamnedest thing," Franco says to me. "Jesus."

"Would you stop cursing!" I phrase it as a question but I say it as a demand. But when I look at Franco, and see his confusion and hurt, not just because of Renato's return but because of my reaction to it, my heart aches for him. Franco will be my husband as of this time tomorrow, and I don't want him to feel anything but happiness. "I'm sorry, Franco. I wish we would have had some warning."

Franco holds me close as Chettie, Elena, and Papa come out of the church.

"He's a priest," Papa sneers as he smooths the brim on his hat and punches the crown. "The town playboy becomes the padre. Only in America."

At dawn on my wedding day, Elena's house is quiet. I go down the steps to the kitchen and put on the coffee. I open the shutters to the side yard and look out. The ground is covered in a light dusting of snow. The sun is starting to peek over the hill, throwing a bright gleam on Dewey Street. It has snowed on my wedding day. I wonder what the old *stregas* would make of this. Either rain or sun is a lucky element for the bride and groom, but what about snow?

I pour fresh milk into the pan as the coffee percolates. I watch the milk as it foams, removing it quickly and pouring it into the bowl. This will be the last time I will fill one cup with milk. How I've loved these mornings when I get up an hour before everyone else and sit in the quiet warmth of the kitchen and have my breakfast alone. This is the last morning I will be alone. From this day on I will make Franco's breakfast, and then, as the years go by, the children will come and I will make theirs. I get a sick feeling in the pit of my stomach.

I don't understand the meaning of Renato's return so close to the day I am giving myself to my husband. And a priest!

Would it have made any difference had he returned with a wife? Yes! Someone would have been chosen over me. At least he's not still a bachelor. What would that have meant on my wedding day?

"Good morning," Elena says softly as she comes into the kitchen. She goes to the toaster and loads bread into the slots. She takes the butter crock from the shelf and the jam from the cupboard. "Are you all right?"

"I'm fine."

"Don't let Father Lanzara ruin your wedding day."

It always amazes me how Elena knows exactly what I'm thinking. "Don't call him 'Father.' "

"But he's a priest now."

"Not to me. He may be your priest. He's Roseto's priest. But he's my ex."

"Nella, you have to let go of all of that. The past. Him. What you used to feel, it's of no use to you now."

"Do I look like the kind of girl who would pine for a priest?" I say.

"No. But if you hold on to what you were to each other, it will get in the way of how you feel about Franco."

"I'm not holding on to anything," I lie.

"I know something about holding on to the past," she says. "It took me a long time to accept Alessandro as my husband and not Assunta's widower. I always felt like I was in second place. Please don't let Franco feel the way I did."

"I would never do that," I say, my heart breaking for the difficult position Elena has been in all these years.

"Sometimes it's subtle. Sometimes you won't even know you're doing it. Lots of times Alessandro treated me as though I should know something or as though I should understand something about him when it was all new to me. And even though we've been married longer than he was to Assunta, I am always aware that he had a life before our life together."

"I'll be careful," I promise her, realizing that I've never been careful with Franco. I say anything that's on my mind to him. I've never stopped to think how my words might hurt him. But I'll be very careful from now on, as tender with his heart as he is with mine.

"You have such a good man. He can make you very happy if you let him."

Elena goes to the cupboard and sets the table for the children's breakfast. I watch her as she effortlessly falls into the morning routine, as though she were born to do it. This is her little corner of the world, and she has made it warm and inviting. She has found her happiness in an unlikely place. I vow to do the same. Nothing about my home life was ever as easy as the work I do in the mill. I always struggled to fit in naturally with the flow of a family. Now, on my wedding day, I feel the obligation to create a new family. I hope I'm up to the task.

Mercifully, Roseto's new village priest did not show up at my wedding. Father Impeciato handled the proceedings with an old-fashioned calm and resolve. The choir sang on cue and Pinto's Hall made sure the orchestra played the extra hour so the millworkers could dance well into their Sunday morning. Franco and I went to a charming hotel in the Poconos for our wedding night. He gave me a strand of pearls and a night-gown. I gave him a new tool set and pajamas.

From our room, we had a perfect view of the Delaware Water Gap, and a featherbed that was as soft and deep as a cloud. We made love and ate chocolates and talked of our future. We made our plans to have children and someday see Italy together. I want to show Franco the world. He just wants me to live in his.

I never mentioned Father Lanzara during our honey-moon week, and neither did Franco. But Renato has remained in the back of my heart like a dull ache for five years, and getting married cannot change that overnight. I don't want to love Renato, I don't want to have these feelings, but for some reason, they persist. I want so badly to rid myself of that dull ache, but my honeymoon was not the time to try. Now that we're home, I know it's time to face the dragon.

I climb the steps of Our Lady of Mount Carmel as I have for so many Saturdays for confession. Usually, I like this sacra-ment. I like to feel that God forgives me for being human and gives me a chance to start anew.

I have never entered a confessional to speak directly with a priest. He is merely a conduit to God Himself. It has never mattered to me who the priest was; if it was Father Impeciato, that was fine, or a visiting priest from Bangor, equally fine, because I am a faceless sinner to the confessor, and he is faceless to me.

But this day I know the face of my confessor. I know his voice. I know his hands. I've held him when he cried. I want a dialogue. It is inappropriate for me to knock on the door of the rectory, or stop in after Mass to speak with Father Lanzara. After all, this man once loved me. I am not the only person in town who knows of our past. I would not compromise his reputation or mine in that way. I will always do what I think is right, and in the dark box of the confessional, the only place we can converse freely, I wish to come clean.

"Bless me, Father, for I have sinned."

Either Renato does not recognize my voice or he pretends not to. He begins the prayer in Latin and I stop him.

"Renato, it's me. Nella."

"Nella?" he whispers.

"Yes, your Nella. Would you care to tell me what happened to you?"

"I wanted to tell you when I entered the seminary, but I thought it was best to leave you alone."

"No, it would have been best to talk to me instead of disappearing."

"I never thought that they would send me back here."

"If they sent you to China, you would still owe me an explanation."

"The bishop had a plan in mind and could not be persuaded to change it. He has a dream to build a Catholic school here. And then a hospital. He looks at me as though

I'm another Father DeNisco. He thought a hometown boy could rally the town."

I almost feel sorry for him as I listen. For all my suffering, this is a real penance for Renato, to return to the place he grew up, to lead the very town that always made him so restless. "The bishop is an idiot. You don't belong here. You have a past here. A past that I'm a part of. Maybe a small part . . ."

"It wasn't a small part," Renato says quietly.

"The letter you left me was an insult."

"I was confused. I didn't want to lead you on."

"If you wanted to be a priest, or marry someone else, or live alone, all you owed me was a conversation. What was I supposed to be thinking these past five years?"

"I'm sorry, Nella."

"You should be."

"Truly. I am sorry for the way I acted."

"You know what, Father? That's not good enough. How ironic that you get to sit in this box and forgive people. Well, I can't forgive you."

I sit back on my calves and try to drink in the truth: Renato has chosen something else over me, as surely as if he had returned on the arm of another woman, and I need to accept it. I loved him more than he loved me, and that is a bad place for a woman to be.

For the first time since I began confessing my sins in this booth, I pull back the velvet curtain without offering an act of contrition. I walk out into the church, and out the door onto

Garibaldi Avenue. I stand there a long time before I walk toward home and my destiny, Franco Zollerano. This is one confession for which I feel no absolution.

CHAPTER TEN

When news comes of Mr. Jenkins's passing in his home in New Jersey, Franco and I are not surprised. By the fall of 1939, Mr. Jenkins had turned most of the daily operation of the factory over to me, with monthly visits by his son, Freddie. Mr. Jenkins tried to work through a heart ailment and then cancer, but he became so frail he could no longer make the drive to Roseto from New Jersey. He counted on me to run his business, and I did, always grateful for the opportunity. Even though Mr. Jenkins was a Johnny Bull, he grew to respect the Rosetans at the end of his life and looked upon me as a daughter he could trust with his beloved mill.

With two children at home, our six-year-old son, Franco

Junior (we call him Frankie), and our two-month-old daughter, Celeste, our hands are full. Franco and I dream of opening our own factory, but while we save as much money as we can, it will be several years before we have the seed money.

Freddie Jenkins has none of the charm of his father, and even less of his vision. Jenkins's operations grew to include four mills in our area—two in Roseto, one in Pen Argyl, and the newest in Martins Creek. Freddie often says that anyone can set up a bunch of sewing machines in the Slate Belt of Pennsylvania and make money. He surely has. Franco and I lie in bed at night and scheme how we too can get in on the boom.

Instead of driving to church for Celeste's baptism, we put her in the pram and walk up Garibaldi Avenue. Papa and Mama live with us now, giving Alessandro and Elena much needed room on Dewey Street for their growing family (Elena had a third baby last year, a daughter, Maria).

We are happy that Papa is with us, because he is a good influence on our son. Frankie thinks that Garibaldi Avenue is his private street, and he runs across to his Zollerano grandparents' house and then home to my parents. My in-laws have been a great help with the children. My parents and my mother-in-law take turns watching the children when we work.

"I like that hat," my husband compliments me. I bought it at Hess Brothers in Easton. It's a wide-brimmed red straw hat with silk roses on the crown. I made a wool suit in magenta to go with it. I saw Myrna Loy in a suit in the movie *Test Pilot* and copied it down to the buttons on the skirt. "I love you in red." My husband kisses me on the cheek. "Frankie, hold the door for your mama." Frankie holds the church door open for us as we enter.

Elena and Alessandro will stand up for Celeste as godparents. We're baptizing Celeste quickly because Alessandro has to leave for Italy in a week. His importing business has prospered, but he must travel a great deal. Elena is very understanding, but as the family has grown, so has her workload. Somehow she handles it all beautifully.

Father Lanzara is waiting for us inside. He invites me to the Communion railing, where I receive a blessing called "churching" that cleanses me after giving birth, and gives me the right to assume the sacraments once more. Renato gives me a candle to light.

Renato looks at me and prays, "*Ingredere in templum Dei, adora Filium beatae Mariae Virginis, qui tibi fecunditatem tribuit polis.*" He leads me to the altar, where I place the lighted candle in a candlestick. I go back to the kneeler. Renato prays the Magnificat aloud; most of the words blur into a hum, but when Renato reads, "He has shown might with His arm; He has scattered the proud in the conceit of their heart. He has put down the mighty from their thrones and exalted the lowly," the words feel like an apology. When he places his hands on mine to bless me, I pull away quickly. When Renato places his hand on my cheek to absolve me, I look up at him, our eyes meet, and I feel a surge of what we used to mean to each other. Like two old lovers, we speak with our eyes. Even though it's brief, the intimacy is real, and it is electrifying. The baby coos, and I quickly look away. I stand up and turn to my family and smile.

"Here, honey." Franco gives me back our daughter now that I have been cleansed.

We follow Father Lanzara to the back of the church to the baptismal font. We watch as Renato blesses my daughter and welcomes her to the fold. I look around at my sisters, my nieces and nephews, my parents and my in-laws, and realize how lucky I am.

"Father, please join us for dinner," my mother-in-law says.

"I'm sorry. I have to prepare for Mass tomorrow."

"But you must eat something!" she insists. Beatrice Zollerano is president of the women's sodality, so she has to look after the priest.

"Don't worry. Mrs. Stampone takes good care of us in the rectory."

"Her sauce is not one half as robust as mine," my mother-in-law sniffs.

"How about we drop off a plate to Father Lanzara later?" I suggest.

"Please, that's not necessary. Thank you for the invitation."

Renato leaves the sacristy and goes out of the church. I watch him go, sad to think he will have dinner alone.

After we put the children to bed, Franco comes to the kitchen for a cup of tea.

"I'll bring you tea upstairs," I tell him.

"No, you have to get up early too." Franco puts the kettle on the stove. "Alessandro had an interesting offer for us."

"What's that?"

"He said he could give us the down payment to buy the mill. But," Franco pauses, "what he would rather do is partner with us."

"My God, really?" I ask, but immediately have second thoughts. "Is it good to get in business with family?"

"I don't think it would be a problem," Franco says.

But my husband does not have a mind for business like I do. I would rather borrow the money from a bank. I don't believe in business and family mixing, I don't see how it can work without problems. What would happen if a shipment went out late? What would happen if machines needed replacing? What would we do if our best operators went to the competition?

"I don't like the idea."

"Then we stay indentured servants to Jenkins's son. Do you think that's a better idea?"

"It's not better, but we're hardly servants. He just gave me a raise."

"It's not enough," he says.

"It will be enough in two more years." I know, I've done the math, I know the figures. "Why don't we wait?"

"I think we should consider Alessandro's offer. I'd rather owe my brother-in-law than continue the arrangement we have with Jenkins."

"I'll think about it," I tell Franco, but my mind is made up.

"Why do you do that?" he asks.

"Do what?"

"Tell me that you're going to consider something when you have no intention of doing what I ask?"

"I don't know what you're talking about. I consult you about everything."

"Nella, you don't trust my judgment."

"It's not that, Franco. Of course I do. But I've been a fore-lady since I was sixteen. I know a little something about how a mill operates."

"Don't patronize me," he snaps.

"I'm not allowed to disagree?"

"Now you're baiting and switching. Another one of your classic tactics."

Franco turns to go upstairs. I stop him.

"What's the matter?" I want to know.

"I don't like how you look at him," Franco says softly.

"Look at who?"

"Renato. You still care about him."

I can't believe Franco is saying this. Whenever I am near Renato, I act indifferent. I barely speak to the man, and if he is performing a service or sacrament, I barely listen to the words. I don't even try to pray. Yet I can't lie to Franco. "I'll always care about him, but it's not like you think."

"You looked upset when he wouldn't come to dinner."

"I wasn't upset. I feel sorry for him."

"Why?"

"He's alone. Look at us. We have all this family around us. We have each other, our children. What does he have?"

"He's a goddamn priest. He chose that."

"Don't you have any compassion at all?"

"I should have put my foot down when Lanzara came back. Now I mean it. We are not going to church there anymore."

"Why not?"

"Because I don't want to see that. You're my wife, and if you can't let go of him, then I have to cut the rope."

"Franco, I've never done anything, anything wrong. I promise you."

Franco gets tears in his eyes. "I believe you." I can see that for all my torment, his is just as real. I thought I had a grip on this, that it was in the past. I haven't given myself fully to my husband because a small part of my heart is forever taken up with what might have been. I don't want to love Renato! I don't wish to be with him. I just want to know how to get him out of my heart, permanently and forever.

"I would never do anything. I don't love him. You're my husband. The father of my children. I love you." I kiss Franco tenderly. "I would never hurt you. Please believe me."

"I love you, Nella. But I know what I'm up against. Because *you* are my first love. And I could never stop loving you."

Franco goes up the stairs, leaving me to turn out the lights and lock the door. Did I choose this terrible place between the past and the present, or did it find me? I resolve to make my husband happy, whatever that takes. And if we must leave Our Lady of Mount Carmel to do it, so be it.

"Nella, Nella, honey?" Franco gently nudges me awake. "Get dressed."

I open my eyes and see my husband with a hat and coat on, and my son dressed the same. "What time is it?"

"Midnight." Frankie giggles and tugs on my arm to get me up.

"Are you two crazy?"

"Papa has a surprise," says Frankie, "and he won't tell us what it is."

"Get dressed," Franco says again.

"Where are we going?"

"It's a secret. Pop and Mama are gonna watch Celeste. We'll be back by morning."

"Okay, okay." For the past month, I've been doing every-thing my husband asks of me. This request is pushing me to the limit, but I'm determined to give him whatever he wants. I climb into my clothes, stockings, and boots and meet them downstairs. Franco has packed a thermos and biscotti in a bag.

"Let's hit the road." He leads us out the door. Frankie looks at me and shrugs, and I shrug right back at him. From our first date, Franco Zollerano has prided himself on surprises, road trips, offbeat destinations. I should complain that he's crossed the line, waking our son in the middle of the night, but I bite my tongue.

Frankie soon falls asleep in my arms. Franco plays the radio and whistles as we drive toward Philadelphia. I cannot imagine what he has cooked up. "Honey, where are we going?" I ask about three miles outside Philadelphia.

"Have you read the road signs?"

"We're in Philly, but what's in Philly that is so important that you had to drag us out of our warm beds in the middle of the night?"

"You'll see." Franco pulls up in a parking lot behind a series of buses and a few trucks. When he turns off the engine, Frankie wakes up. "Are we here?"

"We're here. Come on, son." Franco takes his son's hand and leads him across the parking lot. I follow, and as I move through the parked vehicles, I realize that we are at the site of the traveling circus, the greatest in the world: the Ringling Bros. and Barnum & Bailey circus.

"Don't tell me we're joining the circus," I say to no one in particular.

"There it is, son."

And there, in an open field, is the big top. It lies flat on the ground like a parachute. The orange-and-white-striped tarp seems to cover an acre. Then, with a mighty trumpet, an elephant, guided by three trainers, comes down a ramp and lumbers over to one side of the flat tarp. Soon another elephant comes down the ramp and is positioned on the other side. A third elephant comes down the ramp, this one is the baby, and it too is led to the tarp. A trainer blows a whistle, the trainers holler at each other, and one shouts,

"Lift!" And the three elephants line up. With their brute strength, they pick up the poles with their trunks. The flat tarp is pulled into standing position in moments.

Frankie's eyes, wide with wonder, can barely believe the majesty of what he sees. "They put up the tent, Papa."

"Yep. The elephants do all the work," Franco replies.

I watch my son and his father as they marvel at the sight. My nose burns as my eyes fill with tears. I married a man who sees the world in a completely different way from me. He is full of wonder. I cry, not for my son's amazement, or for how I have been given the gift of witnessing this love between them. Rather, I cry for me. I don't believe in anything except what I can see. If I can't touch it, it's not real. My imagination has always taken a backseat to my practical nature. I don't know how to have fun, I don't know how to let go, and therefore I don't know how to live. I think I love deeply, but I don't. I don't give of myself where it counts. I don't give my husband a sense of flight, or my children a sense of magic.

"Nella, can you believe it?" Franco watches the orange and white tent, now suspended on poles and ready for business.

"It's wonderful," I say softly.

"Was it worth the trip?" he asks, not taking his eyes off the skillful operation.

"I'll say." And then we watch the parade of animals, regal and dignified as they process into the glorious tent. The llamas, the bears, the tiger, and the lion, followed by the hardworking elephants, disappear inside.

"Just like Noah's ark." Frankie counts the animals.

"Almost." Franco puts his arms around his son.

"That was the best thing I ever saw," Frankie says to his father. "Do you think so, Ma?"

"Oh yes," I agree.

"You're not going. You're too old."

"I'm thirty-three."

"That's too old!" I tell my husband, knowing full well that three Roseto men have already signed up to fight against Mussolini and Hitler, and their ages are twenty-nine, thirty-four, and thirty-eight.

"The army doesn't think so."

"I don't want you to go," I plead, but to no avail. Franco's mind is made up.

"You have help here. Your parents won't be traveling to Italy with the war on, and my folks are right across the street. It would be different if we didn't have their help with the kids, but we do. I want to do the right thing," Franco says firmly.

"The right thing is to be safe for your wife and children," I remind my husband. I can see by the way he looks past me and out the window that I am losing the fight.

"They need mechanics badly. There isn't a machine in the world that I can't take apart and put back together again."

"Please, Franco."

"Nella, if there was ever a woman who didn't need a man around, it's you." He kisses me on the forehead. "Now, think about your children and their future."

"I am thinking of them! We can raise money for bonds and help the war effort in other ways."

"I want to show my son how to love his country, and I can't do that staying here and working in the mill. I need your support, honey."

We have been going back and forth about this since December 7, 1941, when the news broke. It is February and Franco is determined to join up. He has already spoken with the recruiter, who gave him hope that they would take him at thirty-three. "I support you." But really, I'm giving up. He's a man on a mission, and no one, not even his mother, can stop him.

The entire family, the Paganos, Zolleranos, Castellucas, our children, and I, all take the ride to New York City to see Franco report for duty. I cry for most of the eighty-mile car trip (we have three cars in caravan, with Franco driving the lead car). I try to be strong for the children, though Frankie thinks his father is a hero already, and Celeste is too young to understand. That leaves me to reconcile my husband's choice. I look over at him and think about what he told me, that I don't need a man, but he's so wrong. I need him desperately, and the thought of losing him is inconceivable to me.

And yet I'm not alone in my heartbreak. Many families in Roseto are giving up their men: Chettie's baby brother, Oreste, Franco's first cousin Paul. Nearly every girl at the mill has a husband, beau, or brother who is shipping out. But no matter how many men go, every woman feels alone, bereft by what she can only hope is a temporary loss. It is not only men that we are losing to the fight; Roseto has two nurses who are shipping out to England. We pray for victory, and soon.

Franco's younger brother has already joined the navy. My mother-in-law faces the possible loss of two sons, yet she doesn't shed a tear. I am amazed at her strength.

It seems so odd for those of us who are Italian to be at war against the country we come from. It is hard to understand turning against your own, but we know the true hearts of the Italian people, at least those from our village. They don't want a dictator. My husband is not conflicted at all about Mussolini. "He must go," Franco said simply.

Franco kisses his mother and father good-bye, then he kisses Frankie and then Celeste, who stuff all sorts of trinkets into his pockets. He takes me in his arms and kisses me last. As I walk him to the entrance, he doesn't say much. For the first time in our marriage, he is quiet and I'm a chatterbox. I try to encapsulate all our dreams quickly, reminding him of what we've meant to each other, promising him that I'll take care of the children, that when he returns we will have our dream and open our own blouse mill.

"I'm not worried," Franco says.

"Good. That means you'll be careful." I try to smile.

"I'll be careful," he promises.

We look at each other, and I no longer see any trace of the young man I met at the mill when I was just fifteen. He isn't simply older, he has grown up.

"You know that I love you with all my heart, all of it," I tell him.

"And I love you."

"Come home to me."

"I will, Nell. I promise."

Franco joins the other recruits in a line, and I see that my husband is by far the oldest. But when it comes to experience and skill, he will have much to offer. As he walks into the building where the recruits will be detained, I turn and walk back to my family. Elena holds Celeste, while Papa holds Frankie's hand. From this moment on, no matter what comes, I will not cry, I promise myself. I will do what my husband wishes and try to live without him. It's not like I have a choice.

Chettie and I spend our lunches at the mill scheming about what it will be like when Franco and I are finally able to open our own factory. It's been nine months since he left. Chettie's brother has been sent to the Pacific theater, and his letters are less frequent now. We hear news that the war cannot go on much longer, but who knows for sure?

Freddie Jenkins has decided to take as much advantage of us as he can while the men are away. (Freddie was deferred due to poor eyesight.) The movie business is booming, and our mill continues to cranks out styles worn by the younger starlets, Lana Turner, Gene Tierney, and the Latin bombshell Carmen Miranda. The design from her image came in, and we all had a chuckle. A floral blouse tied at the waist, perfect with the suspender pants and platform shoes so popular now. The machine operators had quite a time with the voile material, but the results were spectacular.

Frankie writes to his papa once a week. He imagines Franco in bomber jets and on the field carrying a gun. In fact, Franco is working in a munitions plant in England. He is repairing the planes that return from battle. News of the bombings in London always take my breath away, but I pray that Franco is out of harm's way.

When the government car pulls up in front of the factory, the buzzing of the machines goes silent. One girl in our ranks, Mary Bozelli, lost her fiancé, and that was almost a year ago. She left work that day, but returned the next. She dealt with her grief by pressing on, and we all marveled at her strength.

"Oh no," Chettie says. "Bad news."

My heart leaps into my throat as the young officer comes toward us.

"Who are you looking for, sir?"

"Concetta . . . I can't pronounce the last name."

"Marucci?" Chettie asks, her voice trembling.

"Yes, ma'am."

"That's me."

"The United States Army regrets . . ."

I watch Chettie as though we are in a fog; she nods and listens to the officer, her eyes fill with tears, and when he says the name Oreste Ricci, tears roll down her face. The officer turns and goes.

"My poor brother," Chettie cries. "How will I tell Mama?" Then Chettie fishes in her apron and pulls out Oreste's picture. She bows her head and begins to pray the Litany of the Saints, reminding them to welcome her brother into their fold. I bow my head with her, but I'm overcome with the sorrow of it all; I mouth the words, but I'm not really praying. The last thing I would do in a moment like this is seek out God. Why would I pray to Him, when He took my loved one from me? But Chettie is different. In matters of faith she has always been clear and uncompromising. She knows what she knows about her soul as though it were her right hand. It's as real to her as the things in this world, something that I have never been able to comprehend. She slips the picture back into her pocket. "After all that, my brother dies."

"After all what, Chet? The war?"

"No. Losing Papa the way we did. Oreste without a father since he was a boy. I watched as my brother went from a carefree, happy boy to a somber little soldier. And then fate makes him one."

I hug Chettie, who tells me that she must go and tell her mother. She moves down the steps and up Garibaldi Avenue to take the turn onto Dewey Street. She walks so heavily, and the factory is still so silent, that I can hear her footsteps as she goes.

The funeral mass for Oreste Ricci at Our Lady of Mount Carmel brings out all the women and men who have sons, brothers, and husbands in the war. *Homefront* magazine, published in Bangor, Pennsylvania, runs a special article about Oreste. War has erased the lines among Italian, Welsh, Irish, and Dutch. We realize that we are all in this together. We've even stopped using the expression "Johnny Bull."

Renato gives a beautiful eulogy, remembering Oreste as a boy, and chronicles the Ricci family saga. He speaks of their bravery and their common touch, reminding us all of Carlo Ricci, who was our school janitor. Renato is a powerful and convincing speaker, but he too is filled with emotion when the flag is presented to Oreste's mother.

The November wind is bitter cold when we leave the church. There will be no burial today. The Riccis are hoping that Oreste's remains will be found, though he was serving at sea, so the possibility of that is slim.

"Nella, how are you?" Renato comes through the crowd, seeking me out.

"I'm fine. The family's fine."

"Any word from Franco?"

"He's still in London. So far, so good."

"I'm praying for him."

"Thank you."

"Nella, could we talk for a moment?"

"Sure." I look around, and maybe it's my imagination, but I feel eyes on me, all around.

"Come with me," he says. Then, in a gesture that makes me uncomfortable, he guides me through the crowd, across the plaza in front of the church, and next door to the church office and rectory.

"Hello, Mrs. Stampone," I say to the church volunteer who keeps the rectory. Mrs. Stampone looks up and smiles, going about her dusting. Renato leads me into his office and closes the door.

"I haven't seen you at Mass for a very long time. Why is that?"

"We're going to St. Elizabeth's in Pen Argyl now," I tell him. At first we were the subject of some gossip for leaving Mount Carmel, but then a rumor went around that we were thinking of opening a factory in Pen Argyl, so we wanted to stake a claim in the community. Of course, that wasn't true.

"Why?"

"It was Franco's decision."

"Was it because of me?"

I nod that it was.

"I was afraid of that. I should have discussed it with him the first Sunday you weren't in the pew."

"No, no, that's a bad idea."

Renato goes behind his desk and sits down. I can't look at him. Still. I am fine when I don't see him, and completely at peace when I don't think about him.

"Did I do something to offend him?"

I shake my head. "No. I did."

"You did what? You offended him? How?"

"You know, there's that concept in our faith . . ." I begin.

"Yes?"

". . . that love never dies."

"It doesn't," Renato says plainly, clearly not yet understanding what I'm trying to tell him.

"That's what my husband believes. And that's why we go to St. Elizabeth's."

"Ridiculous." Renato throws up his hands as the full meaning of my words finally sinks in. It reminds me of the day he got impatient with me when we were reading aloud and I couldn't pronounce the Latin properly. "To change your home parish over something that happened years ago . . . I don't understand."

Now I do. Renato is completely resolved on the subject. Even though the strings to the past are delicate, I am the only one holding on to them. My husband knows me better than I know myself sometimes.

I hear a thump outside the office door. With my luck, Mrs. Stampone is listening; soon my business will be carried from house to house like a milk delivery. I stand and tuck my purse under my arm. Renato stands. I look him in the eyes, still the same intensity, the same blue, but now they hold a different regard for me. Now almost forty, Renato has the dynamic confidence that comes with experience. In a sense, it makes him more alluring. His quick temper and bombastic opinions are gone, replaced with a quiet and dignified calm that makes him a true leader. Under his leadership, the parishioners have built a primary school and a convent for the Salesian nuns who will run the school. This fall he will break ground for a Catholic high school, to be built across the street from the church plaza. He is working on building a hospital in town. He is tireless when it comes to community activisim. Like Father DeNisco before him, he has rallied the people of Roseto and brought out their ambition and their generosity. He is determined to make the town expand and grow. And yet, when I look at him, I see a poet. "This job suits you, Renato."

"Just as yours must suit you. You are as beautiful as ever."

His comment takes me aback. It is inappropriate, and yet I longed for it. I always want to know what he thinks of me, even if it's years later and a lifetime ago. "Thank you," I whisper.

I leave without saying good-bye, not to him and not to Mrs. Stampone, who dusts the windowsill outside his office. And finally, I bow my head in sincere prayer. *Please, God, bring Franco home soon.*

CHAPTER ELEVEN

"To the left, Franco! To the left!" I shout from the ground to my husband on a ladder. "It's too high." Franco drops the sign, which swings from two chain links, about five inches lower. "Perfect!" I call up, shielding my eyes from the sun. I fish into my pocket for my sunglasses. When I put them on I look up and see NELLA MANUFACTURING COMPANY, EST. 1945 in perfect white script on a vivid red background.

"What do you think?" Franco asks as he descends the ladder and joins me on the ground.

"I think we should have called it Zollerano's Manufacturing Company."

"Too cumbersome. Besides, I like to be reminded who I'm

working so hard for." Franco puts his arm around my waist and kisses my cheek.

Just as we planned, as soon as Franco got home, the First National Bank of Bangor, Pennsylvania, gave us a business loan to start our own mill. Freddie Jenkins was furious, and angrier still when nearly all the machine operators came to work for us. He ended up closing his Roseto mill, but since he opened three more in Jersey, the Jenkins family fortune is secure.

Frankie, now twelve, and Celeste, six, are thrilled with the mill. Papa is home to greet them after school, and Franco's mother will often make them dinner on nights when we're late with shipping. The headaches from the new mill are the same ones we had at Jenkins's but at least they're *our* headaches. Our first order comes from our old friends the Rosenbergs, who have done beautifully with the Hollywood blouses. We go into production on the Jennifer Jones, a white cotton blouse with a breast pocket embossed with an embroidered horse. This one should sell like mad.

"Aunt Nell, I really need your help," Assunta says when she stops by the new mill. She looks so much like her mother at this age that often Elena and I forget it's 1945 and think we're back on Delabole farm. Assunta is tall and slim, with her mother's black eyes and pale skin. She even has the same crease between her eyes. But Elena's influence on little Assunta is apparent. She has largesse and kindness. She has her mother's feistiness, but none of her bad temper.

"Father Lanzara asked me to run for queen of the Big Time," she continues.

"Well, you know we already think you're a queen," I say.

She laughs. "I know, Aunt Nella. But this is a different thing. I get to wear a crown and put one on the Blessed Lady. It's a big deal."

"I know it is. And it has been since I was a little girl. Who else is running?"

"Elisabetta Sartori. Her parents are Enzo and Caterina, they have a farm in Totts Gap. And Ellie Montagano."

"Her?" I remember the bratty little girl with the ringlets.

"She really wants to win. Mostly to beat me, I think."

"Well, what would beating Ellie Montagano involve?" I ask.

"Raising money, lots and lots of money," my husband says as he comes through the office door. I look up at him from my desk. He wears a T-shirt and work pants, and his hands are covered in grease. "The Holy Roman Church Incorporated needs lots of dollars."

"Don't touch anything, Franco." I hand him a rag and ignore his comments. "What do you call that tithe you put in the basket every Sunday at St. Elizabeth's?"

"Fire insurance." My husband shrugs. At thirty-seven, he still has the same strong arms and neck, but his hair has tiny flecks of white.

"Well, will you help me run?" Assunta asks us both.

"Absolutely. But if you're going to run, you have to work hard. A Castelluca-Pagano cannot lose," I tell her.

"I wouldn't worry, Assunta." My husband laughs. "You'd be the first Castelluca to lose. They're a determined bunch."

At the end of the day, when we've counted the tickets and posted the numbers, Franco and I go through the factory turning off the lights.

"Did you get the finishing room?" I call out to him.

"Yeah, hon." He flips the lights and comes through the main room. I stand and look all around.

"Thank you, Franco. I love our mill." I put my arms around his neck. "I love you more, but I love our mill." I know he feels the same way. He loves our independence as much as I do.

Franco kisses me and reaches for the light switch of the main room. He pulls me down on a pile of silk blouses on their way to finishing. He unbuttons my work smock and finds his way to my blouse, kissing me as he goes. I laugh and pull him close. "This is against the rules."

"It's your mill. Change the rules," he says as he slides on top of me.

"What about the Gene Tierneys?" I whisper.

"I don't think she'll mind." He kisses my ears, then my neck.

When Franco was gone during the war, I tried to remember each and every time we'd made love. I didn't want to forget a single detail about our life together.

"How's this?" he says as he lifts me on top of him.

"It's better than a hay ride."

Franco laughs, and there is no sweeter sound in Nella Manufacturing Company.

*

We take my niece Assunta's campaign for queen of the Big Time door-to-door. Once we've covered Roseto, we take the campaign to West Bangor, Bangor, Martins Creek, Pen Argyl, and Flicksville. Every night after work, we load up the car with my sisters, Assunta, and a stack of tickets and fan out in the neighborhoods, covering two blocks at a time. We don't forget the farmers either, making sure we stop in Wind Gap and Stone Church. I can't imagine that Assunta's competition has the kind of manpower that we do. My sisters are as determined as I am to sell every ticket.

I push the kitchen screen door open, exhausted from another night of fund-raising. My dinner waits on the stove for me.

"Don't you think you're going a little overboard with this queen competition? I'm starting to think you want to win more than Assunta," Franco says over his glasses as he reads the paper at our kitchen table.

"You don't understand." I turn the heat up on the pan of *pasta e fagioli* on the stove.

"You're right. I don't understand. Why is it so important that Assunta win this thing?"

"Franco, you didn't grow up on the farm. You grew up on Garibaldi Avenue, *in town*. When I came to Roseto to visit, I never felt a part of it. When I went to school it began to change, but then I had to quit and go to work. I remember when I was a girl, and I'd stand outside Marcella's, and in my head I'd do the math, figuring out how much I'd have to save up to buy my family a box of cream puffs."

"I didn't grow up with money either."

"It's not about the money, it's about being recognized. When I was a girl, my sisters and I never thought we'd be a part of the Big Time celebration. We walked in the back of the procession with everyone else to say the rosary; we were never invited to be on the court or carry the banner for the sodality or march with the schoolkids."

"So you have something to prove?"

"To myself. I want a Castelluca to go from Delabole farm to Roseto's queen of the Big Time in one generation. I don't think there's anything wrong with that."

My husband smiles and goes back to his paper. I spoon the *pasta e fagioli* into a dish and sit down and eat. The Castellucas may have come a long way in a short amount of time, but we still eat pasta and beans on Friday night.

Assunta puts her heart into the final week of fund-raising. The competition is so fierce this year, I take a stack of tickets to our buyers in New York. Franco can't believe that I'd cross the state line to raise money for Assunta's campaign. The Rosenbergs are happy to help and sell them in the Garment District to their vendors and friends. They have no problem supporting our cause, even though the proceeds will go to our Catholic church. "Good deeds are good deeds," Sid Rosenberg tells me when he takes the tickets. We're sure their efforts will help put Assunta over the top.

I'm too nervous to go to the church hall for the counting of the proceeds, so I stay home and wait for a call. How thrilled I am when Assunta calls to tell me that she has won.

The only awkward part of winning queen is that the girls you competed against become your princesses. Elisabetta Sartori, a beautiful girl with long blond hair and deep brown eyes, was a good sport, though her mother, having been denied that front-row seat, was not. Ellie Montagano, small and round like her mother, was very polite on the surface, while her mother had dredged up stories about our family in order to derail Assunta's campaign. Franco encouraged me to let it go (after all, the Rosenbergs put Assunta in the black and in the big crown, so why quibble?). The rest of Assunta's court includes Rosemary Filingo, Angela Martocci, Grace DelGrosso, Mary Jo Martino, Giuseppina Bozelli, Lucy Communale, Monica Spadoni, Laura Viglione, Helen Bartron, Violet Stampone, Kitty Romano, Rosina Roma, Rosemarie Gigliotti, and Eva and Angela Palermo.

"Mama?" Celeste comes into my room.

"Honey, hurry. We have to take Assunta's gown to her." I look up from my sewing; the final fitting required two additional darts in the waist.

"Is this right?" Celeste turns around in her costume. She is one of Assunta's flower girls.

"Where are your leotards?"

"I don't have any. I'm gonna wear anklets."

"You can't wear anklets."

"That's all I have."

"Oh, Celeste." I put the gown on the bed and go into Celeste's room. I rifle through her drawer until I find the package of white leotards. "Here. Hurry."

I go back into my room and cover Assunta's gown with a sheet. Franco and Frankie wait outside. Frankie, against his will, is a page. He wears satin knickers and a hat with a plume.

"Where's Celeste?" Franco asks.

I turn around, but she's not behind me. "That girl." I hand over Assunta's dress and go back in the house. "Celeste?" I call up impatiently. She doesn't answer. I go up the stairs. "Celeste, what is the problem?" I push her door open. She is struggling with the leotards. "Here, let me," I tell her, yanking them up over her knees and up to her waist.

We take Chestnut Street over to Dewey, as Garibaldi Avenue has been sealed off for the parade.

"There's gonna be a big crowd," Frankie says as he looks out the window. "And I have to wear this stupid hat."

"It's very regal," I tell him. "Be a good sport."

When we get to Dewey Street, we jump out of the car with the dress. Assunta is inside, waiting in her slip.

Celeste follows me up the walk. Assunta's hair has been put up in a lovely circle of curls. I help her into the gown, a white satin A-line gown with an embroidered bodice and long fluted sleeves and an overskirt of layered white tulle. The netting looks like a cloud of whipped cream.

Elena, in a chic pale blue suit, adjusts the skirt of Assunta's gown. Mama looks at Assunta and gasps. "You look just like your mother."

"I do?"

"Just as she did on her wedding day." Tears spring into Mama's eyes. Elena puts her arms around Mama.

Celeste fluffs the layers of tulle on Assunta's gown. "Don't touch that, Celeste," I tell my daughter.

"Assunta, I want to give you something." Mama reaches into her pocket and gives Assunta a small black velvet box. "Your mother was my eldest daughter, and someday I would have given her this. . . ."

Assunta opens the box and lifts out the gold locket with the blue sapphire that Papa gave Mama so many years ago. "Thank you, Nonna. I love it."

Assunta leans down as I clip the locket around her neck. "You know, before you were born, your mother wanted you to be named Celestina, for your nonna."

"Like me!" my Celeste says proudly.

"Yes, honey, like you." Elena smooths my daughter's hair.

I look at Assunta. "But when your father came home from Italy after your mother died, he took one look at you and named you after her."

Assunta's eyes fill with tears. "I wish she was here."

"We all do," Elena assures her, even though the story of her own life would have turned out far differently. We gather around Assunta, our queen of the Big Time, and embrace her. We can't make up for her mother's absence, but at least we can help her remember how much she was loved by our sister.

The July sun is hot on the plaza as Assunta crowns the statue of the Blessed Mother. After the war, the women in town donated their rings to make new crowns for the statues, a glittering one for Mary and a smaller one for baby Jesus, who she holds in her arms. I donated a gold signet ring that Franco had given me, and I take great pride in looking up at the gold crowns and knowing that my love for Franco is a part of them. There are some women who gave their wedding bands, but I just couldn't give mine up.

Celeste and Frankie do a wonderful job of carrying Assunta's train as she walks up the front steps of the church to receive her crown. The ceremony is very moving, and we applaud Assunta as she is helped onto the float with a throne. As they parade down Garibaldi Avenue, Elena cries. Our niece, the little girl Elena mothered so tenderly, has grown up tall and strong, and now holds the highest honor a young woman in Roseto can achieve. Never mind she won the American way, selling tickets. She had the honor of crowning our patron saint; surely that means a life of good luck and happiness. I can't help but think how far we've come from Delabole farm, how so many years ago, for one of us to become the queen of the Big Time seemed impossible. But we are outsiders no longer. All those years toiling in the Society of Mary, working in the mill proving my mettle, and defending the family name when Elena married our brother-in-law seem to float away like the white balloons let loose over the church plaza when the parade begins.

One of Assunta's duties as queen is to attend the carnival. I remember so many years ago what a thrill it was when the queen made her rounds. Assunta does a good job, including everyone in the fun.

"Quite a day," Renato says when he stops by Alessandro's

candy stand, which is still set up across from the church every year out of tradition. For several years now, Alessandro has given the profits to Our Lady of Mount Carmel.

"Yes, it was, Father."

"Thank you for all your help selling tickets. You know you made me look good with the bishop."

"It's all for a good cause."

"Yes, I want to put a cafeteria in the primary school. The profits from the carnival will help a great deal."

"Father, you should have been an urban planner. You've changed this town with the new schools and the park. You've done a wonderful job."

"Thank you, Nella." He smiles. "I couldn't have done it without your generosity." Now when I look at Renato, I don't see the face I used to dream about, or the lips I used to kiss. I concentrate on that Roman collar, and it keeps me on the straight and narrow.

"Nella, I wanted to tell you, I have some news. I'm leaving Our Lady of Mount Carmel. I've been assigned to a parish in New York."

My heart sinks a little. Though we don't go to church here, I always knew that Renato was up the street. I might run into him at firehouse suppers and on the street when I take my evening walk. He is so much a part of Roseto that it is hard to imagine the community without him. "I'm sorry to hear that."

"My replacement starts the first week of September. He's a terrific priest. Father Schmidt."

"The bishop is going with a non-Italian?"

"Change is good. The people will like him, I'm sure."

"You did a great job for Roseto, Father."

"I didn't reach all of my goals. I wanted to build a hospital here."

The din of the crowd and the sizzle and shouts from the sausage and pepper stand make it hard to hear. I look at Renato, and he smiles at me.

"I'm thirty-five years old now," I tell him. "I've known you half of my life."

"And I'm still seven years older than you."

"I know. You're an old man," I joke.

He laughs. "Nella, I—"

"You don't have to say anything," I tell him, looking away because suddenly I can't bear to look at him.

"I'll miss you," he says quietly. "I didn't want to leave a second time without saying good-bye."

"Thank you."

"You see, there is redemption. Sometimes we don't have to make the same mistakes twice."

Renato is pulled away by a parishioner, anxious to introduce him to her family. I don't know it for sure, but I feel that this is the last I will see of him for many years.

The fall of 1959 brings big changes in our household. Soon after my daughter, Celeste, has turned twenty, she decides that her November wedding to Giovanni Melfi, a nice Neopolitan boy from Philadelphia, should somehow top the

Queen of England's. Our Lady of Mount Carmel is filled with calla lilies, the Hotel Bethlehem has been festooned with dozens more, and the glamorous New York City boutique Sully of Fifth Avenue has built her a gown with more beads than a Moroccan temple.

"Are you surprised?" my husband says as he hunts for his shoehorn. "Celeste is no farm girl."

"She's a chicken-in-every-pot baby, and, boy, does she act like it. Spoiled rotten."

"I can hear you," Celeste says from her room. "I need some help in here."

I go into Celeste's room. She stands in her slip, stockings, and garter. When I look at her, I am amazed that she is a woman. Where did the time go?

"The train is going to be a problem."

"Because it's eight feet long?" I joke.

But Celeste looks lovely, like one of those carved cameo beauties from the old world. Her brown eyes sparkle under a cap of short black curls. She looks like an Italian movie star. She has her father's strong jaw and my nose. She is prettier than me; in fact, she has the best features of the Castellucas and the Zolleranos. She is far too young to get married, I think, but this is her choice. She was in her first year of college at Marywood and decided it wasn't for her. Giovanni was willing to wait until she graduated, but she wasn't. As we all know, my Celeste doesn't take no for an answer.

"You're beautiful," I tell my daughter.

"You think so?"

"Of course I do."

"You never say it." There is a sudden sting to her voice.

"What do you mean? I say it all the time."

"Ma, you have never said it."

"That's just not true," I argue.

"Oh, please. Let's not fight on my wedding day. Let's make it the one day we don't fight. Okay?" Celeste sits down at her vanity and gently presses powder to her forehead.

"I know we squabble."

"That's a polite word for it." She laughs.

"It's not funny." I put my hands on her shoulders, and she looks up at me.

"Ma, please. Let's not get started. I'm serious."

"I'm serious too." I turn to go.

"You just don't get it," Celeste says to my back.

"What is it I don't get? That you have everything you've ever wanted? That you live in a nice house and went to a good college? That you have a big wedding with three hundred people in the Hotel Bethlehem, a place I didn't set foot in until I was thirty-four years old?"

"Here we go . . . the Delabole farm stories. The poor Castellucas who made good. They went from the cowshed to Garibaldi Avenue."

"And don't forget it."

"Oh, Ma, you don't let anybody forget it."

"Because it's important. What you come from is who you are—it's your starting place. To come from nothing and make something of yourself, to provide for a family, is no small feat. You will see what I'm talking about when you're a mother."

"Oh, please. You want everybody to know how hard you've worked. Well, I'm going to tell you something: You did work hard. You worked so hard you were never home. I barely ever had a meal with you—"

"You were with your grandparents. I never had both sets of my grandparents when I was growing up on the farm."

"Mom, this isn't about what *you* had, this is about *me*. You were never here, which is why I left Marywood. What is the point in getting a degree when I have no intention of leaving my children?"

"I never *left* you, Celeste."

"You didn't have to—you weren't here in the first place. Ask Frankie. I'm not the only one who felt abandoned."

Celeste's words go through me like tiny knives, each one splintering my heart as it sinks in my chest. What is she talking about? Abandoned? She and Frankie were surrounded by family. We worked within walking distance of our children when we bought a mill down the street, we gave them all the things we never had. Celeste traveled! She had vacations; what did I ever know of vacations? She went to Atlantic City and Miami Beach and places I only dreamed of and could never go because I was working. Working for what? For my children. If it weren't her wedding day, I would tell her these things. But I doubt she'd hear them; she is not interested in anything I have to say.

"Nella, come and get ready." Franco pulls me out of the doorway. "Let her be."

I go into our room and dress. Franco goes into Celeste's room and closes the door. I don't want to know what they're talking about. If Celeste knew what it was like to do without, she could never say such hateful things to me.

When Franco returns he takes my hand and says, "Honey, Celeste wants to talk to you before we go to the church."

I go into her room. She wears a glittering tiara and a veil of tulle that surrounds her like a cloud.

"I'm sorry, Celeste."

Celeste's eyes fill with tears, and it dawns on me that she was never much of a crier. "I know, Ma. And I'm sorry for my smart mouth."

"I did the best I could, honey. I hope you understand that someday."

"I do understand it. I just get impatient."

"I want you to be happy. I want it more for you than myself. That was always my dream for you. To do better. To be better."

"And I'll try."

Instead of riding up to Our Lady of Mount Carmel, which we rejoined when the new Catholic school opened in 1952, Franco, Celeste, and I walk up the hill in the bright November sun. Frankie and his wife have gone ahead to make sure the ushers are in place before we arrive. Franco holds Celeste's left hand while I hold her right. This is the last time we will have her to ourselves. Maybe my daughter is right, maybe we didn't have enough of these moments.

"Thank you, Ma," Celeste says to me as I go up the stairs to take my place in church.

I turn to my only daughter. "Be happy." And I mean it down to my bones.

"I'm taking you to Italy for your fiftieth birthday," Franco says from his desk at the mill.

"It's a bad time of year, hon. We have our biggest shipment for the spring line in January."

"If we don't go now, we're never going to go," he warns. "I want to take you to Venice, Florence, and Rome. And then we'll drive south to Roseto Valfortore."

"Okay, plan it." I kiss Franco on his head. "But make sure it's two weeks between shipping and starting the new line."

"You got it, boss." My husband pinches me as I pass.

My husband, always the romantic, wants to see Roseto Valfortore.

"The house is too quiet with Frankie and Celeste married. I can't believe both of my kids left Roseto." Franco shakes his head. "We need some new interests."

"We have plenty to do with this mill," I remind him.

"Why don't we sell it?"

"What? Are you crazy? We're making money hand over fist."

"I know. But how much do we need? We own the house outright, and this building. Who knows what we would get for the business? Probably what we ask. Let's just let it go and see the world."

I sit down on the edge of my husband's desk and fold my arms. "And then do what?"

"Relax." He slides his hand under my skirt.

"Oh, for God's sake, that's only a few minutes of activity a day."

He laughs. "I could make it last longer."

I lean down and kiss the top of his head.

"Aren't you tired of working?" he asks. "You've been doing this since you're fifteen."

"I can't help it. I've grown to love it."

"But it can't love you back."

"Oh, I don't know about that. It does a pretty good imitation of it when the checks come in."

"Okay, you win. Two weeks in Italy. That's it. No early retirement." Franco goes back to his paperwork. I watch him put on his glasses and put his head in his hand as he works. He reminds me of Mr. Jenkins, who must have been around Franco's age when he hired me. Would I ever make a sixteen-year-old girl a forelady? Never. But old Jenkins saw something in me.

Sometimes it seems like it was yesterday, and then there are days when my life feels double the fifty years and I can stop moments in my memory and relive them, actually feeling the things I used to feel. When it's bitter cold on a winter morning, I remember going to the barn at Delabole farm and milking the cows with Mama. When the weather turns to spring, I think of Renato Lanzara giving me books on the shore of Minsi Lake. When the summer comes, I remember

Franco's kisses on the porch on Dewey Street, and then, when it's winter, I remember my sister who died as her baby was born.

The deep wells of desire, the sting of regret, the passion of my youth, all of those things have made me who I am. But I know that what Franco is telling me is true. I am incapable of change. I reach certain plateaus and stay there, out of comfort sometimes, and out of necessity other times. God bless Franco. He brings home travel brochures and I look at them, but places outside my mill and home don't seem real to me. Taking care of business, taking care of my family, these are my ideas of time well spent. And don't we have lots of time to travel? If we work another ten years, my Franco will still only be sixty-two. That's plenty early for retirement.

"I'm going to check the shipment." Franco goes out of the office. I pour myself a cup of coffee. I flip through the brochures of Italy from the travel agent. How lush and romantic it seems. Maybe my husband is right, a trip would do us a lot of good.

"Mrs. Zollerano, come quick!" Donna Mugavero, my collar setter, says, pushing the door open. "It's Mr. Zollerano!" she says in a panic.

I rush out into the main room; the hum of the machines grinds to a halt. The machine operators stand and look aghast at my husband, who lies on the floor. The only time the machines stop in a mill is for lunch or break time, or disaster. I look at their faces and know that something is terribly wrong.

"What happened?" I kneel down next to Franco. "Honey, what's wrong?" I touch his face and squeeze his hand. Nothing.

"I'll call the ambulance." Sally Viglione runs to the office. But it is too late, my Franco is gone.

The cars on Garibaldi are double- and triple-parked as my family and our friends gather in my home. Celeste and Frankie came as soon as they heard the news. They went with me to choose their father's casket, Mass cards, and flowers. We hung on to one another, choosing the best of everything they had to offer at the Fiore Funeral Home.

My sisters are in the kitchen arranging the platters of food that have been dropped off. They laugh, remembering funny stories about their brother-in-law, but I can't listen for long. Franco is not a story to me, he shared my life and my bed, and I can't imagine going forward without him. The widows of Roseto have come in one by one to offer their condolences. The first thing they tell me is that at fifty-two, Franco was too young to die. I can't believe God would take such a young man from us. I suppose I should be praying, but I can't.

The girls at the mill have stopped by to leave notes and see my children. Sally Viglione chastises herself, wishing that she could have done something, maybe seen something different in Franco that would have led her to call the doctor. But I assure her that moments before he died, we were laughing and talking as always. There was nothing to be done.

That night I crawl into bed exhausted. How strange it is to go to my side of the bed and turn to spoon with Franco and find him gone. Celeste and Frankie are in their old rooms. I called my parents in Italy, and they are on their way home.

I haven't shed a single tear. I know there is a river inside me, but so far, I am so closed off that I cannot imagine crying.

"Ma?" Celeste comes into our room in her nightgown, tears streaming down her face. "I'm so sad."

I lift the blanket on the bed and she crawls in next to me.

"What are we going to do?" she asks.

"I don't know," I tell her. But I know the answer, because I've already lived it: You go on. You have no choice, you go on.

"He was too young."

"I know."

"Did he say anything?"

"We were talking about going on a trip. Then he . . . just collapsed. I didn't hear him say another thing."

"Poor Pop. He never got a vacation."

"We went to the shore every summer."

"I mean a real vacation. One of those long months off."

I don't know if Celeste means to, but she makes me feel terrible. And I know she's right. "I wish we would have done it."

"He was happy, though," she says kindly.

"I think so."

Celeste snuggles in close to me. "Ma, he always used to tell me about you."

"He did?"

"Yeah. When you and I would fight, it would upset Daddy, and he'd always come and talk to me. And he'd tell me what you were like when you were young. He said before he kissed you, you were a real block of ice. But he said he just kept chipping away at it. He said he devoted himself to the religion of Nella Castelluca. He loved you more than you ever knew."

"I knew."

"He used to talk about how you ran a factory when you were just a kid. How you acted like you knew what to do even when you didn't. He told me about a fire where you saved people—"

"He saved the workers, I didn't."

"He said it was you."

"That was your father. Always giving credit to someone else."

"He told me that you made him work hard to win you."

"Really?"

"Yeah. He said a man should always have to work hard to win a woman's heart, because when he gets it, it's worth it, and he'll never take it for granted. I remembered that when I got married."

We lie in the quiet for a long time. Celeste blows her nose. "Ma, why don't you cry?"

I think about it for a moment. "I don't know."

*

My husband's funeral was just like he was, warm and down-to-earth. The only royal touch was the Knights of Columbus (the one group my husband was a member of), who wore their plumed hats and tuxedos with sashes. When they formed an honor guard with their swords on either side of the church aisle for my husband's casket to pass, it was a stirring moment. Franco was devoted to their causes, in particular charity work on behalf of children. No one would call my husband a religious man, but he was always involved.

Father Les Schmidt spoke of my husband's generosity to the church, not just financially, but in ways that he gave of himself, helping to build the school and the new rectory. Papa and Mama made it back in time for the service, but not soon enough to change from their traveling clothes.

Alessandro and Elena have been steadfast. Roma came from her home in Philadelphia and Dianna from hers in Pen Argyl. My nieces and nephews were a great comfort. A big family is a treasure at times like these. My in-laws' grief is painful for me to witness. They have suffered the worst fate, losing their son. His brothers are bereft.

Chettie and Anthony showed up with an album of pictures from when we were young. I look at Franco and me; he is so handsome and tall, and I have the steely jaw of a Rosie the Riveter. Perhaps my Franco was right: I'm as hard as a block of ice, and the only person who could ever chip away at it was him.

Back at the house, Celeste goes through the pantry, making

a list of all the cakes, pies, and cookies that have been dropped off. There is a roasted turkey and three honey-baked hams. The phone rings. Celeste answers it. "Just a moment," she says into the phone. She comes into the kitchen. "Ma, it's for you."

"Who is it?"

"Father Lanzara." She rolls her eyes.

I go to the living room and sit down on the edge of the sofa and pick up the phone.

"Nella, I'm so sorry to hear about Franco."

"Thank you for calling."

"How are you doing?" he asks.

"With all your years working with the broken and down-trodden, don't you know you're never supposed to ask a widow how she's doing?" I try to laugh. "It's terrible. I never thought I could be this sad."

"It's a huge loss. And so young."

"Yes. We had a lot of plans."

"I'm sure you did."

There is a silence, but it isn't awkward. "Where are you, Renato?" For some reason I call him by name. It seems silly for me to call him "Father."

"I'm at St. John's University, in Queens."

"Are you chaplain?"

"No, I'm teaching literature."

"That's wonderful," I say.

"Nella, I'm afraid I have to go, but please know that I'll pray for you and for Franco," he promises.

When I hang up the phone and go back into the kitchen,

Celeste and Frankie are sitting at the kitchen table. Their spouses and some friends are on the back porch.

"What did he want?" Celeste asks.

"To express his sympathy." I pour myself a glass of water.

"To ask you out on a date," Frankie jokes.

"That's not funny," I say. What has gotten into these kids tonight?

"Pop always said he liked you."

"We were friends when we were young, Frankie."

"Well, the way Pop saw it, Father Lanzara wanted more than friendship. That's why we went to St. Elizabeth's. Right, Celeste?"

She grunts in response.

"Oh yeah, Pop had his problems with Mount Carmel." Frankie points in the direction of the church.

"Frankie, do you mind? You're talking about the house of God and priests."

"They're no different from you and me, Ma. They have all the same problems. And all the same wants and needs. Our priest in Jersey drives a Cadillac. Vow of poverty? Some poverty. How do you like that?"

"Let's change the subject." I look at my son, who no matter how old he grows still seems like a six-year-old boy determined to test my patience until I blow.

"Okay, Ma."

Our Lady of Mount Carmel Cemetery rests high on a hill above Garibaldi Avenue. As cemeteries go, this one is lovely:

wide roads that separate green fields filled with headstones. Franco bought our plots soon after we opened our own mill. It had always bothered him that he did not make the arrangements before he went off to war.

"It's nice, Mama." Celeste takes my hand as we look at Franco's headstone for the first time.

"What do you think, Frankie?"

"It's fine, Ma," he says, his eyes filling with tears.

The stone is simple. It reads:

Franco Zollerano
Husband and Father
March 17, 1907–November 18, 1959

CHAPTER TWELVE

N ow, don't get your hopes up," Papa says to me as he drives along a dusty back road to Roseto Valfortore. "It's not like our Roseto in America. It's old, not modern."

"Papa, please, don't make excuses. I think it's beautiful already." Papa convinced me to come to Italy with my mother and him. They invited me many times, but this year, since it was one of my husband's dreams for my fiftieth birthday, I decided to come. Franco wanted to see where we came from, and if he were here, he would have loved the winding back roads, the low rolling mountains, and the hillsides covered with wild roses. Roseto has earned its name. Everywhere you look, pockets of red roses, from deep ruby to the palest pink, bloom across the green hillsides.

"Looks like Delabole, doesn't it?" Mama says.

"It does," I tell her. The manicured, plowed farm fields are offset by rough, stony ground. The only difference is that the earth here seems dry and ancient, the fieldstones deeply embedded in it, some so large, you could sit in the shade under them. Fig trees bask in the open sun on hilltops, while groves of olive trees line the road from Biccari. Papa points out the marble mines in the distance. Deep gashes in the earth, surrounded by piles of slag and rubble, remind me of the slate quarries of home.

"Now I see why you like to come here. It is just like home."

I look at my father as he drives, and I am convinced he will outlive me. His life of hard work on the farm has kept him in excellent health. He has even overcome the injuries he sustained in the quarry back in 1925, when I was in school. He gets a pain in his leg when it rains, but that is the only residual problem he has from the accident.

"What's the matter?" Papa looks over at me. "You thinking of Franco?"

"Yes."

"Well, cry."

"I can't cry, Papa. I try. I don't know what's wrong with me."

"It's no good. You must cry. I remember something my father told me."

"What was that?"

"He said that you teach your children everything, even

how to grieve. You must show Celeste and Frankie how to grieve."

"Oh, Papa, they know better than I do." I wish my father knew how much I learn from my children. They are far more astute than me, though they have no idea how deeply I feel things.

As we drive deeper into Bari toward Roseto, the hills turn a deep emerald green.

Papa reads my mind. "It's more green here because of the ocean." I begin to understand how Roseto, Pennsylvania, came to be. The forefathers rebuilt their beloved hill town, and as we drive up to the entrance of Roseto Valfortore, it is not unlike the steep hill of Division Street that gives way to Garibaldi Avenue. As Papa drives down the main street, I feel as though I have been here before. So many of the details are identical. The same two-story houses with their porches on the second story line the main street just as ours do. The look of the people—the dark hair and flashing black eyes, the prominent noses—the features of *our* Rosetan people, are here. As much as the people look like the folks at home, it is their posture and carriage that give them away as Italians from the other side. People who do heavy labor, either on a farm or busting rocks in a quarry, have a strength in their neck and shoulders that gives them an upright carriage. I remember Miss Stoddard telling me to stand up straight. My people came by that posture naturally. Papa has it, Mama too. I worry that years behind a sewing machine, slumped indoors in the mill, took a toll on my bones. I see it in all of us who work in the mill. We aren't what we once were, and it isn't just our advancing age.

"You see why your mother and I come here every year?" Papa points. "It's just like America, without the noise."

I laugh. "Oh, Papa, our town isn't so noisy."

"No? Here they still ride horses. This car is a rare exception in this town." Papa pulls up to a gold stucco two-story house in the middle of the main street. "This is my brother Domenico's house. This is where we stay."

"*Come stai!*" Papa's youngest brother, a compact, sturdy man of sixty with sandy brown hair, comes out of the house. "Nella!" Domenico embraces me. "Agnese, *vieni!*" He throws his arms around Mama. Zia Agnese comes out of the house, and I am stunned at how youthful she is. She is my age, but looks a full ten years younger. Her shoulder-length black hair is pulled back in a ponytail, her skin is golden bronze with pink cheeks. She has full lips and beautiful teeth. She gives me a big hug. "Nella!" Their daughter, Penelope, comes to greet me. She's around twenty, and built like her papa. She is a beauty, but different from her mother in every aspect.

"You come in, you rest." Zia Agnese helps me with my bags. Penelope shows me a breezy front room with shutters that let in the sun. She puts my bags down and surveys me from head to toe. I remove my hat and place it on the nightstand. Then I take off my gloves. "You won't need your hat and gloves here." She smiles. "I hope you brought sandals and skirts."

"I did."

"No stockings, okay?"

"Okay." Well, that settles that, I think, and sit on the edge of the bed. This trip is off to a terrible start. I brought a suitcase full of new clothes: two serge suits, a wool bouclé coat dress, and plenty of new stockings. The only casual clothes I brought are a full black cotton skirt and a white blouse (made at Nella Manufacturing, of course). The white blouse is called the Kim Novak, though the Hollywood connection to our blouse mill grows slimmer every year. Movies are not what they were; their influence has lessened. We turn to brand-name designers now. They seem to be more important than the stars.

I change out of my traveling suit into my skirt and blouse. I forgo the stockings as advised, and slip into a pair of ballerina flats, comfortable for walking. There is a smoky oval mirror over the fireplace, and I lean in and look at myself. My hair, which used to be a mop of curls when I was a girl, is set stiffly in a medium pageboy. Even my bangs are stiff. I didn't notice a hair salon in town. Luckily, like Papa, I don't have gray hair, but in a new room, with new lighting, I see that my hair makes me look old. I run my hands over my face. The powder that I apply is too pink, and that makes me look old too. My lipstick, a light peach, does nothing for me. I look closely at my face, and though it's not wrinkled, I have the overall expression of a pinched, imperious woman. Faint lines that slope south on my forehead give the impression that I'm always looking down on people. My nose is straight, and my lips full, but the set of my mouth is smug, as though

I have all the answers. I look deeply into my eyes. And at last, I see myself. The waxy veneer of the woman I am seems to melt away, revealing the girl I used to be. Suddenly I can't stand myself and I look away. All the things Celeste has said about me are true: I am nothing more than a profit-driven mill owner. I have become old Mr. Jenkins. Or worse, I have become his son, Freddie. I found my purpose in the mill and am driven by its success and profitability. What happened to me? What happened to the girl who loved to read books and live in her imagination? And how did I let it happen?

There is a knock at the door. "Come in," I call out. Agnese walks in, but I turn away.

"What's wrong?" She comes over to me.

"I don't know.

"Tell me." She puts her arms around me, and I don't know why, but her warmth, as a stranger to me, moves me deeply. I begin to cry. It begins like small stabs of pain, deep in my gut, that turn into a great heaving: my husband, our life together, the possibility of our future, and my youth, all gone now. The grief comes pouring out of me. I try to stifle the sound and cannot. "Cry, go ahead. Cry. Let it out," she says. And for the first time since I held Franco on the floor of the mill, I cry. "God help me," I wail through my tears.

When I wake up, I look at my travel clock and can't believe it. It's noon! That means I slept twelve hours. I sit up in bed; the only sound I hear is the curtain, whipping gently against the windowsill. Papa's right, it *is* quiet here. I go down the hall to the bathroom. I listen when I reach the stairs but hear no one. I draw a bath. I sink into the hot water and breathe. I'm not sure why, but I feel good; I almost float. No wonder everyone was worried when I did not weep for Franco; there is great relief in tears.

Usually when I soak in the tub, I wear a shower cap to preserve my hair set. This time, instead of being careful, I slide down under the water, immersing my chin, then my nose, then my entire head. I hold my breath underwater and feel the heat and warmth soothe my eyes. I stay under as long as I can and then sit up. I push my hair off my face and rest against the back of the tub. I look around the white room. There is a long window that overlooks a field in the back. A stack of thick white cotton towels sits neatly on a shelf near the tub. The white ceramic sink has a long antique mirror over it. There is a screen painted in bold peach and white stripes that obscures the toilet. A small white rug lies on the black-and-white-tiled floor. Except for the levers, handles, and drains, the bathroom is every bit as modern as ours in America.

Once I'm dressed, I go downstairs. No one is home, which surprises me; it must be near lunchtime. I push open the front door and go out into the street. People are milling around, but no one I know. I walk up the main street, loving that I don't have to say hello to anyone, just walk and look. The storefronts reveal very little. In America, we try to sell items with fancy displays. Here, it seems, you go in and get what you need. Roseto Valfortore is not a shopper's paradise.

When I make it to the end of the street, I see Agnese and Penelope coming toward me carrying a few small bundles wrapped in brown paper.

"Ah, Nella, you're up." Agnese smiles. "How are you feeling?"

"I feel good," I say. And I do. I feel a mighty burden has lifted off me. I breathe deeply, hoping that more change will come. I have rested for the first time in a very, very long time.

"Where's Mama?"

"She went into Foggia for the fish market with the neighbor. She loves the market."

"Come, we make the meal." Penelope walks ahead.

"You slept well?" Agnese asks.

"So well. Thank you. Where's Papa?"

"He went with my husband. They go looking around. Who knows at what? Your father tells us you have your own factory," Agnese continues.

"We did." That was interesting, I think; why did I put Nella Manufacturing in the past tense? I correct myself. "We do." So far from the pressures, the machines that need to be fixed, the production that needs to be met—it all seems so far away. How could thirty-some years of work slip so easily from my mind?

"Hard work, eh?" Agnese asks.

"Very hard."

"You like?"

"I used to." I smile at her.

I follow Agnese and Penelope into the house. Agnese shows me to a chair in the kitchen. I'm not to help but to sit and talk while they prepare the food. The kitchen is the largest room in the house. There is a long farm table with twelve chairs around it. There is another table and long counter where the food is prepared. The fireplace, which serves as their oven, has cast-iron doors. I watch as Agnese and her daughter unwrap the fresh fish, preparing it with lemon and herbs to be baked in the oven. Penelope puts a large pot of water on the stove to boil macaroni. Soon, instead of being lost in the details of how they are cooking, I watch their partnership. There is no correcting, and no leader. It always seems as if I tell Celeste what to do and how to do it, and then in frustration, when she does not do it to my liking, I get angry and do it myself. Here, a mother and daughter work together, but they truly like each other and respect each other's way of doing things. When I think on the way I handle Celeste, I regret so much. I doubt she has ever felt like we are a team. Now, even when we are bonded by grief, the past hangs over us like a low ceiling in a dark room.

Papa and Zio Domenico return from their rounds. They laugh and talk, and I am reminded how Papa was surrounded by women on Delabole farm. I knew he was missing something, but I never knew exactly what, until I see him here, in his homeland. He thrives in the place where he was born.

After lunch, I slip into my sandals and go over to the mirror. Instead of putting on powder, I put on a little lipstick. Being around Agnese's youthfulness is rubbing off. There's a pink patch of sun on my nose and cheeks. I am starting to look like the happy girl I used to be.

I decide to go exploring, so I take off up the hill, sort of like where Chestnut Street would be back home. The church is at the top of the hill. With the shards of stone surrounding the courtyard, the old stucco structure looks more like a fort than a house of worship. The apostles carved in relief over the door stand in welcome, their large feet almost comical. I push the old wooden door open. There is a small, dark vestibule and then another door. I push through it into the church. Once inside, I see the magnificent frescoes, in faded blues, greens, and pinks depicting the life of Mary. Here, behind the altar, she begins as a girl and the frescoes take her through the crucifixion on the back wall of the church. It makes me smile; this Blessed Mother as a woman is quite a beauty, with ruby-red lips and enormous blue eyes. I slip into the pew and begin to pray the rosary. "Glory be to the Father, and to the Son, and to the Holy Spirit . . ." I get lost in the repitition of the prayers, and when I stop I wonder if the meditative state I've lulled myself into has any spiritual consequences. I wonder, as I always have, Does God hear me?

The village priest comes from the sacristy, genuflecting in front of the altar, and then goes on his way down the side aisle and out the back of the church. I think of Renato, the night before my wedding, when I first saw him in his black cassock. How shocked I was! I could understand if he married a wonderful woman and had a family, but the far-fetched choice of becoming a priest has always seemed so wrong. I feel guilty thinking about him. After all, I lost my husband, whom I built a family, a business, and a life with—why ponder Renato Lanzara? The only thing he ever did with any consistency was abandon me. Maybe his rejection of me has something to do with the wall I've always had around my heart.

I get up and walk out of the church and into the sunlight. I sit down on a bench overlooking the town and marvel at the view, the orange roofs on the stucco houses and the patterns of stone in the old roads. I hear a group of kids laughing and talking as they walk up the hill. I remember those sounds from Delabole School and then the Columbus School, how sweet that youthful laughter sounds, and how I felt I never got enough of it. How I wish I could have been young when I *was* young. It all ended the first day I set foot in Roseto Manufacturing Company.

As the group rounds the corner on their way to the church, I see that they are older, probably college age. The bits of Italian I hear them speak have an American twang. What are they doing here in this village?

A sick feeling churns in my stomach. My instincts, which I usually choose to ignore, gnaw at me. I am being presented with clues, but they're not adding up fast enough. I remember my hair, a mass of fresh curls, and my skirt, simple cotton. I look down at my feet in sandals, no stockings. I want to run in the opposite direction, but there is nowhere to go. The courtyard of the church is a dead end.

"Nella!" A wave of excitement and dread peels through me

at the sound of the man's voice. "What are you doing here?" There is no doubt. It's Renato. I turn and face him and smile. His hair is still thick, but now it's white. He is tall and trim, and wears small wire-rimmed glasses. He is dressed in a white shirt and khaki slacks, but no Roman collar.

"I'm here with my parents. What are you doing here?"

"These are my students from St. John's. I wanted to stop and show them where my ancestors are from. And the frescoes in this church are astonishing."

"Yes, they are."

"How are you?" he asks, without speaking directly of my loss.

"I'm okay. Franco always wanted to come here, so I thought I should."

"It's like home, isn't it?"

I nod in agreement. Renato and I are from the same place, the same people, and the older I get, the more valuable that bond is to me. Renato continues to chatter about the landscape, the vista, and the art, and I realize he's nervous. He's chattering as though he is trying to cover something; he's telling the kids how he knows me, and all about Roseto, Pennsylvania. The students seem to notice how fast and furious he speaks. I put my hand on his arm to slow him down.

"How long are you here?" I ask him.

"A few days, and then it's on to Rome."

I look at the students. "May I borrow your professor this evening?"

The students laugh. One of the girls smiles. "He's a priest, you know."

"Oh, I know all about it," I tell Renato. "I'm at 127 Testa Street."

"I'll see you around seven." He turns to his students. "Let's see the frescoes."

I walk down the hill slowly, afraid to trip. It is so steep; in my mind's eye, I see myself falling on the rocks and rolling like a tire all the way to the Adriatic Sea. What strange fate to see Renato here. What does this mean? As I walk down Primo Street, I catch my reflection in the windows of the grocery. I look at myself sideways and stop. I turn forward. In the sun, with my hair a wavy mess and my skirt gently swaying around my calves, I could be a girl. I know I'm not anymore, but I could almost pass for one.

There's a restaurant at an old inn outside Roseto Valfortore on the Fortor River called Juno. The setting is lovely, an old stone fortress with outdoor gardens. The main dining room has a gravel floor and is under a tent. Renato leads me to a table overlooking the wide blue river.

"How's this?" he says, pulling my chair out for me.

"Fine." I smile.

I borrowed a white linen skirt and a light pink cashmere sweater from Agnese. She insisted, as the clothes I brought were too formal for the inn.

"Where's your collar?" I ask him.

"I don't wear it when I'm traveling."

"That's not a good idea."

"You'd think the collar would be a deterrent. But actually it's the opposite."

I hold my hand up. "Enough! I don't want to know any more." We laugh, and it's as though it were yesterday and we were on the banks of Minsi Lake. "Renato, you've known me since I was sixteen."

"Fourteen."

"Right. Fourteen. How do I look?"

Renato sits back in his chair.

"You'll have to excuse my vanity, Renato, but I just turned fifty. I never felt old before, but now I do. The number scares me. Franco is gone. I'm a widow. I just feel like everything has ended. It's over for me." My true feelings pour out of me. I'm in the company of someone who knew me when I was a girl, and I feel safe. It's almost like the tears from the first night I was here. I can't help myself from sharing my feelings; I need to talk. The waiter comes over. Renato chooses a wine. The waiter speaks to him about the food.

"Just bring whatever is good," Renato says to the waiter. The waiter is happy to take that request to the chef.

"You're not old. You're still beautiful. More beautiful."

"You're just being nice." I run my hands through my hair, which feels thick and soft. Never again will hair spray come near my head. I'm a convert to the natural look, thanks to Agnese.

"I'm being nice, yes. But I'm being honest. You're lucky. You have a face that will always be young."

"Maybe it's just how you remember me."

"No, it's how you are." Renato pours me a glass of wine. "What happened to you?"

"What do you mean?" I sip the wine and feel my face get hot immediately.

"You never asked me anything like this before. You were always a girl without vanity."

"Well, I never felt old before."

"No, that's not what I mean. You're self-aware somehow. You need to understand something, maybe?"

"I'm trying to understand why I've failed at everything. How can anybody be this old and feel so stupid?"

"What do you mean?"

"I've learned nothing. Franco died before we ever had a real vacation. Celeste thinks I was a terrible mother. Frankie jokes about it—like he had a mother who was a stevedore instead of a cuddler. They think all I did was work, that all I cared about was making money."

"Is any of it true?"

"I was always ambitious, Renato. Always."

"So, they had a good life, right?"

"They wanted for nothing. Grandparents all around. They had a wonderful childhood."

"So what are they complaining about?"

"Me."

"They wanted more of you; is that bad?"

"I guess not."

"There are days when I would give my life to have my father back," he begins. "My mother was gone when I was five; I looked for her in every woman I ever knew, and in a sense I still do. We all wish things could be different, but we choose a way to live, a way to be, and you can only choose one way."

I think about this for a moment. "You've heard a lot of confessions, haven't you?"

Renato laughs. "Too many."

"You're never surprised in there? In the black closet?"

"Not anymore."

"Good for you." I smooth Agnese's sweater into the belt of the skirt. "You mastered something."

"I didn't say anything about mastering it. I'm just telling you that it seems that we all have the same demons."

"A man of God talking about demons."

"Let's not talk about me in the context of the priesthood."

"Why not? You're a priest."

"I don't know anything more than the next man, really. I'm flattered that you think I have an inside track, but I don't. I'm as doubtful and full of questions as you are. What do you think about that?"

"I wish I could say I was surprised." I lean back in my chair and put my hands on the arms of it.

Renato laughs. "This is why I always loved you. . . ."

"Oh, for God's sake, Renato!" The word "love" embarrasses me.

"No, I'm serious. I always loved you because you saw through it all."

"Through the charm?"

"Through the charm, the bluster, the intellect, the poetry, the ideas, through all the layers of all the stuff I pride myself on possessing. You, however, cut right to the heart of the matter and force me to be honest."

"Then why did you leave me?" As soon as I say it, I feel a terrible pang of disloyalty to my husband. I wish I could take the words back. I wish I didn't wonder about why Renato left, and I wish I could take back all those times in my marriage when I would get angry with Franco and think to myself, You may not love me in this moment, but I know a man who once did. What a terrible thing to do in a marriage, to turn away from the moment and reach back into the past, where everything seems perfect. "Never mind. I don't need to know."

"But maybe I need to tell you."

"No, it's not right. I loved Franco. I chose him. I don't want to know why you left; it will only make me feel that I chose Franco second, and I never want to feel I did that."

"But isn't that what happened?"

"Dear God, Renato. Please."

"Isn't that what happened?" he presses.

"No!"

"That's what Franco thought. I know that's why you had to leave Our Lady of Mount Carmel for St. Elizabeth's, and I have always blamed myself for that. The day they assigned me to Roseto was the worst day of my life. I begged them to send me anywhere else, but they were convinced I was the next Father DeNisco. For fifty years, the diocese looked for a priest with the talent, vision, and diplomacy of DeNisco. I told them there was only one Father DeNisco, and that man was a saint. They wouldn't hear of it. They were sending me home, to Roseto. No arguments. And you didn't disagree then; you would be thrown out. We did what we were told."

"But you were like Father DeNisco. You accomplished great things."

"Oh, the diocese and their big plans. A school, a hospital, a rest home. They were going to make Roseto the model for their highest Roman Catholic aspirations."

"They succeeded."

"In some ways. But I didn't want to come back. I didn't want to hurt you. I felt like I ruined your wedding."

"You didn't ruin it. I loved Franco."

"Good." Renato sits back, relieved.

"I knew I could keep Franco interested for a lifetime, but you, I wasn't so sure."

"You could have, Nella."

The waiter places small plates of local delicacies on the table. We sample lobster ravioli in truffle sauce, veal sautéed in wine with artichokes, and fresh greens. I ask Renato about his life now. As Renato talks about being a professor, and life at St. John's University, and what it's like to live in New York instead of a small town, I start to feel for him again. My heart, still healing from the deep wound of losing Franco, is longing for connection. I want to push through the grieving and feel like a woman again. But that is not right, and I know it. It would be like the night that Renato and I made love. We would connect out of sympathy and a need for comfort, not real love, not the kind Franco and I had all along. That love was authentic, and it took this long and even his death for me to realize it. Maybe I'm not so stupid, maybe I know a little more about myself than I let on. Maybe this evening at a romantic table in this old Italian fortress is the symbol of what Renato and I ultimately meant to each other; his love was just a flicker in time, a sparkle of a star far away that once guided me.

"Why did you do it, Renato?"

"Do what?"

"Become a priest."

"Oh, that question." Renato smiles. "Well, at first it felt as though I was led to it. I was living a pretty fast life without consequences—"

"Except for me, of course."

"Except for you. And I looked around and wondered what I could do with my life. I prayed about it. For a young man in 1927 who loved to read and write and think, it was a perfect profession. I loved solitude, and yet I like serving people. I enjoy giving a good sermon. I can't explain it; in a sense, it chose me."

"But you could have been a doctor or a politician or anything, really, if leading and serving people is what compelled you. Why that life? The priestly life?"

"When I was in the seminary I would look around at my classmates and wonder what the one thing was that we all had in common. You would think it was a love of God and a desire to serve Him, but that wasn't it. It was a detachment. It was as if we were comfortable being separate. I had my excuse; my mother died when I was a boy. I always felt that I was wandering through, unable to connect because I didn't have Mama to teach me how. I can't speak for my fellow seminarians; they had their own reasons for choosing a life that meant at its very core that you could not have intimacy with another person. That intimacy was reserved for God."

"And you were okay with that?"

"It's all I knew to be true. I learned that I couldn't find myself in the arms of a thousand girls. I tried, but it didn't work. I was never satisfied."

When Renato mentions other girls, I wince. I knew there were other girls before me, and after, but I wanted desperately to believe that I was special. Now I know I wasn't special enough to keep him out of the priesthood. "I found that intimacy you speak of with my husband," I begin. Maybe I shouldn't confide these things to Renato, but I continue. "Franco and I were connected. I didn't value that enough when he was alive. I took it for granted that there was someone to get me an aspirin in the middle of the night, that there was someone at the mill who could look across the desk and understand exactly what I was feeling when he heard a particular sigh. We didn't just share a life, we grew it."

"I envy that," Renato says quietly. "And now I wish I had it. I don't think any good comes from separating yourself from people. Ultimately, it is the least blessed state."

"Celibacy?"

"Oh, it's not just celibacy. It's knowing that for your whole life, you have promised not to become close to anyone because it will interfere with your work, your relationship to God. When I was young, that separation made sense to me. Now it seems foolish."

"Why do you stay?"

"I'm an old man." Renato laughs. "What do I have to offer a woman now?"

"I see what you mean. I feel the same way. I had what I had with Franco, but I feel done. I had one good marriage, two excellent children, and a life. What else is there for me? I had the best. I can't top it." I throw my hands up.

"I love teaching. First and foremost, I'm a teacher. The students are terrific. I take a group from Queens to Italy every year, and they see the real art, the inspiration behind it. It opens up their world." Renato looks away. "But every day when I get up, I think, Is today the day I leave? And then I go on with my day, and there are things about the life that still work, so I stay in."

"I didn't think you'd have such doubts."

"Constantly. That's why I signed up." He shrugs. "Maybe I thought I'd find the answers giving them to others. Not so."

"What about women?"

"What about them?" He smiles. "Do I miss it?"

I nod.

"I'm not perfect," he says slowly. "I've made mistakes."

"Oh." How naive I am. I thought there was some secret ingredient in the holy oil that keeps a priest celibate, but obviously I was wrong.

"You're shocked?"

"No, but I assumed as a priest, you'd give all that up. Don't you *have* to?"

"You try. But that's the whole nature of sin: you try and fail, and try and fail. That's how it works. There would be no redemption without sin." He pours me another glass of wine. "But as time goes on, it isn't the physical contact you miss so much, it's the emotional part. The intimacy. The deepest level of love. The knowledge that someone understands you, is rooting for you, is sharing your life. Even though I feel I've deepened my faith as a priest, I'm well aware of what I've lost."

"If it's any comfort to you, I still struggle. I always feel alone. Maybe that's my cross to bear."

Renato reaches his hand across the table and takes mine. "And mine too."

Renato walks me home to my uncle's house. Maybe at fifty years old, all you get from an old love is a window of what you were when you were young. Maybe a first love exists to reaffirm the best parts of yourself, the choices you made when you didn't worry about the consequences. Maybe a first love exists to remind you to be brave in the moment, to stand up for your feelings, instead of shrinking back in the face of potential loneliness. It's old-fashioned guts that we gave each other, I think as I hold Renato's hand and feel the warmth of him near me. When we reach the doorway, there is a small light on in the window. It is very late, and everyone is in bed.

"Thank you," Renato says to me as we face each other. The moon must be closer to the land in Italy, because it's so bright outside it's like blue daylight. I wish it weren't so, but Renato is still as dashing and handsome as he was in his youth. How difficult it is when you're young to think about being old. When it finally happens, you can't believe it. But we have not changed, not really. I am still trying to let go, and Renato is as elusive a priest as he was a poet.

"You never told me . . ."

"What?" he says after a long pause, searching my face.

"Why you left me."

Renato takes a moment and looks away. "I was afraid."

"Afraid I'd gobble you up and make you work in a mill?"

"No." Renato looks over my shoulder and off into the distance. "I left you before you could leave me."

Renato leans down and kisses me on the cheek. He turns to go, and while I want to stop him, I don't. Now that I understand Renato, I don't need him to stay. He belongs out there in the world doing the thing he loves, and I have to invent a new life alone. If only I had known to treasure my moments with Franco. If only I had known the first day he loaned me his handkerchief that the clock was ticking. Alas, I didn't hear it.

Celeste's fingernails dig into me, making small half-moon impressions on my hands. "Push, honey, you can do it, push!" My Celeste is having her first baby in Easton Hospital. Giovanni is outside in the waiting room with the other nervous fathers. I came as soon as I heard she was in labor. As the contractions came faster and faster, my daughter grabbed my hand and said, "Stay."

The doctor is not happy that I am here. But when I saw that my daughter wanted me, it would have taken killing me to break me away from her. No woman should be alone at this moment, and if at all possible, her mother should be with her. After Assunta died, Mama made sure she was with each of her girls when she gave birth. This modern doctor is not going to keep me from my daughter. "I'm here, honey. I'll never leave you," I tell her.

Celeste is a trouper; she pushes for close to an hour. Then the moment comes. Celeste pushes, then cries out; her belly ripples like the surf of the ocean, and out with another mighty push the baby appears. "It's a girl!" I holler.

The nurses move in and take her, doing a thousand routine things in a matter of moments. "How is she?" Celeste asks.

"Perfect. Just perfect." I hold Celeste's hand and wipe her face with a damp cloth; for an instant, I remember Assunta and her terrible, fateful moment. Not so for my daughter; she is rosy and beaming, as though she just came back from an exhilarating hike up a mountain. The nurse gives Celeste her daughter. Celeste cries as she holds her. "She's so beautiful. Isn't she, Ma?"

"Like you were. Just like you were," I tell her.

"I'm going to call her Francesca. For Papa. Okay?"

I can't help it. I cry. Celeste looks up at me.

"I love you, Celeste," I tell her.

"I love you too, Mama," she whispers. "And you, Francesca."

Who knew it would take the birth of my granddaughter for

me to understand faith? I never had it, but now I see it in her. Even giving birth to my own children did not move me to this place—only the face of my granddaughter. Maybe because she is part of me without being the hardware of me; that makes me see faith in a context. All faith is a belief that life is meant to be, and that beyond it, we never die. We go on and on and on. Francesca has only been here for a moment, but she has given us all an everlasting gift.

I check my watch as I close my front door to walk up Garibaldi to Mary Bert's, Roseto's best and only diner. As I walk up the street, I see that little has changed since I was a girl. Our town is still mostly Italian, though we now have one Greek family of candy makers. Our Lady of Mount Carmel still sits at the top of the hill like a castle; the nearby schools give our town a youthful energy. My friend Barbara Renaldo always says, "Roseto is now for the newly wed or the nearly dead." Sometimes I think she's right.

"Over here, Auntie!" My niece Assunta waves from the back booth. She kisses me as I sit down.

"So, tell me about the wedding plans."

"I know it's corny, but I want Francesca to be my flower girl. I'm not having any other attendants. Just her," Assunta tells me over coffee. "For crying out loud, I'm forty-one years old, I should elope! Fanfare is for youngsters."

"Oh, please. Go for the trumpets and the rose petals and the rice. You deserve a beautiful wedding. And take it from your old aunt who's fifty-six: forty-one is damn young."

Assunta throws her head back and laughs. "It took Joe eleven years to pop the question. Schoolteachers, and I include myself in this generalization, are slow learners."

"But eventually you get it right. That's why God invented erasers, don't forget it."

"Sorry I'm late." Elena joins us at the table. My sister is heavier than she was when she got married, but she still has the same sweet countenance. "Did you tell Aunt Nella about the Hotel Bethlehem?"

Assunta turns to me. "We booked it. Ma, you got the small room, right?"

"The President's whatever it's called . . ." Elena hands her the brochure. How natural it is to hear Assunta call Elena "Ma."

"I want everybody there, Aunt Dianna, Aunt Roma, all the cousins. I want to do something special to honor Nonna and Grandpop."

On a bright and perfect morning, April 26, 1966, Assunta Maria Pagano marries Michael Castigliano at Our Lady of Mount Carmel before a small but happy group of family and friends. She asked my parents to precede her and Alessandro down the aisle. They were so honored to be a part of the wedding processional.

How proud I am of my niece, a schoolteacher at our parish high school, Pius X, and now a new bride. My four-year-old granddaughter, Francesca, drops her rose petals on cue, and watches the service with rapt attention.

Papa and Mama dance at the Hotel Bethlehem until the

orchestra calls it quits. They are back in Roseto for the summer, splitting their time between Italy and Pennsylvania, as they have done since Papa retired. They would not think of missing the annual Big Time at the end of July.

"Papa, I have an idea," I tell him over breakfast the next morning. "Your tenants are leaving Delabole farm."

"We can't keep anybody out there. What's the matter with people? I'll tell you what. Nobody wants to work like that anymore," Papa grouses.

"I'd like to move out there."

"What? All your life you wanted to live in town."

"I know, but I've had enough. I miss the quiet," I say.

"What about the mill?" he asks.

"The Menecolas made me an offer."

"A good one?"

"The best I'll get. I want to take it. I want to sell this house and move back home to Delabole farm. I'd like you and Mama to live out there with me, too, if you'd like. What do you think?"

Papa smiles. I can see that he wants to go home. "It's what Mama thinks that counts."

The farmhouse needs an overhaul, so I take a little money and have the wiring redone and the whole place painted. It needs a new furnace, so I put that in too. The bathroom was never big enough, so we renovate and put in one of those deep, four-legged tubs like Uncle Domenico had in Italy. My parents are so happy to move back in. We put everything where it used to be, and we laugh about where the television set should go. We never had those worries when I was a girl.

The creek by the front gate still gurgles; it's not as deep as it once was, but the stones in the water still glitter like coins. When I walk the fields collecting dandelion leaves for salad, and yank Queen Anne's lace to fill the vases, I think of Assunta and how she loved nice things. The old barn needs some shoring up, but with the cows gone, it's just an old red monument to what we used to be around here.

With a nice cushion in the bank, I can be a full-time grandmother, running to Allentown whenever I wish to be with Francesca. Sometimes I go to Jersey and spend the night with Frankie and his wife, Patricia (they have two sons, Frankie the Third and Salvatore, for Papa). Patricia is of Welsh descent, and I couldn't ask for a better daughter-in-law. When my son gives her trouble, she teases him and lets him know that she's a Johnny Bull.

I am so happy that my parents have a secure old age. They have Italy in the winter and their girls back home the rest of the year. Their grandchildren and great-grandchildren have brought them pride and peace, both of which they richly deserve after a lifetime of hard work and caring for their daughters.

I had new soil brought in to cover the strawberry field where Mama and my sisters and I used to pick berries. I've made a garden of tomatoes, lettuce, carrots, and basil; when the fall comes, I grow pumpkins. I love getting up early in the morning like I used to when I ran the mill. I make my *gabagule*, eat a crusty slice of bread with butter, and head out to weed and hoe and water as the sun comes up.

I still analyze the sun just as Papa taught me to do when I was girl, taking every hue and slight change as a signal: pink sun for planting, yellow sun for picking, always trusting it, as all good farmers do, to bring the right amount of light and warmth to the garden. It is a wonder to me as I grow older that living things, small living things like the plants I grow, and the stray mutt that came to stay (we named him Rex), show me how to live. Like Rex, I rest a lot, and like the plants in my garden, I press on.

I miss my husband more as the years go by, not less. It's a secret we widows share. I still pat his side of the bed expecting to find him there, and imagine what his kisses would feel like now. In memory they are so sweet, I can taste them. I miss his skin, especially when I buried my head in his neck, which smelled of vanilla and thyme. I never forget how lucky I was to be his wife, and how hopeful I am that I will see him again. I try not to be greedy. I had him for twenty-seven years, and that's a nice stretch of road.

EPILOGUE

Sunlight streams into Our Lady of Mount Carmel through the stained-glass windows, throwing a gold hue over the Communion railing. Four altar boys prepare the church for the funeral Mass. It is a warm April day, so they prop open the windows, stack the prayer books, and place programs on the end of each pew.

Two ladies from the sodality lift starched white linens out of a long dress box and carefully place them on the altar. The florist arrives from the back of the church carrying a large crystal vase of three dozen long-stemmed white roses. The arrangement is so lush, he has to peek through the bouquet to see where he is going. Two of his workers follow with identical vases overflowing with roses. The sodality ladies take the flowers, placing two vases behind the altar and one at the foot of it.

"Somebody should ask Father about the candles," an altar boy says to the sodality volunteer.

"I'll take care of it." The woman goes behind the altar to the sacristy, where she finds the priest sitting in his vestments, with his face in his hands. "Excuse me, Father?"

The priest looks up. "Yes?"

"The altar boys want to know about the candles."

"They can go ahead and light them," he tells her.

Father Lanzara looks in the small mirror on the wall and shakes his head. He is close to seventy, but his blue eyes still have the sparkle of a much younger man. He looks around the sacristy he knows so well: the closet with the crisply pressed vestments, the wooden bench under the window, the statue of the Blessed Lady on the sill. He opens his well-worn leather prayer book and reads. He can hear the shuffle of the mourners as they take their seats in the church. They are expecting a standing-room-only service. He hears the sweet strains of a violin and smiles sadly. There is a knock at the door.

"Father, I don't know if you remember me . . ." Celeste Zollerano Melfi extends her hand. Tall and slim, the brunette has familiar brown eyes, large and almond-shaped.

"You're Nella's daughter." Father looks at Celeste and sees Nella in her countenance and expression. He has to look away.

"I found something I think Mama would want you to

have." Celeste gives Father Lanzara a letter. He looks down at it and recognizes his own handwriting. "It was in her jewelry box."

Father nods his head and puts the letter in his prayer book.

"There was one other thing in the jewelry box . . . this poem." She gives him the faded folded paper. "I don't remember Mama ever reading it to me, but it was there, alongside your letter, so I was hoping you would know what it meant."

"I'll look at it," he promises.

The altar boy pushes the door open. "Father, Mr. Fiori sent me. The hearse is outside." Father takes a moment to remember that time has passed. The John Fiori he knew as a boy is long gone. The current one is his grandson.

The mention of the hearse makes Celeste cry. She buries her face in her hands. Father Lanzara comforts her. "She loved you with all her heart," he tells her.

"I know," Celeste says, and, pulling herself together, she goes.

Father Lanzara opens the letter. When he reads the words, his words, written in his own hand, telling Nella that he could no longer see her, he cries. He tucks it in his prayer book. Then he unfolds the poem, in a handwriting he does not recognize. The familiar words of a Yeats poem—"When you are old . . ."—are written in perfect Palmer penmanship. He never read this poem to Nella, but it must have had some significance to her. He puts on his sash over his robe, picks up his prayer book, and goes, closing the door of the sacristy behind him. He follows the altar boy, who waits for him, out the back of the church and to the street.

When he sees the family gathered at the foot of the steps on the church plaza, he is overwhelmed, but does not cry. He sees many familiar faces in the crowd, Chettie Marucci and her husband. He flashes to their double date to see a Garbo movie. The Maruccis, like him, are powdery with age.

Father goes to the back of the hearse and sees a mahogany coffin resting there. He places his hand on the wood and bows his head in prayer. But he doesn't pray; what he says to himself is "I'm sorry, Nella. I did everything wrong."

A group of handsome young Italian men, who Father Lanzara assumes are grandsons and nephews, stand by in suits and white gloves to take Nella Castelluca Zollerano into the church. He instructs them about how to process, and they listen carefully.

The church is filled to capacity, with several generations of millworkers, family, and friends in attendance. The choir loft is filled, and there is standing room only in the side aisles.

Father Lanzara has never seen such a crowd in the church, he thinks as he approaches the altar to begin the service. His heart is heavy, because this is not just any funeral Mass, it is the Mass of Resurrection for a woman he once loved. It is hard for him to reconcile his priestly duties with the personal loss he feels, yet as he recites the familiar prayers, he finds comfort in the repetition and reassurance in their meaning.

When it comes time for the eulogy, he approaches the lectern slowly, putting his hands, which are folded in prayer, up to his lips, hoping to find some way to tell the people gathered in the church what Nella meant to him.

"I'm as shocked by Nella's passing as you all are," he begins, and then stops, looking out over the crowd. "She died suddenly in her garden on Delabole farm. If you're like me, you believed she was so strong and capable that she would live forever. Alas, that was not to be.

"Nella was a woman who struggled to find her faith all of her life. Many years ago Father Impeciato asked her to start the Society of Mary in this church, and she did it, even though she had doubts. When I asked her why she took on the responsibility, she said, 'I was asked.' She never found any answers in church, and made a point to tell me this when I became a priest."

A small wave of laughter ripples forth from the pews filled with Nella's machine operators, who look at one another and smile.

Father Lanzara continues, "Nella shared with me that she finally found faith in the hospital room where her daughter, Celeste, gave birth to her first grandchild, Francesca. She understood then that life goes on.

"Many of you in this church today know that I loved Nella Castelluca. . . . I did love her when we were young, but typical of Nella, she had a mind of her own, and wisdom in all important matters, and in the end, she found a better choice for a husband. Franco Zollerano was her true love, and with him she had two wonderful children.

"Many of you worked for or with her in the blouse mill.

You know her standards were high, but she would never ask you to do anything she wouldn't do herself. And she was always grateful for the opportunity to work, and never took prosperity in its fleeting moments for granted. She was generous and kind and a pillar of this community. What she wasn't was envious, a gossip, or a phony. She never put on airs or held herself above others.

"She was an Italian girl who never forgot she was happiest with her bare feet in the dirt at Delabole farm. She loved her parents, who survive her, and was never less than grateful for their guidance and experience. She grew up to be brilliant at business, though her dream was to be a teacher. That dream was not to be, because she had to go to work in the mill when she was fifteen, when her father was hurt in a quarry accident. Everything about her determination and persistence was informed by that accident. That's how her drive and ambition came to help the people of Roseto.

"Nella and Franco gave me the money to build the school. She would not want me to share this with you, but I feel we must give credit to them. No one knew where the money came from, and while we raised a good sum with fund-raisers, when I went to her and Franco, they gave me the balance. When Franco died and she moved out to the farm, she gave her home to the town for conversion into the public library. She was not only unselfish, she was a visionary who knew what Rosetans needed to achieve the kind of success for their children that she enjoyed.

"When she lost her sister Assunta in childbirth, it was

another turning point in her life. She mourned her sister until the day she died. Years later, she mourned the loss of her husband, and yet soldiered on. We often take determination and will to live as a given, but I assure you, there were times when Nella was so brokenhearted she wondered if she would live through it. The lesson we can take away from her life is to be open to wonder, to look at the world as she did at the end of her life, as a garden of possibility. She told me Franco woke her up in the middle of the night once when Frankie was small, and they bundled him up and took him to watch the circus tent being raised in Philadelphia. She remembered that night always because it reminded her how important it is to be spontaneous and look at the world through a child's eyes.

"When I saw her in Italy in Roseto Valfortore, she confided that she wished she had traveled more. She wished she had taken more trips with Franco instead of working and waiting for retirement. She learned to love solitude and quiet, two gifts that eluded her in her youth in a big family and in her adult life when she was surrounded by the constant hum of sewing machines at the mill. She found them, at last. She wrote to me in a letter: 'If I knew what a tonic the farm would be, I would have moved here with Franco years ago. But I was a foolish girl who loved the clamor of Main Street, and the buzz of the mill. How I wish I would have had my dear Frankie and my darling Celeste on the farm, where I came from. It would have been just us. For all my life, it was never just us. And when Franco died, with him went the dream that

I could fix it.' Sleep gently, my dear Nella, and . . . wait for us."

Father Lanzara goes behind the altar and continues forth with the Mass, relying on rote memory to get through the old prayers, but his heart is broken, and everyone at Our Lady of Mount Carmel knows it.

The funeral procession down Main Street to the cemetery is the longest anyone can remember. The line moves slowly as it passes all the places Nella held dear: Marcella's bakery, Columbus School, the Zolleranos' house, her own home with Franco. As the hearse turns at the end of Garibaldi, it passes the mill she and Franco founded together. Celeste looks back from the lead car and cannot believe how many people came to honor her mother. She takes Frankie's hand.

"Remember when Mama made us walk in the procession at the Big Time?"

"The rosary in the hot sun—how could I forget it?" Frankie smiles. "She'd point to the statue of the Blessed Mother and say, 'That's the real queen of the Big Time.' "

Frankie and Celeste laugh, remembering.

Father Lanzara gathers the mourners around the grave site for the final prayer. Nella's stone is already engraved:

Nella Castelluca Zollerano
Wife and Mother
January 23, 1910–April 10, 1971

He turns to the crowd. "Remember always what Nella meant to you. Love never dies. I promise you."

As the sun burns west over Garibaldi Avenue behind the Blue Mountains and the hillsides of slate slag, it throws a pink glow over the town, reminding everyone who knows that this is a good week for planting.

ACKNOWLEDGMENTS

I have so many wonderful memories of my grandmother Yolanda "Viola" Trigiani. She told me great tales of life working in the blouse mills and on the farm in Pennsylvania. My favorite times were when we'd gather at her house for a visit and my mother, sisters, and I would hang out with her in her room, telling stories and laughing until the wee hours. So much of the weave of this novel is from her, and the rest comes from her son—my father, Anthony, who died in 2002. They were amazing storytellers, never short on color and texture, and I miss them every day. My great-uncle Don Andrea Spada of Schilpario, Italy, provided the spark for this novel, so I am also indebted to him.

At Random House, I thank my editor, Lee Boudreaux, who

has heart and a brilliant intellect, both which come in handy in this enterprise; the effervescent Todd Doughty, who works harder than ten men, with glorious results; the high-energy visionary Gina Centrello; and the perfect team: Laura Ford, Anna McDonald, Jennifer Jones, Allison Saltzman, Vicki Wong, Libby McGuire, Janet Cook, Anthony Ziccardi, Patricia Abdale, Karen Richardson, Beth Thomas, Allyson Pearl, Kim Monahan, Lauren Monaco, Carol Schneider, Tom Perry, Sherry Huber, Ed Chen, Maureen O'Neal, Stacy Rockwood-Chen, Johanna Bowman, Allison Heilborn, Kim Hovey, Allison Dickens, Candace Chaplin, Cindy Murray, and Beth Pearson.

If you need someone in your corner—in fact, every corner and the middle of the room—I hope it's my agent Suzanne Gluck, whom I admire and love professionally and personally. Also at William Morris: Jennifer Rudolph Walsh, Cara Stein, Alicia Gordon, Tracy Fisher, Karen Gerwin, Eugenie Furniss, Erin Malone, Michelle Feehan, Andy McNicol, and Rowan Lawton. At ICM, my love and gratitude to my champion, the fabulous Nancy Josephson, and beloved Jill Holwager. In Movieland, thank you, Lou Pitt, Jim Powers, Todd Steiner, Michael Pitt, and Susan Cartsonis, and at Deep River Productions, Julie Durk, Missy Pontious, Amy Schwarz, Felipe Linz, David Friendly, Marc Turtletaub, Michael McGahey, and Megan de Andrade.

Thank you, Mary Testa, the world's best sounding board; Lorie Stoopack and Jean Morrissey, for your eagle eyes; Jake Morrissey, for your insight, expertise, and laughs; Karen Fink, for keeping everything on track—I am lucky to work with you; and June Lawton, for your counsel and advice, both of which I treasure. Father John Rausch provided many facts of pre–Vatican II Roman Catholic dogma, for which I am eternally grateful. Thank you, Pat Bean, for the research materials for 1920s fashion.

Elena Nachmanoff and Saul Shapiro, Dianne Festa, and Stewart Wallace provided inspiration, support, and humor, all of which I cherish, as well as their friendship. Michael Patrick King, your footsteps on the stairs is my favorite sound, second only to the whistle of your teapot.

Every Italian family, if they're lucky (and we were), gets one great Irish uncle. Mine was the Honorable Michael F. Godfrey, the beloved husband of my mom's twin sister, Irma, and father to Michael and Paul. Uncle Mike was dignified and decent and had a great sense of humor. He served brilliantly as a circuit court judge in St. Louis, Missouri. He left the world better than he found it, and me better for having known him.

My gratitude and love to: Ruth Pomerance, Sharon Watroba Burns, Nancy Bolmeier Fisher, Kate Crowley, Elaine Martinelli, Emily Nurkin, Adina T. Pitt, Eydie Collins, Tom Dyja, Pamela Perrell, Carmen Elena Carrion, Jena Morreale, Rosanne Cash, Ian Chapman, Suzanne Baboneau, Nigel Stoneman, Melissa Weatherill, Jim and Jeri Birdsall, Ellen Tierney and Jack Hodgins, Sally Davies, Dolores and Dr. Emil Pascarelli, Charles Randolph Wright, Bill Persky and Joanna Patton, Stephanie Trinkl, Larry Sanitsky, Debra McGuire, John Melfi, Grace Naughton, Dee Emmerson, Gina Casella,

Sharon Hall, Constance Marks, James Miller, Wendy Luck, Nancy Ringham Smith, John Searles, Helen and Bill Testa, Cynthia Rutledge Olson, Jasmine Guy, Jim Horvath, Craig Fissé, Kate Benton, Ann Godoff, Joanne Curley Kerner, Max Westler, Dana and Richard Kirshenbaum, Sister Jean Klene, Daphne and Tim Reid, Caroline Rhea, Kathleen Maccio Holman, Susan and Sam Frantzeskos, Beàta and Steven Baker, Mary Ellinger, Eleanor Jones, Drs. Dana and Adam Chidekel, Brownie and Connie Polly, Aaron Hill and Susan Fales-Hill, Karol Jackowski, Christina Avis Krauss and Sonny Grosso, Susan Paolercio, Greg Cantrell, Rachel and Vito DeSario, Mary Murphy, and Matt Williams and Angelina Fiordellisi.

Jim Burns, please continue to keep an eye on us from heaven.

To the Trigiani and Stephenson families, thank you all.

And to my husband and daughter, the best companions I could ever hope for on this joyful journey, all of my love.

POCKET
BOOKS

Also by Adriana Trigiani

Big Stone Gap

Big Stone Gap, Virginia, is the sort of sleepy
hamlet in the Blue Ridge Mountains where kids
get married and start families at eighteen, and
stay forever. So thirty-five-year old Ave Maria
Mulligan is something of an oddity. A self-
proclaimed spinster, as the local pharmacist she's
been keeping the townsfolk's secrets for years.

Now Ave Maria is about to discover a scandal in
her own family's past that will blow the lid right
off her quiet, uneventful life.

With an unforgettable cast of characters and a
heroine with an extraordinary story to tell, *Big
Stone Gap* is a wonderfully vibrant, unashamedly
feel-good debut.

'As warm and sweet as Southern Comfort' ELLE

ISBN 0 7434 4012 9
PRICE £6.99

POCKET
BOOKS

Big Cherry Holler

Adriana Trigiani

It's been eight years since Ave Maria Mulligan married Jack MacChesney. With her newfound belief in love and its possibilities, she has made a life for herself and her growing family. What she hasn't counted on is that the ghosts of the past will return . . .

Here we have the story of a marriage, the deep secrets, the power struggle, the betrayal and the unmet expectations that exist between a husband and wife. And here too we have the story of a wonderful community and an extended family, the people of Big Stone Gap, Virginia, who are always there for one another.

Full of humour, honesty, drama and local colour, *Big Cherry Holler* has at its core two lovers who have lost their way and struggle so compellingly to find each other again.

'A charming, moving and beautifully observed tale'
DAILY MIRROR

ISBN 0 7434 3034 4
PRICE £6.99

POCKET
BOOKS

Milk Glass Moon

Adriana Trigiani

A daughter's first love, a mother's heartbreak, an enduring marriage facing its own ongoing challenges, and a community faced with seismic changes, all are deep at the heart of Adriana Trigiani's third novel. As she faces the joys and demands of motherhood, Ave Maria continues her life story with her trademark humour and honesty.

Reaching into the past to find answers to the present, Ave Maria is led to places she never dreamed she would go, and to people who enter her life and rock its foundation. *Milk Glass Moon* is about the power of love and its abiding truth, and captures Trigiani at her most lyrical, affectionate and heartfelt.

'The warmth seeps out of the pages . . . Trigiani's talent is not so much writing page-turners as writing page-lingerers . . . you won't want this to finish'
DAILY MIRROR

ISBN 0 7434 5088 4

PRICE £6.99

POCKET
BOOKS

Lucia, Lucia

Adriana Trigiani

'The perfect feel-good read' GLAMOUR

Lucia Sartori is the most beautiful girl in Greenwich Village. Never short of suitors, she is sought after as a potential wife by the best Italian families in New York. But it is 1950, a time of great opportunity for ambitious girls with dreams of a career, and Lucia is no exception. She has a glamorous job in a chic Fifth Avenue department store, which she's not yet ready to swap for a role as wife.

Until a handsome stranger comes into her life and she falls desperately and passionately in love at first sight. But in order to be together, they must first win over her traditional family. Their love affair takes an unexpected turn as secrets are revealed, Lucia's family honour is tested, and her own reputation becomes the centre of a sizzling scandal.

ISBN 0 7434 6226 2
PRICE £6.99

**POCKET
BOOKS**

These Adriana Trigiani titles are available from your local bookshop or can be ordered direct from the publisher.

☐	0 7434 4012 9	**Big Stone Gap**	£6.99
☐	0 7434 3034 4	**Big Cherry Holler**	£6.99
☐	0 7434 5088 4	**Milk Glass Moon**	£6.99
☐	0 7434 6226 2	**Lucia, Lucia**	£6.99
☐	0 7434 6227 0	**Queen of the Big Time**	£6.99

Please send cheque or postal order for the value
of the book, **free postage and packing within
the UK**, to: SIMON & SCHUSTER CASH SALES
PO Box 29, Douglas, Isle of Man, IM99 1BQ
Tel: 01624 677237, Fax 01624 670923
E-mail: bookshop@enterprise.net
www.bookpost.co.uk

Please allow 14 days for delivery. Prices and availability subject
to change without notice.